"Jenny gets teens. And teens are definitely going to get this book, with its realistic characters and compelling plot. I give this teacher/writer an A+. Way to go, Jenny!"

—MELODY CARLSON, author of the TrueColors and
Diary of a Teenage Girl series

"Go ahead and just try to get to know Katie Parker. She might make it hard for you at first—life's been tough—but despite her best efforts, she'll still win your heart. I know she won mine."

—SARAH ANNE SUMPOLEC, author of the
Becoming Beka series

"I suspect *In Between* will be the first in a long line of hits for Jenny B. Jones. I enjoyed every delicious word!"

—EVA MARIE EVERSON, author of The Potluck Club series

IN BETWEEN

A KATIE PARKER
PRODUCTION
ACT 1

jenny b. jones

THINK

TH1NK
P.O. Box 35001
Colorado Springs, Colorado 80935

TH1NK is an imprint of NavPress.
TH1NK and the TH1NK logo are registered trademarks of NavPress. Absence of ® in connection with marks of NavPress or other parties does not indicate an absence of registration of those marks.

ISBN-13: 978-1-60006-098-4
ISBN-10: 1-60006-098-6

Cover design by Kirk DouPonce, www.DogEaredDesign.com
Cover photos by Superstock and Masterfile
Author photo by Leslie Zachry
Creative Team: Nicci Hubert, Karen Ball, Reagen Reed, Arvid Wallen, Kathy Guist

This novel is a work of fiction. Names, characters, places, and incidents are either the product of the author's imagination or are used fictitiously. Any resemblance to actual events, locales, organizations, or persons, living or dead, is entirely coincidental and beyond the intent of either the author or publisher.

Unless otherwise identified, all Scripture quotations in this publication are taken from the *New American Standard Bible* (NASB), © The Lockman Foundation 1960, 1962, 1963, 1968, 1971, 1972, 1973, 1975, 1977, 1995.

Jones, Jenny B., 1975-
   In between : a Katie Parker production (act I) / Jenny B. Jones.
      p. cm.
   Summary: Soon after moving to a small Texas town, fifteen-year-old Katie Parker's rebelliousness complicates her life at home and school, but when she is accused of vandalism, she finds hope through a new friendship, involvement in a play, and her foster family's faith in God and her.
   ISBN-13: 978-1-60006-098-4 (alk. paper)
   ISBN-10: 1-60006-098-6 (alk. paper)
   [1. Foster home care--Fiction. 2. Interpersonal relations--Fiction. 3. Conduct of life--Fiction. 4. High schools--Fiction. 5. Schools--Fiction. 6. Theater--Fiction. 7. Texas--Fiction.] I. Title.
   PZ7.J720313In 2007
   [Fic]--dc22
                          2006103298

Printed in the United States of America

1 2 3 4 5 6 7 8 9 10 / 11 10 09 08 07

FOR A FREE CATALOG OF NAVPRESS BOOKS & BIBLE STUDIES, CALL
1-800-366-7788 (USA) OR 1-800-839-4769 (CANADA)

To my mother.
This still is not enough to thank you for your love and sacrifice.
I hope when you see a cover with my name on it you think to
yourself, *That girl wouldn't be anywhere without me.* Because I
sure wouldn't. Love you!

Acknowledgments

FIRST AND FOREMOST, THANK YOU, God, creator of all things, including opportunities. I am amazed and humbled by what you have blessed me with. I pray your hand would continue to be with me as you expand my borders Jabez-style. Sometimes it's scary to get what you want.

I would like to thank every teacher I've ever had, even the bad ones (like the one who gave me detention), but especially the good teachers—the ones who encouraged me (translation: the ones who didn't find me totally annoying).

A big shout out to my students, past and present (especially those Blackhawks). Remember, dream big, and don't settle for less than everything you want. Don't forget Jeremiah 29:11-13.

Thank you to Madison, Annie, Taylor, Emily, and Tara for previewing the book and being my sounding board. But seriously, girls, it hurt me to remove the word *incontinent*. Get a dictionary. You're gonna need to know this word one day. . . .

To Mike Daniels and Dr. Ronnie Floyd, thank you for being such hard-nosed pastors and pushing me. I have grown so much in the last five years. This book never would've happened had I not heard you teach the Word.

Kristin Billerbeck, may God richly bless you for placing me in the hands of NavPress.

Thank you to my friends for putting up with me and supporting me—even when you didn't know what I was up to. (See, it was a book. I *told* you it wasn't illegal!) And thanks, Buffy, for the forks in my yard.

A giant amount of appreciation goes to Erin Valentine and Erin Marshall. You guys are the best. Thanks for giving it to me straight, providing accountability, and letting me know when my writing was worthy of being litter-box liner. God totally put us together.

Much love goes out to my family. You're so blessed to be related to me. Oops, I mean *I'm* so blessed to be related to *you*. Seriously, but for the grace of God, I could be a Katie. I'm so lucky to have your love and support, your faithfulness, and your willingness to move heavy furniture.

Thank you, Ninny, for telling me stories as a child. Look what you started!

I am profoundly grateful to Nicci Hubert. Bless you for taking a chance, believing in me, and going with your temporary moment of insanity when you said, "Hey, let's sign her on."

Muchas gracias to Kate Epperson. I don't know how you put up with all my questions, but you do, and you do it with style. I am in major debt to you for all the help.

God bless all of NavPress. I appreciate how you guys are taking care of me and Katie.

Finally, thank you to the fabulous Karen Ball. I am so honored to have worked with you. I have learned so much. Though I quake in fear of your red pen, I am so thankful for your encouragement, your fun spirit, and that sense of humor. And that you really got Katie (and me). God bless you, girl.

Chapter one

I'M WHAT YOU CALL AN orphan, I guess. Officially, I'm a ward of the state of Texas. Knowing that your greatest achievement to date is becoming a dependent of an entire state can totally blow a girl's confidence.

Life can change so fast. One minute I'm living the single-wide-trailer dream with my mom and a few stray cats, and the next I'm sleeping in a room with eight other girls at the Sunny Haven Home for Girls. And just as soon as I get my sock drawer organized and figure out which girls at Sunny will do me the least amount of bodily harm, I find myself shipped out again. It was just last week Mrs. Iola Smartly, the director, laid the news on me. I would be leaving.

Leaving.

And how did I feel about that? Scared, confused, worried. Oh, and don't forget nauseous. I mean, I have been a resident of Sunny for six months, and then Mrs. Smartly tells me I'm getting new parents. Foster parents.

Pretend-o-parents.

Fast forward one week, one nail-biting week, and here I am, with Mrs. Smartly at the wheel, riding in the finest on-four-wheels the Texas Department of Child Services has to offer (translation: one nasty minivan), zipping down the highway, bound for some hole in the earth called In Between.

"You're going to love In Between, Katie." Mrs. Smartly adjusts the volume on the radio so I can hear her.

I turn my head and look out the window. "Great. I'm going to live in a town inhabited by citizens not even smart enough to pick a decent name for their city. Why couldn't I be going to Dallas?"

Dallas—now those people know what they're doing.

"You're going to live with some wonderful people."

"I guess it gets me out of the state home."

She gives my knee a playful shake. "Now, Sunny Haven is a fine establishment. It wasn't that bad."

My jaw drops. "Are we talking about the same place? The very name is sheer irony. *Sunny* Haven?" I laugh. "Puh-lease. There is not a single sunny thing about that place."

Mrs. Smartly dismisses me with a snort, which ticks me off even more.

"And what particular aspect of the home do you find so endearing, Mrs. Smartly? Could it be the dingy gray walls? And I mean ick gray. That's not a color Lowe's is carrying these days. Or maybe you're all about the lights that run up and down the halls? You know, the ones that hum and whine at decibel levels bound to disturb the local dog population."

"Tell me how you really feel." Mrs. Smartly turns on the windshield wipers to swipe some bug guts away.

Well, since you asked . . . "The floors are always cold. My tootsies are too sensitive for that. And in line with the whole prison décor theme, the floors are a color that tends to remind me of vomit."

She pulls out her directions for a quick check. "Go on. Don't hold back now."

"Okay, Sunny Haven a *home* for girls? What*ever*. That place is an insult to the word *home*."

Many of us girls at Sunny may not have had a real accurate sense of what home should be, but if Sunny Haven is it, please find me a pack of wolves or some killer bees to reside with instead.

"You had a roof over your head, you were fed, and most important, you were safe." She slaps my feet off the scarred dashboard.

"Safe? Are you kidding me?"

Mrs. Smartly takes her eyes off the road for a brief moment and looks my way. "You appear fine to me. When, Miss Parker, did you think your well-being was in question?"

"Okay, I offer up exhibit A: Trina." Enough said.

Trina, one of my roommates, would just as soon slit you with the knife she hides under her King James Bible as she would befriend you. Mrs. Smartly knows this.

See, Sunny Haven houses twelve- to seventeen-year-old girls, like Ms. Prison-Bound Trina or just plain ol' strays like me, who have been taken out of their parents' custody for one reason or another.

I like to say my mom and dad ran off and joined the circus, and due to the fact that I'm allergic to spandex and heavy stage make-up, I could not join their trapeze act. Sometimes I add that I'm just hanging out at Sunny until I can perfect my fire-eating routine.

"Even though we may not be up to your Pottery Barn standards, Katie, I think we provide a pretty good home for girls who don't have one of their own."

I bristle at this. My mother happens to be in prison right now. The only bright side about that is she is probably getting better food than I have been. My mother was one of those high-rolling entrepreneurs. She was doing so well, and it just all caved in on her. One of those dot-com businesses, you might inquire? Corporate takeover, perhaps? You know, those are all really great suggestions, but the fact is Mrs. Parker (a.k.a. my mom) found not everyone liked her products or appreciated her business skills.

Funny how the police just don't see all the potential in drugs that people like Mrs. Bobbie Ann Parker do.

If my mom had pushed Mary Kay cosmetics with as much zeal as she had the narcotics, I'd be living the pink-Cadillac life and never have darkened the doors of Sunny Haven Home for Girls. And I sure wouldn't be on the way to Nowhere, Texas, to live with two complete strangers.

Mrs. Smartly's comment bothers me, but I'll run naked at high noon through my new hometown before I admit it.

I rest my head on the window, getting sleepier by the minute. I was a little worked up last night and didn't exactly get all my beauty rest. I could've counted sheep, but even they don't dare visit Sunny.

"This is some pretty country, isn't it, Katie?"

Pieces of Texas pass us by. Restaurants, shops, houses. I don't know any of them. I guess I don't get out much.

After my dad left, I wrote a letter to one Miss Reese Witherspoon, asking her to come get me and let me live with her in Hollywood. While she did mail me a nice eight-by-ten glossy, she never sent a stretch limo to my house to pick me up. I really think we would've gotten along quite well. It's not like I carry knives in *my* King James Bible.

I clear my throat and decide to broach the topic of my new guardians. "So . . . Mrs. Smartly. James and Millie Scott?" (That's who read my file and said, "We'll take her.")

It's like I want to know about these people, but I don't want Mrs. Smartly to think I'm too interested. Or scared. The thing with foster care is you have way too much uncertainty. I knew where I stood at the girls' home. I knew who to be nice to, who to totally avoid, and what the lumps in the dining hall mashed potatoes really consisted of. But foster care? Ugh. I don't know.

"Are you worried?"

"No," I mutter in my best *duh* voice.

"Okay, then." She returns her attention to the road and bobs her head to the beat of the radio, completely dismissing me.

Well, how rude. She could tell me a bit more about the Scotts. You know, just for the sake of small talk to pass the time.

Mrs. Smartly shoves her big, totally unfashionable sunglasses down and stares at me for a few seconds. "You sure? No fears at all?"

I shake my head and raise my chin. "Not even a little."

She turns the radio up a few notches and begins to sing.

I lurch out of the seat and punch buttons until the music is off. "Okay." I take a deep breath. "First, Mr. and Mrs. Scott could be total lunatics. Kooks. They could be scary, scary people with evil, evil plans." All right, let's not even delve into that line of thought.

I keep on babbling. "Next, there is the idea they only get foster children for slave labor. I mean, I am their temporary kid, and since they will be my temporary parents, I am expected to obey their every command. Like 'No dinner for you until you've cleaned the refrigerator!' Or how about 'No water for you until you've filed our taxes, waxed our vehicles, washed the dog, patched the roof, and given Grandma Scott her pedicure.'

"Or maybe they are do-gooders who think *I'm* the evil one, and they'll try to mold me into some goody-goody freak of nature, who never stops smiling, sings show tunes, and says crazy stuff like, 'Yes, ma'am, I'd love to watch more public television tonight.'"

The possibilities are endless.

"Are you done?" With one hand Mrs. Smartly turns the tunes back up, then reaches into her purse between the seats and grabs a pack of gum. She holds the package out to me.

I shake my head, refusing her pity gum.

I close my eyes for a moment, embarrassed at my little outburst. Inhale . . . and exhale. Okay, I'm better. No more freak outs from this point on.

Wait, is that Ricky Martin on the radio? Is Mrs. Iola Smartly belting out Ricky Martin at the top of her lungs? Oh, no way. I'm sticking some tissue in my ears and forcing myself to go to sleep.

Maybe when I wake up, this car ride will be over, and the sight of Mrs. Smartly shaking her bon-bon in her bucket seat will be just a dim memory.

"KATIE," A VOICE CALLS from the driver's seat.

I'm ignoring this voice.

"Katie, wake up. We're almost to the Scotts' house."

The fog in my head clears as I wake up, and I remember I'm in a shabby minivan bound for a life of sheer bliss and sunshine at my new "parents'" house in Wacko, Texas. Mrs. Smartly nudges my leg, trying to wake the sleeping beauty I am. I give her my possum routine. Plus, I've been asleep in the same position so long I can't seem to move my head.

"Katie Parker, you're drooling on your seat belt. Now wake up."

Ew. Gross.

After I readjust my neck, which got stuck in that awkward sleeping-in-the-car position, I tidy up my ponytail and remove all traces of saliva from my face. I arise to see we are zooming past a big red sign indicating we have arrived in good old In Between, Texas. It says, *Welcome to In Between. At the center, you'll find we're all heart.* They may be all heart, but they're certainly not all brainiacs. Did a first-grader come up with that slogan?

"Well, Miss Parker, what do you think?" Mrs. Smartly takes off her sunglasses to look at me.

What do I think? I think she has some ketchup on her chin from her lunch value meal, that's what I think.

"Are you excited? Nervous? Scared?"

She regards me with genuine interest and concern. If it weren't for the fact that I'm probably gonna be right back at Sunny Haven within six weeks, I would miss Iola Smartly. The poor woman was given the job of operating a run-down orphanage in a building that hasn't seen improvements since a guy named Abe Lincoln was in office. Mrs. Smartly had to contend with one ornery building, plus make sure none of us girls skipped school, ran away, or robbed any convenience stores. No wonder she has so much gray in that dark hair she keeps piled up on top of her head.

"Katie, I'm talking to you." My driving companion wears her exasperated look. She is quite used to my daydreaming and my tendency to ignore people.

I search my brain for a response and give her what I've got.

All I've got.

"I don't know, Mrs. Smartly. I just don't know."

We pass a park where children are playing and running. I try not to think how lucky those children are. Moms to push their swings. Dads to wipe the dirt off scraped knees.

Beyond the park there's a water tower just suffering for a paint job. Mrs. Smartly and I eye the tower and can't help but simultaneously read aloud the poorly painted lettering on it, *Home of the In Between Chihuahuas.* Oh, this is getting worse by the minute. Their school mascot is the Chihuahua?

"Well, Katie, you'll be a Chihuahua, it seems," Mrs. Smartly says with a friendly smirk. The last school I was at, their mascot was a tiger. Tigers eat Chihuahuas.

"Maybe my foster parents will be into homeschooling."

"No such luck, sweetie. I'm sure you'll adjust."

City hall. May's Quilt Shop. Gus's Getcher Gas. Tucker's Grocery and More. In Between Public Library. Bright Mornings Daycare. Micky's Diner. I'm in a small town nightmare. Can you call it a town if there isn't even a McDonald's? How does a person survive without easy access to chicken nuggets?

Mrs. Smartly squints hard at her directions and passing street signs, making lefts and rights with her prized minivan. As we wind through the town, my panic builds with every new sight. Are we going too fast for me to jump out of the van? I think I could live with a broken arm. But on second thought, what if she's going at the speed just prime for a broken neck?

Deciding I like my neck right where it is, I resign myself to the fact that In Between is where I'm at.

Where I'm staying.

Ready or not.

Chapter two

AS WE PULL INTO THE driveway, the gravel path crunches under the tires of the green machine. Suddenly I do not want to get out. I want to stay in the minivan and drive and drive forever. Mrs. Smartly will be the pilot and I, her trusty navigator. We can see the world from our vinyl seats, and nothing can stop us from our life of adventure—and many, many convenience store hot dogs.

My Cruisin'-America dreams come to a screeching halt as I spot what must be the Scotts standing at the end of the drive.

Waiting for me.

The green beast lurches then shimmies to a stop, as does my stomach. Mrs. Smartly looks at me, shoving her Hollywood sunglasses (circa 1985) on top of her teased updo. Oh, no. She's giving me the sympathy. I can't stand the sympathy. But her heart is in her eyes, and it's like I'm receiving her telepathic messages. She feels sorry for me. She'll miss me. She believes in me. I am the wind beneath her wings.

"Katie?"

Here it comes.

I sigh. "Yes, Mrs. Smartly." Tell me what's on your heart. Just get the gooshy stuff over with.

"You have a french fry stuck to your leg."

I swat it off. Couldn't she at least manage one tear? One measly tear?

"Out you go. Time to meet the Scotts."

I peel my legs off the vinyl seat and prepare to take my first step out of the vehicle and into who knows what.

"We could've been so good together," I utter miserably to the van, giving the seat a final parting pat.

"Welcome! Welcome!" The woman who must be Mrs. Scott yells, waving her hands like she's trying to signal a B-52 in for landing.

"Behave, Katie. Put your sweet-girl face on," Mrs. Smartly whispers in my ear. So little time spent with her, yet she knows me so well.

Taking Mrs. Smartly's cue to ignore my bags, I dutifully walk toward the waiting couple. They appear trim and tan and look to be in their forties, but I know from sneaking a peak at their paperwork that James and Millie Scott are both in their fifties. They are probably counting the days until they get their senior citizen discount at Gus's Getcher Gas. Mrs. Scott's chin-length, highlighted blonde hair spirals and curls in various directions, and the slight breeze seems to make her hair dance all over her head. She is thin and slight, and her brown eyes look at me — expectant, hopeful. Like I'm a big surprise package unwrapping before her layer by layer. *Don't get too excited*, I want to tell her. *Katie Parker is just passing through.*

This woman before me, who exudes kindness, has me wrapped up in her delicate arms before I know what hits me, before I can inform her of the Katie Parker no-hugging policy. My temporary mom smells of potting soil and fabric softener, and for a moment I allow myself the luxury of breathing it in.

"Your picture didn't do you justice. You are just as cute as you can be. Isn't she, James?"

Millie Scott takes a step away from me, keeps her hands on my shoulders, and holds me out for further scrutiny. I have to wonder what my new mom and dad (insert sarcasm here) are thinking about me. I'm not so unsightly that I need to wear a Tucker's Grocery bag over my head, but I also don't presume to be Miss Teen USA material, either. As I stand there in all my sixteen-year-old glory, I hope they see my overly-processed hair as strawberry blonde and not an unfortunate battle between red and yellow (with no clear winner). My Madonna T-shirt is vintage, not garage-sale castoff. I hope they know this morning I had some decent looking makeup on, but now it's probably streaking down my face, all goth-like. I want them to look at my five-foot-nine frame and see potential, and I don't mean for the Chihuahua basketball team. I want . . .

Oh, forget it. Enough of the "Let's gaze upon our new teenager time." Enough of the inspection. If they ask to look at my teeth, I'm so out of here.

Her husband smiles at me and luckily opts for a shoulder pat instead of a hug. James Scott stands at least a foot taller than his little wife and looks like the football player to her cheerleader. He is broad and solid, and there is something about him that gets your attention. I notice he has khakis on, and I'm proud to say he doesn't have them pulled up and belted below his armpits. His short-sleeve polo shirt has an insignia over the left pocket, and I read *In Between Community Church.*

Mrs. Smartly mentioned he worked for a church in some capacity. *Nice uniform*, I want to say.

As he smiles at me, I notice his dark gray hair, eyes settled behind oval glasses, leather shoes that scream out "I'm comfortable, but stylish too." But mostly I notice his caution. As I quit my assessment of my would-be dad, I stare straight into his face. His blue peepers meet mine, and in this moment I know. I know that, number one, James Scott is carrying around some hurt of his own; and number two, he's not really sure he wants me around to see it.

"Hey, let's get your bags, young lady, and we'll show you around, get you all settled in." Mr. Scott drops his hand from my shoulder and walks to the van to collect all my worldly possessions.

Mrs. Scott's arm snakes around me as I'm led toward the house. We walk up a cobblestone path with flowers on either side. The house in which I am now to live looms before me. It doesn't look scary, but my stomach does a triple flip anyway. The cream-colored home is anything but new. My new digs have obviously been around for a long time and have seen much TLC and restoration, unlike a certain girls' home, which will go unnamed.

Aside from some pretty scary looking yard gnomes, my own mother never really got into home maintenance, so I am reluctantly impressed by the Scotts' home. Black shutters hang at every window, and the two-story abode is topped off by a tall brick chimney. I'm sick at the thought of staying here, but I've been in the system long enough to know things could be worse.

"We're so excited you're here, Katie." Mrs. Scott gushes with enthusiasm, and I wait for her to add a sporty "Yay!" I offer the woman a weak smile but find I don't really have anything substantial to say.

With a brief look at Iola Smartly, Mrs. Scott tries again. "We have a room for you all set up, but it needs a teenager's touch. So later in the week we can go shopping for things to make you feel more at home, okay?"

She's trying really hard. I've got to give her that.

Mrs. Smartly clears her throat and jerks her head, signaling me to acknowledge Mrs. Scott.

I shrug a shoulder. "Yeah. Thanks."

Mrs. Smartly's eyes roll around and she shakes her big, poofy head.

Look, until I know the Scotts' motivation, until I know I'm here for upright reasons and not to clip their dog's toenails on a daily basis or be the resident toilet scrubber, I have got to play it cool. Sure Mr. and Mrs. Scott look like nice people, but I hear a lot of psychopathic serial killers are quite charming too. If there is one thing I learned from Trina, the Knife Wielder, it's always be on your guard.

We enter the house, and I instantly get a whiff of homemade chocolate chip cookies. Do these people think they can woo me with cookies? Do they really think I'm that weak?

I hope they don't have nuts in them.

Various antiques surround me, but surprisingly not in a "don't touch me" sort of way. The Scott home is cozy, with overstuffed furniture, walls adorned with decorative plates, the occasional botanical print, and family pictures spanning decades. I scan the perimeter to make sure the heart of any home is here—the television. Luckily, it's not an antique, but it's not exactly a sixty-inch flat-screen either. I'm keeping my fingers crossed for cable. That's right, I hope these people don't do me bodily harm, and I hope they have VH1.

Mrs. Smartly is looking this place over like she's committing it to memory. I hope she's doing this for caution's sake and not with the thought that I'm gonna steal that blue and white platter hanging over the fireplace.

"So, Miss Katie, you're awfully quiet. How are you feeling

about all of this?" Millie Scott asks.

Mrs. Smartly looks at me with such intensity I'm afraid her eyes are going to laser through mine.

With a bored (yet artfully haughty) glance at the house I mutter, "It's okay."

I know my face is speaking volumes, though. I know my face is saying, "You people don't impress me. I don't want to be here. Your efforts are useless." Apparently, I need to come up with a "Yes, I will take milk with my chocolate chip cookies" expression too. I mean, seriously, when is the woman going to break out the baked goods?

"Maybe we could see Katie's bedroom?"

A light enters Millie Scott's eyes at Mrs. Smartly's suggestion, and you can tell she thinks that's a grand idea. My room had better not be upstairs. If I need to make my great escape, I don't know how I would get down. Let's be realistic. That bit of tying a bunch of sheets together can't possibly work in real life. *"Girl falls to her death—insufficient thread count to blame."* Plus I am *not* hoofing it up and down stairs all the time.

"If you'll follow me upstairs, I'll show you your room."

Sheesh, can't an underprivileged, displaced ward of the state ever catch a break?

At step number 260 (okay, okay, it was step number seven) we are met by the largest dog I have ever seen in my life. I'm throwing mental daggers at Mrs. Smartly. She said nothing about a dog. I don't like dogs. They slobber and they smell, and this one looks like a giant, mutant horse.

"Now get out of the way, Rocky. Oh, look, he's excited to see you, Katie."

We are forced to stop and observe the dog out of respect for Mrs. Scott, and the dog takes this moment to sniff me in ways I find totally inappropriate and surely should be documented in that file Mrs. Smartly is carrying around with her. Mrs. Scott watches me with her dog, hoping no doubt for a connection. With a polite pat on the head to her little snookums, I continue up the stairs. Rocky decides we are racing and darts ahead of me, taking the stairs three at a time. Their mongrel had better not be going to my room. A girl's gotta draw the line somewhere.

"Here we go. This is your room, Katie."

Millie Scott leads us into my bedroom, and for the briefest of seconds my breath catches and time stops. It's like I'm a character in a Hilary Duff movie. I'm surrounded by pink walls—not a Barbie pink, but a spunky, rockin' pink, with crisp white trim outlining the room. There's a bookshelf, filled from top to bottom with books (I guess a bookshelf filled from top to bottom with *People* magazines was too much to hope for), a white shaggy rug stretched over the worn wooden floor, and a dangling crystal light fixture that boldly declares sophistication and class. (Granted, what do I know of sophistication? But I'm betting that light doesn't respond to a clapper.)

In a corner stands a white wooden desk with an empty bulletin board hanging over it. On the opposite wall is a bed. My bed. It's white and big and covered with various floral quilts someone with patience, skill, and a whole lot of free time must've pieced together and stitched.

"What do you think? I did the best I could, but it definitely needs a teenager's flair." Mrs. Scott fluffs a bed pillow.

The room is amazing. I've never seen anything like it. I've never *had* anything like it. I would like to say I'm not touched by the effort Millie Scott put into creating this space for me, but I am. This bedroom looks, well, safe. I look at this room, and I think, *I could make a home here.*

But I'm not.

"Did you buy all these things for me?" I drag my hand across the desktop.

Mrs. Scott looks at the floor. "Ah, well, not all of it. A lot of this furniture we already had, and I just spruced it up a bit. A little paint and polish, you know." Her eyes sweep the room. A hint of sadness steals across her face just before the serene smile returns. Interesting. I tuck this information away.

My attention returning to the room, I turn in a circle to make sure I'm taking it all in. Just for good measure, I twirl in another circle, seeing the paint, the fluffy bed, the big, fuzzy rug, my desk, the curtains, the lights, the pictures on the wall, the starched pillowcases, the—

Oomph!

The underside of a dog.

"Rocky! Get off her! Oh, Katie, I'm so sorry."

I'm dying. This is it. I'm flat on my back with Rocky, the two-hundred-pound canine freak show on my chest, his tail wagging every three milliseconds and hitting my leg like it's going to break the skin any minute now.

"Rocky, off! My goodness, he just came out of nowhere! Sweetie, I'm so sorry!" Mrs. Scott tries in vain to remove her dog. "Really, he's never a problem, Mrs. Smartly. I hope you don't think we would ever let Rocky endanger Katie."

From my spot on the floor, I look up at Mrs. Smartly, my beloved guardian angel these past six months, and give her my best pitiful look. *Please, oh, please don't leave me here with Mr. Slobbers.*

"I'm not the least bit worried, Millie. I think Katie's going to be just fine." Mrs. Smartly has the nerve to give me a wink, like I, too, think this is just a precious Polaroid moment.

The dog, apparently deciding we're all playing a super-nifty game, plants his whole body on my legs, sitting patiently, waiting for what comes next.

Can't.

Feel.

My legs.

"Yes, Katie's definitely in the right place," says Mrs. Smartly with a parting nudge to my leg with her orthopedic shoe.

Chapter three

THE REST OF THE HOME tour moves at Mach speed. Mrs. Scott talks and draws our attention to various things in the home, and Mrs. Smartly jots down a note or two in her file. It's all over much too quickly. I am not ready for Mrs. Smartly to leave. I'm sure not ready to be left alone with Mr. and Mrs. Scott.

I clear my throat. "Maybe we could look at the laundry room one more time?" Mrs. Smartly cuts her eyes at me. Doesn't it mean anything to the woman that I would rather be in her company?

My guardian reaches for her car keys. "Katie, it's time I left."

Isn't this the part where she should be crying? Delicately wiping her tears on a handkerchief? Letting me know how much I will be missed? At this point, I'm even okay with the kind of crying that involves heaving sobs and lots of snot. Come on, Mrs. Smartly!

Genuine panic races through me. I'm going to be alone with total strangers! And their dog will probably suffocate me in my sleep tonight or drown me in drool. No, no, no! Think, must think.

"Did you pack my switchblade, Mrs. Smartly?"

Mrs. Smartly doesn't even blink.

Millie Scott sure does.

"No, Katie, I left it back at the home, along with your rat poison collection." Mrs. Smartly smiles evenly. "Our Katie has quite a sense of humor."

Mrs. Scott isn't sure whether to be calmed or not by Mrs. Smartly's indifference. Oh, yeah, Millie Scott, you'd better be scared. You'd better fear this. I am dangerous. I do dangerous, risky, life-threatening things all the time.

Oh, who am I kidding? The most dangerous thing I've ever done is sit on a public toilet.

"Walk me out to the van, Katie. I've got something for you." And with that, Mrs. Smartly shakes hands with my new mom and pop, throws out some final instructions, and pulls me out the door with her.

The two of us walk silently down the driveway to the green van. The path stretches before me like some sort of melodramatic symbol of how far I am from home. In this moment, I am overwhelmed with a powerful sadness. I miss my mom, my old trailer house, the stray cats. Right now I even miss that ugly, redheaded kid across the street, who threw worms on me.

Don't cry. Don't you cry, Katie. Deep breaths now.

I drag my feet along the gravel in a deliberately annoying way, which, of course, doesn't faze Mrs. Smartly in the least. Leaning her ample frame into the driver's side of the van, she pulls out a small box.

"What is it?" I say it as if I already cannot stand the gift or her.

"It's stationery."

Stationery? Well, sure. Nothing says "have a nice life" like paper products.

"Great. Thanks, Mrs. Smartly." I don't know why I'm mad, but

I am. "Maybe I can write the governor and thank him and social services for placing me in the Chihuahua capital of the world. Maybe I'll write Trina and see if she's moved on to nunchucks yet. Or hey, I know, maybe I'll write Dave Letterman and tell him me and my new dog have a super-cool trick we like to call 'Kill Katie.'"

Mrs. Smartly snorts, and the next thing I know, I'm plastered to her polyester, paisley dress, enveloped in my second unsought hug for the day.

"Katie Parker, you are something else."

Mrs. Smartly's chest shakes with her chuckling, and to my utter shame, hot tears fall down my cheeks. Oh, this day will live in infamy.

We move apart, and before I can turn my head, she has a tissue in my hand. Iola Smartly—prepared for anything. Clearly she was a Girl Scout in her youth.

"This paper is for writing letters to whomever you want, Katie. You can write the governor if you so choose, but if you don't write me at least once every week, I will be telling Mr. and Mrs. Scott you already think of Rocky as your flesh-and-blood brother and would love for him to sleep in your room."

Now that's just cruel.

"And you can write your mama and update her on your life."

Oh, to be the author of prison letters. It's a young girl's dream come true. "I'm not writing my mom. She totally ditched me. Left me for *this* place." I jerk my head toward the house.

"She's in prison, Katie. It's not like she took off for Honolulu."

"The day she calls is the day I'll write." I know she can make phone calls in that place. And do I ever receive one? No.

"Fine. Then you can just write me."

Mrs. Smartly gives me her I-mean-business look, and I obediently bob my head in agreement. "Okay. I'll write you." I clutch the stationery and the soggy tissue to my chest, wishing I were anywhere but here.

"Katie, I know this is scary. And it's not fair." Here come the waterworks again. "But the Scotts are good people. They're going to try their hardest to make you a home, and I want you to behave and be nice. They are not your enemy."

Again, I nod my head. Which causes my nose to drip.

"I believe in you, Katie Parker," Mrs. Smartly says with such force I can't help but to look up at her. "You have something. I don't know what it is, but you have got to know you are special and your life is meaningful."

Another tissue magically appears out of nowhere. Does the woman pull them out of her ear? Where does she keep those things?

"I do believe, Miss Parker, you are just a blessing unfolding by the day. God's got big plans for you, and it may not seem like it now, but he's taking care of you, and In Between, home of the Fighting Chihuahuas, is where you are supposed to be."

God-schmod, I want to say. I'm practically an *orphan*! How special is that? How blessed is that? If God blesses me any more I'll be living on the streets, digging for my dinner in a certain hamburger restaurant's McDumpster.

"One of these days really soon, you're going to be able to say, 'I know what it is to be wanted, what it is to be loved. I know what home is, and I'm right where I'm supposed to be.'" Mrs. Smartly smoothes her big hand over my hair, and the gesture is so motherly—and so unlike her—that my eyes fill up again.

God, if you are up there, just take me now.

She hugs me again (three and counting) and hoists herself into her awaiting coach. I swipe at my eyes, like that ever does any good.

"Mrs. Smartly," I cast a sorrowful look back at the house. "Are you sure you want to leave me here?" My voice catches, and I'm all too aware of the plea in my tone. I expect a wisecrack from Mrs. Smartly, but her face softens, and she suddenly gives me something I know I don't ever want from her—pity.

"No, Katie Parker. I don't want to leave you here. But I do want to do what's right for you, and just as sure as I know this engine is going to overheat at some point on my way home, I know taking you back with me to Sunny Haven would be the wrong thing to do. Now I'll be checking on you, so if anything goes wrong, I'll be back." She sees the hope in my puffy eyes. "But I really don't think that's going to be necessary. Katie, you have a chance to have a good life." She pokes a stubby finger in my chest. "Don't screw this up."

The van door gives a mournful creak as it shuts, and Mrs. Smartly starts the reluctant ignition. The van, *my* green van, slowly backs out of the driveway. I would give in to my urge to chase the vehicle down the driveway, but I'm sure Rocky the Wonder Dog would join the chase and come after me like I'm his latest dog biscuit. Mrs. Smartly slowly brakes the van and rolls down the window. "I will miss you, Miss Katie. You're one of my favorites."

"I'll miss you too." I'm just blubbering now.

"And if you tell anyone I said that, I'll be bringing your new sister, Trina, out here." And with the engine choking and hacking, Iola Smartly, director of the Sunny Haven Home for Girls, drives off, leaving me standing in the middle of the drive, more miserable than I've ever been in my sixteen years.

I am Katie, the Lonely Girl.

Lifetime should do a movie about me.

Chapter four

"KATIE, WOULD YOU LIKE TO come in?" Mrs. Scott stops a few feet away from me, clearly uncertain how close is too close. "You've been standing out here over an hour."

Well, time flies . . . when you're miserable!

"Dinner is going to be ready in about an hour. And I have some chocolate chip cookies in the kitchen if you'd like some. You probably already sniffed those out though, right?" Mrs. Scott's grin is a clear invitation for casual banter.

"Cookies? No, I hadn't noticed."

Mrs. Scott looks around the yard, probably trying to figure out what I've been staring at for the last hour. I did find the shapes of the Alamo and Justin Timberlake in the clouds, but they rolled on by about thirty minutes ago. Other than that, I've just been stationed in one spot out here in case Mrs. Smartly changed her mind and decided she couldn't face Sunny without me. I'm guessing I'd probably stand out here and weather a lot of bird poop and other elements and that still wouldn't happen.

"Katie, are you afraid to come inside the house?"

Afraid? Is she talking to *me*?

"No, ma'am, I told my boyfriend I was moving, and he said he'd probably hop on his hog and come by." Where did *that* come from?

"Oh." Mrs. Scott picks a weed from the yard. "You have a boyfriend then?"

"Yeah." I wait a few seconds, acting like I'm not going to say anything more. More suspense, you know. "I got a boyfriend. His name is . . . um, Snake." Did I really just pick a reptile?

"Snake. What an . . . interesting name."

"Yeah, well, the shorter the name, the easier it is to get it tattooed on your—"

"Okay, why don't we go see about those cookies now." Mrs. Scott paints a smile on her face. "And you can tell me all about it. I have a few boyfriend stories of my own."

Excuse me, Mrs. Fancy Pants?

"No, what I mean to say is, when I was your age I had lots of boyfriends. No, I don't mean lots, I mean a couple. You know, I didn't have boys lined up at the door or anything."

My new mom is unraveling right in front of me. Maybe I should show her some deep breathing exercises I learned in PE last year.

"I wasn't that type of girl. Not that it's not okay to be that type of girl, well, I mean, it's not okay, but I would never judge someone if she . . . if she . . . Um, will you be drinking skim or whole milk with those cookies?"

DINNER IS A QUIET affair. At least on my end. Mr. and Mrs. Scott do all the talking, and I do all the eating. Actually I don't really eat. I just shove things around on my plate until I finally discover a use for Rocky the horse. It seems he's mighty fond of Mrs. Scott's pot roast with potato-and-carrot medley. Part of my brain is marveling over the food before me, the taste and appearance, as well as the care that went into making it. My own mother thought variety in your diet meant eating a different Hot Pockets sandwich than you did the night before. But the dinner table scene is just too awkward and foreign for me to be able to do anything but sit here with a stomach full of nerves. I sneak a glance under the table at Rocky making a big production of licking the gravy off his mammoth chops.

First off, Mr. Scott began the meal with a prayer and thanked God for me. Mrs. Scott chimed into this brief prayer with a few quiet "Yes, Lords." I'm not real up on my prayers, so if this was supposed to have been a three-part harmony, I wasn't prepared. Then Mr. and Mrs. Scott proceeded to make small talk between themselves, giving me many opportunities to jump in. I remained mum, instead using the time to build little forts out of my potatoes and carrots.

"So, Katie," — Mr. Scott clears his throat, as if to communicate the small talk is over, and now it's time to get down to business — "you'll be going to school Monday. Are you nervous about a new school?"

How about scared spineless.

I shrug my left shoulder. "I dunno." Maybe the Scotts will want to return me to Sunny when they realize the kid they got didn't pack her personality.

He tries again. "Well, what is your favorite subject?"

I pretend to think about it for a second. "Shop class I guess."

"Really?" Mr. Scott leans in. "Do you enjoy working with your hands? Making something out of nothing? Maybe putting your hard work into something and having the satisfaction of completing a project?"

"Nah, I just like working with sharp objects." I feel some small measure of satisfaction as Mrs. Scott looks at my meat knife, and I know she is making herself a mental note to keep the cutlery out of my reach.

The truth is I don't know why I'm baiting the Scotts. Just habit, I guess. This is what they expect of me, so this is what they will get. It's always been this way. People look at me, look at my scholastic record (or lack of it), look at my mom's rap sheet, and see who they want to see. It's like a coat I have to put on every day, even though it doesn't fit. I'm the poor, homeless kid with a druggie mom from the worst trailer park in Texas. I must be stupid. Surely I'm a deviant. No doubt I'm a troublemaker.

I've found it's much easier to go with the flow and play the part than to try and prove none of that is me—or none of that should be me. I just want to grow up, get out of foster care, and be on my own. I want to go where no one knows me or where I came from. I can't wait to start over and be whoever I want to be. I might even change my name. You know, like Madonna did when she went all Kabbalah.

"Katie, I thought we'd go shopping tomorrow for some school clothes and maybe some clothes to wear for church Sunday."

Mrs. Scott is hoping this will be the golden ticket, I can tell. She's hoping the word *shopping* will make this poor girl come alive.

"Thanks, but I have clothes." Oh, that one hurt. I hate my clothes! My clothes hate me right back. We're terrible together. I *so* need new clothes, but I cannot give in! Must. Not. Give. In.

"Well, sure you do, honey, but you would be doing me a favor by letting me buy you a few things. Our daughter, Amy, is all grown up now, so I haven't had the pleasure of buying for a young lady like yourself in a long time."

Now Mrs. Scott is shoving her potatoes around. Maybe I could let her buy me a shirt or two. But church clothes? No, I don't need those.

"I guess we could look around if you really wanted to." I think I just broke my record for most words in a sentence since arriving. "But I don't need no church clothes." Yes, yes, I know that was a double negative and horrible English, but I'm wearing the coat right now. Remember the coat? Mr. and Mrs. Scott exchange a look.

"Katie, you do know we work for a church, right?"

"I did read something about that," I deadpan, with a pointed look at his shirt. Yeah, *so* not impressed. I take a drink of milk, hoping someone will change the topic.

"Mrs. Smartly told you all about us, didn't she? You know I'm the senior pastor at In Between Community Church, right?"

A spray of milk flies out of my mouth and nose, jetting across the table. Rocky takes two giant leaps, and he's out of the room, instantly fearful of the girl spewing the two percent.

Did Mr. Scott just say *pastor*? You have *got* to be kidding me!

9-1-1, I'd like to report a murder.

The dearly departed goes by the name of Iola Smartly.

Chapter five

AFTER A FITFUL NIGHT OF staring at the ceiling, I am awakened by the sound of Mr. Scott downstairs yodeling "Oh My Darlin'," as Rocky, dog in residence, howls along. Rocky's attempts at singing sound more like he's trying to communicate the depth of some inner pain, like a spleen hanging out or the discomfort of swallowing the neighbor's cat whole. And Mr. Scott is no melodious treat either.

I roll over. 7:00 a.m. I don't think I fell asleep until 6:59.

I sigh and rub my eyes, then scan the room. Am I really here? And how can I *not* be here? I have got to get out of this place. The Scotts and I are so different; it's just a matter of time before they send me back.

Throwing the covers aside, I slink out of bed, and dread unsettles my stomach. My black suitcase sits on the floor, and I open it and get a clean pair of jeans. They're my favorite ones. The knee is ripped out but not in a cool, Abercrombie and Fitch sort of way. I grab some other things and head for the bathroom.

I take a quick shower, wondering how long I can stay in there before someone comes to get me. Have I mentioned I don't want to be here?

My hair still damp, I inch my way down the stairs into the kitchen. The dog is still howling, and his shrill outbursts rock my sleep-deprived head.

Mrs. Scott sees my grimace and greets me with a big smile. "Good morning, Katie!"

Mr. Scott sticks his head around the corner from the living room. "Morning, Katie!"

Great. My foster parents are morning people. Could this get any worse?

"Oh!" I jump at the intrusion of a wet dog nose.

"Rocky, get back. He's just smelling your clothes, trying to get to know you." Mrs. Scott gives the dog a command, and he charges back into the living room with his duet partner.

That dog's way of getting to know me is scandalous and totally unnecessary. If I greeted people like that at school Monday, I'd be arrested.

"Take a seat, sweetie, and I'll get you something to eat." Mrs. Scott guides me to the breakfast nook table and puts silverware in front of me. "Did you sleep well?"

Choosing to ignore her question, I barely hold onto a smart remark about my lack of sleep. First of all, I don't do mornings. And second of all, I don't function well on zero sleep. I just don't feel I'm at my best when the bags under my eyes are beyond the power of foundation, concealer, or spackle.

Mrs. Scott brings me my breakfast—a giant stack of smiley faced pancakes. Okay, not bad. I like pancakes. At least it's not lumpy oatmeal or some cereal with the word *fiber* in the name.

My new foster mom flutters all around me, handing me more pancakes, plus fruit, hot chocolate, and juice. Milk is noticeably absent. I guess no one trusts me with that drink anymore. In between handing me syrup every few minutes and refilling my juice glass, she talks nonstop of where we'll shop and what we'll hunt for. Mrs. Scott is just a ball of uncontained energy this morning. Clearly she's had her Ovaltine.

I can hardly hear her for the torturous sounds of her two favorite guys in the next room. I do catch snippets, such as "I hear UGGs are out," "pink is the new black," "cashing in the 401K for name-brand jeans," and "fun, fun, fun." It's a crying shame to have a headache before you've even had a chance to brush your teeth.

I hold my ears like I'm four. "Could you please ask them to stop?"

Mrs. Scott rambles on, sharing what she discovered while flipping through a *Seventeen* last night. A full minute passes before it registers I've spoken.

"Stop what?"

"Whatever Mr. Scott and Rocky are doing. Please make it stop."

"Oh, James works with Rocky every day on a new trick or command. He really is a brilliant dog."

Mr. Scott and Rocky reach a shrill crescendo that makes my eyes cross.

"Oh my daaaarlin' Clementine!"

Mrs. Scott drops her own breakfast of a grapefruit onto her plate. "Oh, yes, I see what you mean. Sorry."

My faux mom speeds out of the kitchen, and I hear her say something to Mr. Scott about scaring me with his shenanigans. Okay, I know shenanigans. Shenanigans is sticking two hundred plastic forks in your neighbor's yard or shaking up someone's canned pop so it will explode when he opens it. What I'm experiencing now is called torture. Pure and simple. Mr. Scott could use that tactic during war interrogations.

Mrs. Scott breezes back into the room with a serene smile upon her face.

"Sorry, Katie!" Mr. Scott bellows from the living room.

"Okay, so where were we?" Mrs. Scott continues, picking at her grapefruit.

I think we were at the point where ear plugs were to be placed on the shopping list.

"Ah, yes, then after we go to the shoe stores on Fourth and Main, we'll head to the mall and do some damage there. And then, of course, it's on to Macy's."

"As in *the* Macy's department store?"

"As in Betty Macy's clothing store."

I roll my eyes. *So* not enjoying this.

"But she has some really unique handbags in there."

Oh, sure she does. They're probably made of doilies.

"Are you finished with your breakfast?" Mrs. Scott is eyeing the clock, and I can tell she is beyond excited to get this shopping frenzy started. She barely even touched her grapefruit. No wonder she is so cheerleader skinny. "It will take us about an hour to get to the mall."

Great. An hour alone in the car with Mrs. Scott. Nothing like having to travel to an entirely different county to find an Old Navy.

"Who needs the mall?" My eyes widen, all innocence. "Maybe I could find a new T-shirt or two at Gus's Getcher Gas?"

"I don't think a *Monster Trucks Rev Me Up* T-shirt is what all the girls in your class will be sporting Monday morning." Mrs. Scott winks, and I am fleetingly impressed by her early morning wit. "Now, unless you want something else to eat, go upstairs and get ready. We have miles to cover today. I have a stack of teen and style magazines for you to look at on the way."

I scoot out of my chair and drag myself up the stairs. There isn't enough pancake batter in the world to fortify me for this day.

"I even have a few pages marked of items I thought you might like!" she calls after me.

Great.

My new mother works for the fashion police.

Chapter Six

"IF YOU LOOK ON PAGE sixteen of the October issue of *Teen Scene*, I believe you will find this exact shirt on that Simpson girl. Which one is it, Jessica or her sister . . . oh, what is her name, Mary Kate?"

As Millie Scott cross-references her teen magazines, I try on the millionth shirt she has handed over the dressing-room door. This is torture in the extreme. I'd rather have my finger nails pulled out one by one. I'd rather suffer one million paper cuts, then jump in a pool of lemon juice. I'd rather watch anime. In Japanese.

I'm tired.

I'm cranky.

And if I have to strip down again for "one more shirt" or "last pair of jeans, I promise," I am going to scream my head off.

We have been at it for over six hours, and while my haul has been substantial, let's be real. These are things that will just be left in that nice big closet when the Scotts send me packing. It's hard to get too excited about buying new clothes, most of which I will never get around to wearing.

I am not going to get attached to any of these clothes Mrs. Scott throws at me. Not the five pairs of jeans, including the ones that make me look like I actually have a butt. Not the hoodie with the extremely obvious, but beautiful brand name on the back of it. Not even the new winter coat the sales girl said makes me look like a smart, yet chic college student.

Though the two new padded bras will be with me forever. *Now that I have found you, my pretties, we shall never separate.* Show the orphan girl a Wonderbra, and suddenly life is worth living.

"Oh, my goodness!" Mrs. Scott cries.

Super, she probably realized there are still some jeans left in Texas that we have yet to try on.

"It's after three o'clock! We've forgotten to eat lunch!"

Forgot to eat lunch? This girl docs *not* forget about meals, Ms. Half-a-grapefruit-for-breakfast. Lady, around noon I ate a pair of those Mary Janes you pushed on me. Of course I'm hungry! I'm a growing child! Well, except in the Miraclebra area, but I think we've already established my great shortcoming.

"I'm so sorry, Katie. I've only had you one day, and I've already managed to starve you. I got so caught up in all of this, I just lost track of time."

I know she is envisioning me tattling to Mrs. Smartly. Like I would. I'm a lot of things, but I'm no snitch. Those kinds of girls get beaten up.

"Well, Mrs. Smartly doesn't like it when I skip meals. She believes my nutritional health is directly proportional to my mental, physical, and emotional development." I have no idea what I just said, but I know it was on a test I took in health class last year.

I fling open the dressing room door, and Millie Scott is before me, surrounded by a sea of bags and packages, wringing her hands.

"Katie, truly, I had no idea it was so late. We'll leave right now and go get something to eat. Anything you want. You name it." She looks so distraught I can't help but try and use it to my advantage.

"I wondered why I was feeling so faint this last hour. Food would be very nice, ma'am."

"Anything."

"And dessert."

"You got it."

"Appetizers too?" I'm reeling her in.

"Of course."

"And a strawberry virgin daiquiri with a little pink umbrella floating in it?"

Millie Scott's brow furrows. Oops, too much. But if I don't get at least a hot fudge sundae out of this, I'm going to be thoroughly put out. I tried on everything ever hung on a rack! I deserve chocolate!

As I strike a pathetic pose, I realize I have never addressed Mrs. Scott by her name aloud. What do I call her? Millie? Mrs. Scott? Woman Who Is Not My Mother?

"You must be starving. What was I thinking?"

I'm thinking you've sniffed one too many perfume samples in those fashion magazines.

Mrs. Scott continues her nervous chatter, putting a supporting hand under my arm, which is quite a feat given all the packages she is carrying. She leads me out the door, and we make our way to the exit.

Where the blinding light of day nearly brings me to my knees.

Oh, sun, I forgot you existed. I have been in a cave we mortals like to call a shopping mall, and I have missed you.

Remembering my new sunglasses with the cool pink rhine-stones, I slip them on, and my vision is restored. I dutifully follow behind the Queen of MasterCard and Visa.

It takes me, Mrs. Scott, and two strangers who were dumb enough to stop and help thirty minutes to pack the car and get every bag in. I told Mrs. Scott if we needed to sacrifice any of the purchases due to lack of room, that the underwear could go since I liked to go au natural anyway.

So far Miss Millie just does not appreciate my jokes.

Five minutes later we are parked at a restaurant. At least I assume we're at a restaurant. All I can see in front of me is a solid wall of packages and boxes. We're so tightly packed in this sedan, if Mrs. Scott left me in here, I think I'd only have about an hour's worth of air supply. Suffocation by JC Penney is *not* a cool way to go.

"Katie, are you ready to get out?"

I hear her door open.

"Mrs. Scott, is that you?" I say this weakly, hoping she'll notice she's lost me in this avalanche of shopping bags.

"Katie? Katie, where are you?" She digs around me, trying to latch onto some part of me she can safely drag out. "Is this you?"

"Nope. I think that's my coat."

"How about now?"

"Nuh-uh. I can see your hand though. I'm two Marshalls bags to your left and down a Dillard's."

"Yes, just a second, I think I—gotcha!"

"Ow! That's my nose!"

Mrs. Scott manages to find my arms and with a good tug, I'm finally sprung from the vehicle.

Ah, air.

French fry scented air.

Freedom never smelled so good.

Chapter seven

"KATIE, ARE YOU READY TO ORDER?"

Millie Scott and the waiter have been waiting for me to give my dessert order for the last two minutes. For the first time in my life, I am in a restaurant that has its own separate dessert menu, and I just want to savor the moment and take in all my choices. This menu has pictures—a centerfold of chocolate cake, New York style cheesecake, strawberry shortcake, and a few other decadent items I've never seen before. Feeling pressured, I select a chocolate concoction that has ice cream, brownies, hot fudge, and a whole list of candy shop items sprinkled on top. Maybe this foster care thing is working out; I get a padded bra *and* ooey-gooey dessert, all in one day.

Mrs. Scott interrupts my chocolate fantasies. "I thought maybe we could hit the salon next week if you wanted."

I run a hand through my shoulder-length hair. What's wrong with my hair? Granted, it's currently not a color existing in nature, but still. First all new clothes and then new hair? What next, a brain transplant? A personality transfusion? Is there anything else you'd like to alter about your new foster child, Millie Scott? What are you trying to do, turn me into Paris Hilton?

"It would be fun to go together and get pedicures. While we're there, we can flip through magazines and see if there are any new hairstyles we want."

Well, it's hard to be mad at the lady when she puts it like that, like she just wants to hang out and have fun. But if she suggests we do some Internet research together on plastic surgery, I'm on the first bus to Sunny Haven.

The waiter delivers my long-awaited dessert, and Mrs. Scott drops the salon topic.

I stare at the restaurant's chocolate creation in a few moments of reverent awe before attacking it with my spoon. I notice the waiter has mistakenly brought two spoons, and Mrs. Scott's hand reaches for one. Her spoon targets my dish, coming closer and closer. I sit in horror as I realize I am expected to share. Did Millie Scott sweat right through *her* deodorant by trying on every shirt in the mall? No. Did Millie Scott cram her feet into every pair of shoes in the great state of Texas? I don't think so. Did Millie Scott spend the majority of *her* day trapped in one tiny excuse for a dressing room after another? No. I did! Me! Back away from the chocolate! Drop the spoon and no one will get hurt!

I repress my inner Trina and watch as my nonMom helps herself to my brownie fudge sundae. It's just not fair. I worked hard for this dessert! She's coming in for bite number two. And now three? This is too much.

"Get your own." I hear myself say.

"What did you say?" Mrs. Scott asks, as a ringing goes off in her purse.

"Um . . . get your phone?"

"Hello? Yes, mother. Yes, I know I haven't been by in a week.

You know we've been extremely busy. I thought you would be getting ready for your singles' cruise. Right, I can see how that would be a problem. Yes, I know you need your Floaties and nose plugs for the pool. Fine." Mrs. Scott sighs into the phone. She looks stressed. "I'll pick some up at the store." Her brown eyes shift to me. "Yes, she's here. She's just beautiful."

Mrs. Scott grins then rolls her eyes to show me she is not enjoying her phone conversation. Well, I am. It's given me just enough time to eat all my dessert. If she stays on a few more minutes, I can run my tongue over the plate. Very ladylike, I know. But who knows when chocolate and I shall meet again?

"Yes, mother. Okay. I'll pick up your stuff and bring it over. No, no, you are not going yourself. We've talked about this. I will be right there." And with a quick "love you, bye," the phone call is over.

"Katie, there's someone I'd like you to meet this afternoon. My mother." Mrs. Scott stops talking, and there is a long pause, as if she is trying to think what to say next. "My mother is, um, different. I don't want her to scare you, but she's been compared to Judge Judy."

"Judge Judy?"

"On crack."

I knew there was a crazy grandma in their closet somewhere. I knew it! I'm still not going to rub her feet.

"Mother is going on a cruise with the single senior citizens in the church and needs a few things. So we'll just stop at the store then take them over."

"Your mother doesn't drive?"

"Oh, she can drive. But the town has asked us to not let her anymore."

"The town?"

"Yes, she's such a horrible driver that they had a town hall meeting last year and voted unanimously to start a campaign to get her car taken away from her." Her head nods. "They were right. We haven't had to replace a stop sign in over six months. And the *Say No to Mad Maxine* T-shirts were quite catchy."

The corners of Mrs. Scott's mouth turn up, and I find myself smiling back.

"The town really is safer." My foster mom dabs at her lips with delicate hands, removing all traces of *my* brownie. "Except for the incident last month, things have been going much better."

"Last month?"

"Mother bought a bicycle—a tandem bicycle, no less—and had a little accident, wiping out in the street. Luckily though, the chicken truck stopped for her. After it hit a fire hydrant." She shakes her head and laughs. "It rained feathers and naked chickens for an hour. But Mother says she is close to perfecting her wheelie."

A BMX granny. That is awesome. Her mother sounds like someone I'd like to know. If she's Mrs. Scott's mother, she must be sweet, too. A little eccentric, but probably the sweetest, kindest, most gentle-tempered woman ever.

Chapter eight

MILLIE SCOTT'S MOTHER IS EVIL.

Maxine Simmons is a gum-smacking, energy-drink-guzzling, wheelie-popping demon.

And we arrive just in time to see her trying on bathing suits for the cruise. Ew. I know when I close my eyes tonight, I will still see her parading around in various styles of spandex one pieces. She was going to show us her bikini possibilities, but Mrs. Scott stopped her. I'm already scarred for life. Seeing this woman in a two-piece would have sent me right over the edge.

"Mother, when we went shopping last week, we bought you a few cover-ups. Where are those?"

Mrs. Scott and I are both staring at the black number her mother is modeling. The suit is all black, except for a huge orange tropical flower on the front. It looks like an orchid is getting ready to swallow Mrs. Scott's mom at any moment.

"Hah! Cover-ups are for old people. I got good legs. No need to deprive the world of these gams." The woman does some sort of Rockettes kick, then looks at her audience for affirmation and

JENNY B. JONES

realizes for the first time during this fifteen-minute glamour show that I am in the room.

"Who are you?"

"Mother, this is Katie. Katie Parker. She's the girl we've been telling you about."

Mrs. Simmons, or Mad Maxine, as I think I will refer to her, plants her bathing-suit-clad body right in front of me and looks me in the eyes for a full minute. One uncomfortably long minute. A weaker girl would be crying at this point. She's that intimidating.

Or crazy.

"Like I told you, Katie arrived yesterday, and we got her all settled in. Then today we went shopping. We've had a great time, haven't we Katie?"

Mrs. Scott tries to make casual conversation, but her mother ignores her. Mrs. Simmons's eyes pin me in place.

"I got these legs from dancing. I was a Vegas showgirl back in the day. I've danced with Sinatra, Ol' Blue Eyes himself. When I was not much older than you, I could dance the tango with a forty-pound headdress on my head."

Mrs. Simmons looks at me like *top that*, and I honestly have no response. Um, one time in the third grade I ate glue? I mean, seriously, what do you say to this?

"That's great, Mrs. Simmons."

"Later I'd go on USO tours, and I'd dance on stage for the soldiers from dawn 'til dusk, with no rest in between."

Her face is now even closer to mine. I can smell her spearmint gum. I nod a few times then look over at Mrs. Scott for help. I see my foster mom is now on the other side of the room, taking things out of Mad Maxine's suitcase and replacing them with other clothing choices. I try to will Mrs. Scott to look my way and make eye contact. I send her telepathic messages. *Save me. Save me from your crazy mother.*

"And I met a soldier and married him. Davis Simmons knew a good thing when he saw it." Mad Maxine backs up just enough to pop her gum. "And I had three children, Millie being my third, and you know what, little girl?"

"Um . . . " I gulp. "No."

"I still got it. That's right. The body is a temple, and I have got myself a tem-*ple*. And until I am wearing adult diapers and being spoon fed, I will clothe myself in whatever I want. Are we clear?"

And before I can respond, Mad Maxine snaps her head toward her daughter. Mrs. Scott's eyes bug out. She shuts her mother's suitcase and wisely takes a step back.

Smart woman, my foster mother.

"Do I look like I need help picking out what to wear for my cruise, Millie?"

Oh, no. Please don't fight. Not in front of the child.

"What about you, little missy? Do you think I look like I don't have enough sense to dress myself?"

Oh, if I could only click my heels together and be home. Before I know it, Mad Maxine has my chin in her claw like hand.

"Well, do you?"

"No, ma'am."

"Ha!" With a satisfied cackle, she releases me to take a swig of her nearby energy drink. The label reads: *Super-Charged Cola*. This woman shouldn't even be allowed to be within sniffing distance of caffeine.

"Mother, I just think you should pack more of a variety of clothing. You never know what the weather will do. Remember that time you went to Jamaica, and there was a hurricane?"

Yeah, and she probably jumped on her broomstick and rode right out of it.

"I am sixty years old. Don't you think I know how to pack by now?" Patting her crayon yellow hair, Mad Maxine walks over to inspect her modified suitcase.

"You are not sixty." Mrs. Scott's index finger flies out to point at her mother. "Katie, she is not sixty. Don't ever let her fool you. She's seventy-six, and that's being generous."

I don't know why Millie and James Scott wanted a foster daughter. It looks like they have their hands full with psycho granny here.

"Mom, we're not here to talk about *you*. I wanted you to meet Katie, and all you've done is show her how you can throw a tantrum."

"I am sixty-two years old. If I want to throw a tantrum, then that's what I'll do." And with a *humph*, the woman turns back to me. Great.

"Where did you come from, Katie Parker?"

Is this a trick question? I'm so intimidated by this woman, I don't want to get the answer wrong. Does she mean what town? Does she mean on a deep, emotional level, like *I come from heartache, Mrs. Simmons, heartache.* Or does she mean where do I think I originated from in terms of my beliefs on creation?

"Sunny Haven Home for Girls," I squeak out.

Mad Maxine stares at me for a long while, like I'm supposed to add more to it. As she keeps her piercing gaze on me, I notice her hands. Her nails are perfectly manicured and painted a shiny, scarlet red. She has rings on nearly every finger, giant, sparkling rings shimmering and dancing on her hand. She probably stole them from a pirate.

No, she probably *was* a pirate.

"I know something about homes," Mad Maxine says finally and looks at me like we are two kindred souls.

Cue the violins. This woman knows drama.

"I know what it's like to be thrown in with a bunch of people you don't even know. I understand what it's like to not see your family, and to have to depend on others."

"Now, just a minute, Mother." Mrs. Scott steps in between us. "Katie, before you go feeling sorry for her, my mother sold her home in Las Vegas to come and live with her children. She lived with my sister first, then my brother, and then landed on my doorstep. Even though we waited on her hand and foot, she left my home and bought this little apartment at Shady Acres Retirement Village. Live with a bunch of people you don't know? She's the *president* of the social committee! And as for her not seeing her family, I'll have you know she carries around a PDA and makes James and me schedule our visits with her so we won't interfere with *her* activities."

"That's right. And I see you're not penciled in for today, so don't let the door hit 'cha where the good Lord split 'cha. If you want to talk to me anymore, I won't have an opening until four o'clock this afternoon. I have a Pilates class." Mad Maxine waves her hand toward the door, clearly dismissing us, and we move on cue.

Just a few more steps and this will all be over.

"Oh, did you get the nose plugs and Floaties I asked for?"

"Yes, Mother, they are in your suitcase." Mrs. Scott kisses her mom on the cheek. "Have a good time. And remember, unless the captain asks you to, you are not allowed to steer the boat."

"Bah! That's my daughter! Always the spoil sport."

And in the midst of more cackling, Mad Maxine grabs me and pins me against her tropical disaster of a bathing suit in a hug. I think of a praying mantis, and hope she doesn't try to suffocate me while Mrs. Scott's not looking.

"You come back and see me, Katie Parker. You and I have a lot of catching up to do. I can tell you need family, and I've decided you may think of me as your grandmother." She leans in closer to my ear and whispers, "You just remember I know people. If you steal the silver, we will track you down." And with a pat to my flaming cheek, Mad Maxine gently shoves me and Mrs. Scott out the door.

Safely outside, Mrs. Scott and I both take a few deep, cleansing breaths.

I try to think of something to say. "Well . . . she seems nice."

We look at each other, simultaneously sigh, and share our first real laugh together.

Chapter nine

DEAR MRS. SMARTLY,

It's me, Katie. I'm tied up in the Scott's basement. I haven't eaten for days, and there has been talk of feeding my withering carcass to the mammoth dog. Please don't blame yourself.

Okay, O Wise One, things are fine here. As fine as could be expected for being in a strange town, in the home of people you've known for only three days.

Today I had to go to church with the Scotts. It turns out someone "forgot" to tell me Mr. Scott is a pastor and the Mrs. is his secretary. The last time I was in a church was for some Bible school thing that a neighbor dragged me to. I was five. The Kool-Aid was watery, the cookies stale, and the teacher snapped at me for finger painting a mustache on Jesus.

Yeah, so church. Hmm. Interesting place. I like how it's acceptable in their religion to stare at me. All heads turned my way when I walked in with Mr. and Mrs. Scott. Their eyes stayed on me when we sat down together. And you better believe those churchies were watching me like eagles when the collection plate came my way. What do they think I'm gonna do, grab a handful of checks and make a break for the door?

We know I couldn't do that.

No one is gonna cash a two-party check to a sixteen-year old girl with no ID.

We sang some songs that were kind of lame. And then Mr. Scott got up at the podium and preached (why couldn't he be something normal, Mrs. Smartly, why? Like a doctor, a lawyer, or even one of those plumbers who show way too much backside?). Everyone seemed to really get into Mr. Scott's sermon. There were *amens* firing off all over the place. Then there was a time called an invitation, according to Mrs. Scott. That took forever. Come join the church! Come give your life to Jesus! Come pray at the altar! I think they should've passed out snacks during this portion of the service because I got a little hungry sitting there all that time. Maybe have a hotdog salesman come through the pews, like at baseball games.

But it gets worse. At the end of the service, Mr. Scott introduced me to the whole church and made me stand up there in front with him and Mrs. Scott. (Maybe we should've invited Rocky to the service.)

To add to the fun, everyone came up and shook my hand or hugged me. (Hugged me! Are you writing all of these things down in that file of yours?) I've never been so squished and shaken in all my life. I'd rather be yelled at for giving Jesus facial hair.

You and I will be discussing this church business soon, Mrs. Smartly. Isn't this infringing on my rights? My First Amendment rights? My Constitutional rights? My rights as a Texan? Didn't they fight over the Alamo to secure my right to choose? I choose to not go to church! Remember the Alamo! Okay, so maybe I have the wrong battle in mind, but there has got to be some historical event or law that backs me up. This was never part of the deal. But of course, neither was a drooling, two-hundred-pound dog, but we will address him another day.

So tomorrow is school. Can't wait. You have got to know I'm eaten up with excitement over Monday morning. You can't contain this kind of enthusiasm. This kind of spirit belongs on the Chihuahua cheerleading squad.

What if everyone hates me? What if someone shoves my head in a toilet and gives me a swirly?

Mrs. Smartly, I think I just want to come back. I don't think I can do this. Maybe tomorrow will be such a catastrophe they will send me back. You know deep in your heart you want us to be reunited.

Okay, maybe you don't, but I still would like to get out of here.

Did I mention Millie Scott has been pretty cool? You would like her. And frankly, she could teach you a thing or two about fashion. She knows it all. She has my wardrobe completely trendy. But I did find out for sure those cushy-soled lace up shoes you wear are definitely not in this year. Thought you should know in case you'd like to update. I say that because I look out for you, Mrs. Smartly.

Just like you should look out for me and get me out of here.

So Millie Scott is okay so far and has been sticking pretty close. But Mr. Scott (you know, the preacher), he doesn't really have too much to say to me. I guess he's just really busy, but we women know when we're getting the brush-off.

Well, I'm getting tired. This is more writing than I did all last year in school. I thought I should update you on everything though. I figured you'd probably had some sleepless nights, being worried about me and all, so I wanted to let you know how it was, and also let you know I can be packed and at the end of the driveway in two minutes and seven seconds. I've timed it.

I will let you know how my first day of school goes. If I survive it. I do have something special picked out to wear to school tomorrow. I want to make quite an impression.

Okay, so hugs and kisses to Trina and her knife set.

> Counting the seconds until I see
> your polyester dress again,
> *Katie Parker*

Chapter ten

MORNING. UGH. MY ALARM CLOCK is so loud it sounds like the town's tornado siren is in my room. I was awake most of the night. Again. I did a lot of tossing and turning, as well as a good amount of thinking and worrying. My first day at In Between High.

With a big sigh, I heave my body out of bed and grab my new fluffy pink robe. Maybe I could fake a fever? How hard would it be to conjure up a case of chicken pox? I think I could do a fine imitation of a whooping cough.

My slippers go *whish, whish* as I drag my feet across the hardwood floor to my closet. It's time to mentally prepare for my clothing selection for today. Ah, there's that white shirt with the cool sleeves that look so chic. And the short plaid skirt is just calling my name. *"Katie! Put me on, Katie! I show off your calves and accentuate your waist!"* Oh, and what about the jeans with the recognizable design on the pocket that just shouts *"Even though I was probably made by a five-year-old in a third-world country, I am ultra trendy and super expensive!"*

I run my hands along the rows of clothes hanging proudly in my closet. Not today, pretty things. There is work to be done. If my goal is to leave, it's time to kick start *Project: I Want to Go Back.* (Yeah, I know it's a lame name, but it was all I could come up with at 3:30 a.m.)

I bypass the many hangers of new clothes, move toward the back of the closet and pull out today's uniform. Black shirt, black skirt, and a black trench coat. I step over my new running shoes, my brown slingbacks, and the cutest leather sandals ever and pick up a sturdy, although mighty ugly pair of black lace-up boots.

In the bathroom adjoining my room, I quickly get dressed, hoping Mrs. Scott won't check on me before I get myself all ready. The look I am going with today is one you must take in all at once and not in stages.

I spend another twenty minutes crafting my hairstyle for my Monday premiere. I straighten my hair as flat as it will possibly go, so it falls limp and clings to my face. My bangs hang over my eyes like a curtain, and it isn't lost on me that I resemble a sheep dog. I hope I don't walk into walls or accidentally venture into the men's room with this hairdo. Reaching into my cosmetic bag, I take out some purple cream hair tint, and run it through sections of my hair, creating a few obnoxiously bold stripes.

Now for the pièce de résistance. My makeup is my medium, my face the canvas. I paint black eye shadow over my eyelids, outlining with ebony kohl eyeliner, and adding layers of cakey, dark mascara. With a swipe of some extremely dark lipstick in a color somewhere between gross and disturbing, I survey my finished product.

I look absolutely horrible.

The boys will not be flocking to this girl. But that's okay. I am not here to think about boys. The plan is to get out of this Taco-Bell-less town. Today I am Goth Girl. Like a superhero gone bad, I will roam the halls, looking for people to intimidate and striking a scary pose here and there.

When Millie and James Scott see this, they will be so scared they will have me packed up before my spiked dog collar is fastened.

"Katie! Time for breakfast! Are you awake?"

Speaking of the wonder parents, there's my cue. For a second I hesitate. Would it be so bad to roll with it and play nice? I could have all those clothes and a home for a while. But I know it's only a matter of time before they change their minds and send me back anyway. I've heard all sorts of horror stories from girls at the home—girls who are moved from one foster home to another, never allowed to stay in one place. Yeah, well, not Katie Parker. I won't travel from town to town like some sort of concert roadie. (Unless I could actually be a concert roadie. Totally different.)

My boots make loud thuds on the stairs as I charge down to the kitchen. Propelling off the last step, I hold back on my impulse to yell out "ta-da!" and land right in the doorway of the room. Smack in front of the awaiting Scotts.

Mrs. Scott's mouth opens, and her coffee mug hangs midsip.

Mr. Scott squeezes his eyes shut then opens them again.

Rocky yelps and scampers behind Mr. Scott, peeking between his legs.

Mrs. Scott clears her throat. "Um, Katie . . . "

"Yes, Mrs. Scott?" I fasten the last buckle on the dog collar. Ouch, how do people wear these things?

"I . . . um . . . " My foster mom takes one more absorbing glance at me then shakes her head, as if to clear the new Queen-of-the-Night-Katie image out of her brain.

"Katie." Now her voice is back to normal. Now that's not right.

"First of all, you must call us by our first names. We're going to be spending a lot of time together, so no need for formalities. And second . . . "

Yes? Here is comes. The yelling. The disappointment. The realization I'm too much for you.

"Do you want sausage or bacon with your waffles?"

What? Sausage or bacon? You're supposed to tell me I can't wear this; and then I will yell back, oh yes I can; and then you will call Mrs. Smartly and tell her to come and pick her goth kid up!

I take a deep breath. (Wow, it really does smell awesome in here. Those waffles must have blueberries in them.) Okay, this isn't working. Time to kick it up a notch.

"Oh, I don't care which. Bacon or sausage, it all comes from the pig. The dead pig. Death . . . that's so cool."

Mr. Scott raises a single eyebrow. "Death is cool?"

"Yes, death. I write poetry about it all the time. My people celebrate it."

"Your people?"

Drat. Mrs. Scott doesn't look scared, only confused.

"I'm what you call goth. See, my people know life is just a celebration of loneliness, heartache, darkness, and . . . " Think! Think of another adjective! "Other dark things."

Mrs. Scott plops bacon *and* sausage on my plate. She fills my glass with grape juice, which I grab like an inspiration piece.

"This grape juice—I like it. It resembles blood, like the blood that seeps out of our souls during a lifetime of wandering and searching." I have no idea what I said, but I'm losing my grip on this situation. Mr. Scott is back to reading his paper, and Mrs. Scott returns to the kitchen counter to cut some fruit.

"Well, maybe you can do some searching at school today. Like searching for your classes and searching for some new friends." Mr. Scott doesn't even drop the sports section when he says this. Hello, at least look at me when you are brushing me off.

"I don't need friends. Loneliness and pain are my friends."

Wow, these waffles are excellent.

No! Focus, Katie! Focus!

"Katie, where is all of this coming from? This is the first I've heard of any interest in the Gothic and, um, dark."

Mrs. Scott cuts a grapefruit into sections and carries it over to her husband. I would swear the two exchanged a look. You know, a meaningful look. And not the kind that says, "You get the car. I'll get her bags."

"Mrs. Smartly told me to behave or I'd be sent back. So I tried to be on good behavior these last few days. But I just can't deny who I am any longer. This"—I sweep my hand over my black garb—"is who I am. It's what I am. When we deny who we are, we . . . aren't who we . . . really, uh, are."

This is not how the script in my head went at four o'clock this morning.

And now to close the deal. "So, Mrs. Scott, I—"

"It's Millie."

"What?"

"Call us by our first names."

"Uh-huh." Whatever. "Well, as I was saying, I guess now that you know the dark, dark truth, you'll want to send me back. I'm sorry this didn't work out, Mr. and Mrs., er, I mean James and Millie."

"Katie, we have no intention of sending you anywhere. We're here for you, and we support you."

No, you don't! You can't! *Project: I Want to Go Back* is disintegrating right in front of me, faster than Rocky can make bacon disappear.

"Okay, now go get your jacket and let's get you to school!"

Millie grabs my shoulders in a brief hug and heads toward the living room.

"Right." That went well.

"Oh, and Katie?" My foster mom stops at the edge of the kitchen, the morning sun accenting her perfect highlights.

"Yes?"

"You have lipstick on your teeth."

Chapter eleven

"KATIE, WE'VE SAT HERE FOR five minutes. You don't want to be late on your first day, do you?"

Millie Scott pats my knee as we sit in the car outside my new school. Do I want to be late? No, I want to be absent. There was no way to get out of wearing this black monstrosity I just had to call an outfit this morning, so I'm stuck looking like a vampire wannabe. Add that to the list of reasons I want to hurl.

When I walk through those doors I will become two things: the new kid and a Chihuahua. Neither prospect pleases me. On the short drive to school, Millie wouldn't hear of my ideas for her to homeschool me. I even offered to go to military school. Mrs. Scott is a big supporter of public education. How fortunate for me.

I taste my defeat. "Okay, let's go."

We exit the car, but not before I trip over my own feet. I just *had* to wear the combat boots. I right myself in time to see about twenty-five kids hanging out outside the building.

Staring.

At me.

"It's going to be fine," Millie places a hand on my back and guides me into the building.

"WELL, MISS PARKER, YOU come with quite a personal file. Light on academic achievement and heavy on the behavior issues," the counselor says sharply, as Millie and I take a seat.

It's true. I have quite the rap sheet. But mostly it's instances of being with the wrong crowd at the wrong time. I don't really cause trouble, but it seems like the people I choose to hang out with do. Kids like me, kids who have been tossed around some, we just want to be accepted. And who is the most accepting group on a school campus? The troublemakers. It may not be right, but sometimes it's as close to right as we can find. But as Mrs. Whipple, the counselor, pointed out, it doesn't make for an impressive personal file. (But it does make for good reading.)

"We do not tolerate misbehavior at In Between High, Miss Parker. Understand that right now." Mrs. Whipple glares at me over harsh bifocals.

Millie tenses beside me. "Mrs. Whipple." My foster mom scoots to the edge of her seat, her posture like that of a cat on the verge of a good pounce. "Katie Parker has traveled a long way, geographically and emotionally, to get here. She starts today with a clean slate and without any judgment placed upon her, no matter what her personal file says. Are we clear?"

Mrs. Whipple and I both turn to stare at Millie in stunned silence. My black mouth forms an *O*. Millie Scott is coming to my defense?

"Mrs. Scott, please understand it is my job to make sure Katie is clear on our rules and most important, our expectations. We run a tight ship here at In Between High, and we want all of our

Chihuahuas to be as safe and successful as possible."

There's a quote for the yearbook.

Millie reaches over and grabs my hand, her glossy, manicured nails a stark contrast to my black nail polish.

"We all want that for our children. But I want Katie to know she is supported here. I want her to begin at this high school with every opportunity to succeed. No labels, no preconceived ideas. Katie is a beautiful, intelligent girl, and she is not here to cause any trouble or be a disturbance." Millie gives my hand a squeeze. And I don't even mind.

Mrs. Whipple takes a slow perusal of my attire, her buzzard-like eyes absorbing every black detail. Yeah, okay, so my outfit is a disturbance. A fashion disturbance.

Mrs. Whipple clears her throat. "Well, of course, we will do everything to make sure Katie is acclimated to our school. I am here to help. But that doesn't change the fact that Katie comes with a list of past offenses. Like this one, 'food fight in the cafeteria.'"

I remember that one. I learned a lot that day. Like it's dumb to tell the principal you were involved just to get the real instigators to like you. I also learned that if you are going to have a food fight, pick chicken-nugget day. Not meatloaf Monday.

"And it says here that in the eighth grade you and a group of kids were caught throwing water balloons off the top of the school building and hitting students."

In my defense, Luke Hardy told me we were getting an early start on our science project. Lessons learned that day: Luke Hardy lies—he has never gotten an early start on any school project ever (or ever turned one in, for that matter)—and should a water balloon happen to drop from your hands while you're on the roof of the school, make sure the principal's son isn't standing directly beneath you.

"At the end of the seventh grade you were sent to the office for turning a bird loose in class."

Now *that* one I did. I will defend that action until my last breath. Mr. Feathers, our class pet, wasn't happy in that cage. He was sad and he never sang. So I set him free. Of course, I didn't realize he wouldn't know the window I left open for him was his exit. Is it really my fault he dive-bombed the room for thirty minutes before he finally found the window? I've taken a lot of heat for Mr. Feathers. He owes me big.

Does Millie know the full extent of all my misdeeds? Maybe after having all of my dirty laundry aired in front of her, she will go home and convince Mr. Scott I need a one-way Greyhound ticket back to Iola Smartly and the girls. I sneak a look at my foster mom, but she isn't paying attention to me. Her eyes are fixed on the counselor, and she looks mad again. This really is interesting.

"And I see here last April you were among a group of students who—"

"That will be quite enough, thank you, Mrs. Whipple. I am sure you will give Katie every benefit of the doubt. You and I don't know the circumstances surrounding each of those items you so graciously regaled us with, so neither of us will hold that against Katie, correct? I have every confidence you will be fair and open minded and reserve all judgment on Katie Parker unless she actually does something to deserve any harsh opinions. Now, if you could go over her schedule for this semester, Katie is ready to get her day started."

Millie rolls her shoulders back and her small chin lifts. My new foster mom is not one to be trifled with. And she took up for me. I don't know if she meant any of it, but she sure sounded sincere. And mad! For me—she was mad. And she wasn't disappointed because of my rap sheet.

I must be in a parallel universe. These things just don't happen in my world.

Mrs. Whipple prints a draft of my schedule. I have a full load. All core classes, except for one elective, which I get to choose.

"There's band, basketball, debate, newspaper, drama, choir. What are your interests, Katie?" Millie reads off more choices from a pamphlet.

My interests? Well, I like to eat. I'm interested in clean clothes. Recently, at Sunny Haven, I've been into self-defense. I've been so busy majoring in survival the past few years I really haven't gotten to broaden my list of hobbies.

"How about we put you in band? Have you ever wanted to play an instrument? Our band director can turn anyone into a musician. I think that would be very good for you."

Millie looks so pleased with this idea that I find myself nodding. I mean, come on, the woman really went to bat for me today. I would probably agree to rappelling off the water tower for her right now.

So, band it is. I guess I will be a marching Chihuahua.

"Band. Very well. We have an excellent music program at In Between High." Mrs. Whipple picks a piece of lint off her *Educators Are Sew Loved* quilted vest, then prints out the final draft of my schedule.

"I have another meeting to go to, but I've arranged for a student peer helper to show you around, Katie."

Mrs. Whipple's gaze is fixed on me. Her expression says, "I know your type. You will be in the principal's office before the week is over, and I will be waiting." Maybe she just needs one of Millie's big hugs.

"Mrs. Scott, thank you for coming in. I hope Katie finds In Between High to be just the place for her." The counselor's face isn't the least bit convincing. She should take drama as her elective.

"I don't see any reason why she wouldn't."

My nonMom hugs me, then gives me a one last pep talk before she heads for the door.

"Bye, Millie." And like she did, I squeeze her hand, making a lame attempt to communicate my appreciation.

Millie winks in reply.

"Good-bye, Mrs. Scott."

"Yes, good-bye, Mrs. Whipple. I'll see you in church Sunday."

The door shuts behind Millie.

Mrs. Whipple lowers her bifocals. "Young lady, my eyes will be on you."

Ew, sounds painful.

With a growl, the counselor heaves herself from her chair. "I'm late for a meeting. Your peer helper will be here shortly. Don't steal anything."

Like a personality? For you?

"I smell trouble on you." She yanks the door open. "I dare you to prove me wrong."

Chapter twelve

"WELCOME TO IN BETWEEN HIGH! I'm here to show you around."

A stunningly beautiful girl of some sort of Asian descent sticks her hand out like a well-trained used-car salesman.

I put my hand in hers, and she shakes it like she means it. I study her, taking note of her almond-shaped eyes alight with curiosity and interest, her flawless olive skin, her glossy raven hair (when it's that beautiful, you can't call it black), and her model-thin frame. If it weren't for the blatantly sincere kindness plastered all over her face, I'd have to dislike her immediately.

"You must be . . . " She scans a copy of my schedule. "Ah, yes, Katie Parker. Well, welcome Katie Parker. I'm Zhen Mei Vega. But you can call me Frances. Like you, I'm in the tenth grade. I am student council reporter, yearbook photographer, first chair flautist in band, though sometimes I play clarinet too; then I'm assistant editor of the school newspaper, secretary of the Future Scientists and Engineers of America, and Fellowship of Christian Athletes leader. I also run track, take piano lessons, and sing in our church choir. I'm sure we have lots in common."

The girl said that all in one breath, and of all the stellar accomplishments she listed, that impressed me the most. And no, even though there are plenty of options for me to choose from, we do not have anything in common.

"Oh, did I mention Spanish Club?"

"I don't think so. I kind of got lost after the band thing."

"Right. Well, let's take a look at this schedule. You'll have English with Ms. Dillon; she's in room 200. You've got biology with Mr. Hughes. It's in room 104, right by the cafeteria, which kinda gets gross during dissection time. Then there's PE with . . . "

Frances's voice becomes a buzz in my head as she gives me a commentary on all my classes, teachers, and room assignments. When she begins to walk down the hall, I follow. She is dressed in a funky T-shirt and skirt, and even though it looks like it might be her own creation, I think Millie the fashionista would approve.

The halls of In Between High could belong to any high school in America. Old tile and red lockers decorated with dents, graffiti, and padlocks abound. Event and club posters adorn the mostly beige walls. Trash cans are tucked in every corner. We pass the occasional fire alarm, which is a personal temptation of mine. Those things call my name. Ever since the first day of kindergarten when I spotted my first shiny red fire alarm, I've longed to pull down that handle and be personally responsible for sounding the hideous noise that follows. But in civics last year I learned pulling a fire alarm is against the law and can get you jail time. A little detention is one thing. A mug shot at age sixteen? Now that's another.

We arrive at the entrance to my first-hour class, which is English. I can't remember what my tour guide said about this teacher, but I've never minded English too much. When I want to be, I'm good at it. I can't solve for x to save my soul, but I can easily race through the pages of a book. And when you're left alone as much as I was, you need something to keep you company. Math? Not much of a companion.

"So, as I was saying, if you have any questions, just let me know. I'll meet you at your locker after your math class, and we can eat lunch together in the cafeteria. I'll show you how to get to the cafeteria and which foods to avoid."

Frances really takes this job seriously. I hate to hurt her feelings, but I'm not ready to eat lunch with a perfect stranger. She can't be too excited about it either. I've been in quite a few different schools and I have a strategic plan for the first week or two of lunch.

"Yeah, thanks, but I think I have lunch under control." I almost manage to look her in the eye when I say that.

"Oh, okay. Well, this is English. Ready or not, here we come!" And with that chirpy exclamation, Frances bursts into the room with me in tow. "Good morning, Ms. Dillon. This is Katie Parker. She's a new student."

Thirty pair of eyeballs shift in my direction. For the millionth time today, I am painfully aware of my poor clothing choices. Hi, I'm from the Addams family.

"Thank you, Frances. Welcome, Katie. Everyone, say hello to Katie Parker."

The teacher, Ms. Dillon, looks to be about twenty-five. She is like a younger version of Millie—thin, blonde, cute, and stylish. No quilted vests for this educator.

Ms. Dillon guides me to a seat and hands me a literature book. I flip through it, absorbing the pictures, recognizing some of the short stories. Kind of sad to get excited over a lit book.

Most of the students have gone back to their work, totally

dismissing me. Two classmates, a guy on my left and a girl two seats in front of me, do look over at me and nod or throw up a hand up in greeting. The girl has a purple Mohawk. And the guy is wearing my black skirt.

Ms. Dillon moves the class on to the next assignment, which is writing a haiku. I love those things. Five syllables in the first and third lines, seven in the second.

> I'm dressed like a goof.
> Where was the bathroom again?
> Can I skip PE?

AFTER ENGLISH, I FOLLOW Frances to World History. She drops me off at a vacant seat and promises I'll enjoy the class. Before Frances flutters off to her own seat, she hands me a map of the school to study up on. She enjoys her job as student peer way too much.

History ends up being an incredibly long period, taught by some guy named Mr. Patton, who should've retired about thirty years ago. I could hardly hear his lecture above the sound of his hearing aids whining and humming. I'm betting his notes on the Egyptian pyramids are pretty accurate. I mean, the old man was probably on the pharaoh's payroll.

Like my last school, In Between High runs on block scheduling, so my next class will be my last one before lunch. Frances waits by the door and falls in beside me as I leave history. She doesn't take Algebra II, being the brainiac she is, so I'm left to fend for myself in there. Algebra proves to be even more boring and tedious than history. I was aware of every single second. Math is so not my thing, and it doesn't help I've moved just enough to get thoroughly behind. I'd blame it on my mom, but nobody cares when it comes to those standardized end-of-course tests. There's a bubble for answers A, B, C, and D, but never a bubble to mark "I don't know the answer, but since Bobbie Ann Parker is my mother, you can't count it against me."

After an eternity passes, I hear the beautiful sound of the bell ringing for lunch.

Then I remember I told Frances not to worry about me.

Why did I do that? I could have at least let her show me to the cafeteria. I am a directional idiot—I get lost in my bedroom at the Scott's house. I don't remember where the cafeteria is!

Time to implement my "New School Lunch Strategy." I grab my backpack, which contains the lunch Millie packed, and head to find a quiet place to eat.

Chapter thirteen

THERE IS SOMETHING SO UNAPPETIZING about eating ravioli while perched on the lid of a public toilet.

And yet here I sit — Indian style, atop the best commode in the joint, napkin tucked into my collar, and a cool juice box balancing on the toilet paper holder. Millie packed my lunch — ravioli in this thing that keeps it warm all day, chips, carrot and celery sticks, a few chocolate chip cookies, and an apple.

So far this is a good place to hang out. No one has been in here in fifteen minutes. Even if they did come in, my feet aren't visible, and I'm eating so quietly they would never know I'm here.

Today has been rough, but not completely unbearable. Sure everyone stares at me like I'm weird, but by far, I'm not the biggest freak on campus. I would need many more tattoos and piercings to even be a contender. Once I considered getting a tattoo, but then I thought —

Creeeaaak!

Wait.

Was that the door?

Great. Someone's in here.

I hear the gurgle of the sink running, so it's probably safe to quickly get the apple out of my bag. Millie thinks a growing girl needs her fruit servings.

My backpack hangs by a hook on the back of the stall door. I'm just gonna grab it without letting my feet down—a small balancing act—but I've had practice.

Almost have it . . . just a little bit more to the left and . . .

Crash!

In a big production of arms, legs, a squirting juice box, and one falling backpack, I tumble onto the floor in a tangled heap.

Ow.

"Hello? Hello? Are you okay?"

That voice sounds familiar.

In fact, those shoes peeking under the door look familiar.

Frances Vega.

Maybe if I just sit here absolutely still, she'll go away.

"Is everything okay in there?"

I won't move so much as a black fingernail until she leaves.

"Well, hey, Katie."

And before I can say pass the toilet paper, Frances Vega's face appears over the top of the stall partition to my left.

Now that's just rude.

"Everything okay? I couldn't help but overhear your fall."

I would imagine the students in the next town heard my fall. I peer up at Frances, not really sure where to go from here. "Uh, yeah, I'm okay. You know, checking things out, making sure the floor is clean and all the sanitation codes are being met." I brush the carrots off my skirt. "I don't want to get too invested in a school that's just going to be shut down by the health department."

"Really? Because it looks to me like you were having lunch in the john."

There's just no way out of this one, is there?

"I wanted some peace and quiet. I thought I might find it in here." Hint, hint. Go away.

"Did you get lost on the way to the cafeteria?"

"No, I didn't."

"Katie?"

It hasn't occurred to Frances we could come out of our respective stalls and have this conversation.

"Yes?"

"I know it's hard being the new kid at school."

Yes, it is. Really hard. And today has been stressful, and it feels like years before three o'clock will roll around, and you have no idea what it's like to be me.

Frances's face disappears, and I can hear her climb off her toilet seat. Now what?

Knock. Knock.

"Katie, it's Frances."

I swing the stall door open. "Of course it's you. I knew that!"

Frances blinks. "I was making a joke."

Great, now I've hurt her feelings.

"Look, I really appreciate all your help today. I do. I just wanted a little alone time. Thanks for checking up on me, but I think I'll get out of here and walk around a bit." And where will I go? I don't have the slightest idea.

"Great. I'll introduce you to some people. Come on."

I barely have time to zip my backpack before Frances is dragging me out of the ladies' room toward the cafeteria.

"You were smart to bring your lunch today. The cafeteria is serving chicken fried steak with gravy. You need to avoid anything they cover up with gravy and try to pass off as meat." Frances chatters away as the lunchroom comes into view.

There are lots of tables. And lots of kids.

We walk past rows and rows of students, but no one casts a welcoming glance in my direction. These are the moments I hate the most. I don't have to deal with the awkward new girl moments like where to sit and who to sit with if I eat lunch in the ladies' room. Granted, the bathroom doesn't score any points for aromatherapy, but you can't beat it for privacy.

Frances steers me toward a group of students who must be her friends, as they are waving and motioning to her. I'm probably walking into a meeting of the overachiever club.

My palms are starting to sweat. My dog collar is suddenly too tight. I can't hold a conversation with these people. If they are Frances's friends, their lunch-time conversation probably consists of playing Guess My Favorite Element on the Periodic Table, solving quadratic equations between bites of French fries, and debating which president had the strongest foreign policy.

I cannot hang out with these smart people. I must find an escape route. Oh, no, getting nearer. We're closing in on them.

Wait—

There's the guy in the skirt. And there's the girl with the Mohawk two tables over. The skirted one nods his head in greeting. That's as good as any invitation I'm gonna get.

Saved!

"Frances, I see people from class. Gotta go, bye." And with the world's fastest brush-off, I leave Frances Vega and practically run to the table where my fellow misfits are seated.

Mohawk girl salutes me with a fry. "Hey."

"Hey," echoes skirt boy.

"Hey," says some dude in a trench coat, his mouth full of nachos.

"Hey." This from skirt boy's overly tattooed girlfriend.

Alert the English department—these people are in desperate need of a thesaurus.

"Hi." I'm probably wowing them with my expanded vocabulary.

"You the new kid?" Mohawk girl checks out my hair.

"Yeah, I just moved here from upstate. I'm Katie. Katie Parker."

Mohawk girl nods. "I'm Angel. This is Vincent. She indicates the skirted friend. Angel introduces the whole table, and Jackson, the guy in the trench, gets me a chair.

"So what's your story, Katie?" asks a girl whose name I've already forgotten.

"Oh, you know, typical stuff. My mom's in prison, I'm currently in foster care, and I'm just passing through." See, I could be tactful and subtle with other people, but with this group, I know there's no need. The worse my story is, the more they'll like me.

"You have a rap sheet?"

"A rap sheet?" I think I know what they mean, but I'm hoping I don't. Do I have to have done time to get my membership card to this table?

"Yeah, you ever been arrested?"

"Um, no." The group doesn't look too impressed, but no one's asking for my chair back either.

"Me neither," one of them says finally, and three or four more chime in in agreement.

"You ever get in any trouble though?" Angel asks.

"Well, yeah. But nothing serious."

Okay, this is a weird conversation. Should I change the topic? Maybe ask them about their hobbies, where they live in town, who their favorite teacher is—what *they* think about foreign policy?

"You're gonna find out real quick this town's boring. Nothing to do here. You have to make up your own fun. You know what I'm saying?" Vincent strokes his bleached goatee.

"Yeah, I guess." No, not really.

"Tomorrow, you sit with us. We'll show you the ropes around here. Right, Angel?"

"Yeah, Vincent. We sit here every day, so we'll see you here."

The bell rings, signaling the end of lunch and the end of one uncomfortable discussion. Angel, Vincent, and their mismatched posse bid me goodbye and head off to their respective classes.

I'm still sitting at the table, reviewing the last ten minutes, when Frances taps me on the shoulder.

That girl is everywhere.

"Did you have a good lunch?"

"Sure."

"Great! Guess what time it is now?"

Time to pretend like she isn't getting on my nerves just a wee bit?

"I don't know."

"Time for PE!"

Physical education right after lunch? I assumed that was a typo on my schedule. What kind of madness *is* this?

Oh, well, I ate lunch on a toilet, nearly broke my neck falling on the floor, and was made to feel inferior by Vincent and Angel due to my lack of a criminal past.

It can't get any worse.

Chapter fourteen

"TODAY WE WILL BE DOING push-ups, pull-ups, squats, lunges, sprints, medicine ball passes, and, if you're lucky, line drills!"

My day just got worse.

"In honor of our new student, Katie Parker, we'll be starting with twenty-five extra push-ups! Get to it! Get to it! Nose to the floor!"

With a groan, I drop to the floor and do push-ups until I'm shaking.

Can't go much longer. My arms are Jell-O. Nineteen, twenty, twenty-one . . .

"I'm Coach Audrey Nelson, and I'm here to turn you into a lean, mean, athletic machine," a sinister voice whispers near my ear.

In my peripheral vision, I see Sergeant Evil squatting next to me, watching my progress—or lack of it.

"How you doin', new girl? You think you're ready for this class? Did you think PE meant you'd be walking laps around the gym? Did you?" Coach Nelson's voice escalates for all to hear, and if I weren't so intent on reminding myself to breathe, I would be embarrassed.

How many more? I spy girls to my left and right rolling over in defeat, clenching their abused arms. I will endure. I will out push-up these Chihuahuas.

Sweat is dripping off my face like rainwater, and my arms and shoulders are on fire.

Anything, I'll do anything to make this insanity stop.

"Twenty-five more, ladies!"

After another grueling set of push-ups, plus some pull-ups, crunches, squats, and other torturous activities, Coach Nelson blows her shiny whistle and demands we get into pairs. I'm so exhausted I just want to drape myself over the bleachers like a wet spaghetti noodle and wait for the feeling to come back into my arms and legs.

"Wanna pair up?"

Angel with the Mohawk. I was so busy burning off a year's worth of calories I didn't even notice she was in the class.

"Yeah, sure."

The whistle blows again, this time with a command for us to toss the medicine ball to one another. I don't know if I can. I think I left my arms back there at half court.

"Gimme twenty-five good ones, or we up it to fifty!"

Coach Nelson weaves through the pairs, assessing the quality of work.

"She's a sweetie," I say in a whoosh, as the ball is torpedoed into my hands.

"Today is Meltdown Monday. It's our hard day." Angel shares this tidbit in between the grunts and groans accompanying her attempt to stay upright.

"So Wednesday will be better?"

"Yeah, that's washed-up Wednesday. We do laps in the pool all period."

Oh, well, that sounds easy. Sure. Laps for ninety minutes. No problem.

I'm afraid to ask, but I must. "And Friday?"

"Fried Friday. The class is forty-five minutes long on Friday, and Coach Nelson devotes the entire time to abs. You won't be able to sit up until Sunday."

"Can't wait." I heave the ball to Angel.

"Gimme ten laps then head for the showers!" As if screaming her orders isn't enough, Coach Nelson blows the whistle hanging so proudly against her In Between Chihuahua polo.

As I'm entertaining visions of the coach choking on her Gatorade, Angel drags me along beside her, and we run our first lap around the gym.

"So what are you doing this weekend?"

"Uh . . . " I can hardly breathe. I think I'm going to die. I'm not going to make it. "I . . . uh, I guess nothing. Hanging out at the house." Inhale. Exhale.

"Some of us are going to get together Friday night and hang out. You should come with us."

I will be dead by then. Death by cardio. Overdose on strength training.

"Yeah, I'll check my schedule."

"Tomorrow, when you sit with us at lunch, you can get to know everyone."

"Sure. Thanks."

One. More. Lap.

"We'll fill you in about Friday night."

"Uh-huh." I meant to say "Thank you very much. That sounds

like a lot of fun, and I'm glad to have someone to eat lunch with," but I couldn't get enough air for all those words.

"Get those knees up! You sissies! I see you dragging! Who do you think you are? Do you think you can get away with that laziness? I want to see champions in my gym! Do you understand me? I'm training champions, not couch potatoes!"

Coach Psycho roars out a few more orders and insults. She is really wearing on me.

"She's harsh," I murmur to Angel as we finally approach the end of our last lap.

"Yeah, tell me about it."

"I think you like to run! I think you want me to tack on more laps! Okay, then, ten more laps! Get those knees up!"

No way.

"Can you believe her? She's evil. I hope she swallows that stupid whistle."

"Yeah," Angel replies heatedly. "I hope she trips over her Nikes and splits her khaki shorts."

"I hope her athletic socks cut off her circulation and her hairy legs turn purple."

This is fun.

Angel laughs. "Or I hope she develops a condition where she pees her pants every time she yells."

"Angel, five more laps for you! If you can talk, then you're not working hard enough! Do you hear me, girl?"

"She is such a drag," Angel says in between breaths.

"I'm talking to you! Did you hear what I said?"

"Yes, ma'am!"

Tweeeeeet! Tweeeeeet! Coach Nelson dismisses the rest of us to the showers.

As I'm contemplating the countless joys of showering in front of strangers, a frizzy haired girl I recognize from Algebra II class walks beside me.

"Mondays are hard, but it does get easier."

"Yeah, today . . . was . . . tough." I'm still trying to catch my breath.

"Just don't get on Coach Nelson's bad side, or it's even worse."

Worse? How can it be any worse? If today is a demonstration of how she treats those she likes, I'd hate to see the torture she reserves for her enemies.

"So Angel isn't one of Coach Nelson's favorites, I take it?"

"One of her favorites?" The girl laughs. "She's her daughter."

Chapter fifteen

"SO, HOW WAS YOUR DAY?"

This from Mr. Scott—er, James.

The three of us, James, Rocky, and yours truly, are sitting in the breakfast nook in the kitchen as Millie busies herself at the stove preparing dinner. We've been sitting in awkward silence for the past twenty minutes—me pretending to do my homework; Rocky gnawing on some rag doll that's had the life slobbered out of it; and Mr. Scott, who once again has his face in the paper, this time reading the stock report.

"Um, it was okay."

"That good, huh?"

And then this amazing thing happens. James puts the daily news down and looks at me—like he's really interested.

"Yeah, that good." I hate to ruin the moment and not give him any details, since he was participating in this conversation, but what am I supposed to tell him? Hey, James, today I wrote a haiku, met Frances Vega, who is the most perfect perky person in existence, sat through Algebra II with kids like me who have math issues, had history with a teacher who probably knew your Moses dude, ate lunch on a toilet, met Angel and her merry band of eccentrics, and put on five pounds of new muscle mass in a single class of PE. Good day.

"Who was your student buddy who showed you around today?" Millie stirs something on the stove that smells beyond good. I offered to help earlier, because it seemed the right thing to do, but she shooed me away.

"Her name is Frances Vega."

"Oh, Frances!" the Scotts sing in happy unison.

"She's wonderful, Katie. Don't you think Frances is wonderful, James?"

"Wonderful. Great, great kid."

Yeah, she's super duper. Spectacular. Fabulous.

And she's everything I'm not—good student, head of her class, well rounded, smart, sweet, good dresser, beautiful. Need I go on?

My two foster parents look at me, expecting me to comment on the golden child, Frances Vega.

"She was nice." That's all I'll give them.

"Katie, Frances would be a great friend. She goes to our church. She's very involved in the teen ministry. Right, James?" Millie pops a carrot in her mouth and begins to rinse her lettuce with vigor.

"Absolutely. Great girl."

Yes, I think we've already established that Frances is great. I guess it's going to be up to me to change the subject. "I also met another girl, Angel Nelson."

James clears his throat. He and the Mrs. exchange a look.

"Millie, is she Audrey Nelson's girl?"

Hmm, I'm not hearing the same enthusiasm here as I did for

Frances.

Millie stops chopping her lettuce. "I think so. Katie, is this girl Coach Nelson's daughter?"

"Yeah, she is. Funny thing—Angel and I were in PE today and this crazy coach is trying to kill us with squats and push-ups, right? So then we both start talking about . . . " The Scotts look a little serious. I don't think they're going to appreciate the punch line to this story. "Well, anyway, I found out Coach Nelson is Angel's mom." Never mind. I don't want to waste the irony on them.

"Does Angel still have the purple Mohawk?" James's voice is as dry as a saltine.

"Yeah? So what?" What is that supposed to mean, Preacher Man?

"James— "

"Does your church not accept people with purple hair?" It slips out before I can stop it.

James Scott's face turns a shade of pink. "Of course we do. We accept anyone, Katie, just like Christ did. I didn't mean that the way it sounded."

"He didn't mean it that way, honey," Millie soothes as she rips apart some spinach leaves.

"Is your God not into people with purple hair?" There I go again. I'm taking up for Angel Nelson and I don't even know her. But I know her type. Her type is my type, so James might as well be criticizing me.

"Katie, I'm sorry. I shouldn't have said that. God is into purple hair, yellow hair, no hair. I'm the one being judgmental here. It's just that Angel Nelson has been in and out of trouble in the last few years, and I'm slightly concerned with you spending time with her. And that has nothing to do with what the girl's hair looks like."

James takes off his glasses and cleans them with his shirt. He lays his hand over mine, which is resting on the loathsome algebra book.

"We just want you to be as safe as possible here and make good choices—especially in friends."

I'm oddly touched by James's fatherly gestures. This is the most attention he's paid to me since I've been here. Sometimes I don't even know if he remembers I'm here. You can't just order up a kid and then forget about her.

"Well, Angel seemed nice to me. It's hard to make friends, you know?" I'm laying down the sympathy card, I know.

"Oh, honey, of course it's hard to make friends at a new school. James, get the plates, would you?" Millie leaves her post in the kitchen and stands beside me. "Maybe Frances could introduce you to some people, too? She knows lots of kids around here."

Frances, Frances, Frances!

"Everybody needs a chance. Maybe you've underestimated Angel. Just because she's not president of every club at In Between High like your girl Frances doesn't mean she's going to be wearing prison stripes and making license plates before she's eighteen."

"Well, we never said she was prison bound. Really." Leaving me with one good eye roll, Millie is back to her salad preparations.

Time to get on their good side. I get up and grab glasses to set on the table. Four days here and I'm already proving myself useful, right? "So, anyway, Angel mentioned she and some of her friends were going to do something Friday night and I was invited. Cool, huh?"

"I don't know, Katie." Millie hesitates. "You've barely settled in here."

And here's where I work some Katie Parker magic. "I couldn't believe it when she invited me. I mean, me. New girl, you know?

I've just felt so lonely here, and to think this girl wants to be my friend. It's more than I could've hoped for."

"Give us some details. What would you be doing, going to her house? The movies? You know we're going to need a lot more information." James says all this in his best protective-father voice. That's not an immediate no, though.

"I'm not sure. She just mentioned it today. I'll find out. It's probably something like watching movies or, you know, hanging out—girl talk and all."

"We'll see." James does not look too convinced.

"Do you think because she has a Mohawk she'll probably want to go steal a car or spray paint the water tower?" Although spray paint to *that* water tower could only be an improvement.

"No, of course not."

"James and I are not that judgmental, Katie. Just find out more information and we'll talk about it, okay?"

Millie, I am finding, is the peacemaker. She just wants everyone to be happy and content. And to eat their vegetables.

"Now, let's eat. I've got spaghetti, French bread, corn, salad, and for dessert, my special chocolate mousse pie."

"Millie is famous for her spaghetti sauce, Katie."

"Oh, yeah?" It's gotta be pretty hard to beat the stuff out of the can if you ask me. Actually, I thought that's all there was. So you can make spaghetti sauce yourself? My mom really deprived me. Next they'll be telling me you can make pizza too.

"Yes, I won the blue ribbon at the county fair last year for best spaghetti sauce."

"And for best chili. Don't forget the chili."

We eat this prize-winning spaghetti and I hesitantly drink it all in—the conversation that's getting easier, the incredible food that didn't come out of the microwave or a box, and this feeling of being a part of something, even if it's temporary.

"Heard from Mother today." Millie says to her husband as we finish up dessert.

"Oh, and how is she?" James helps himself to seconds.

"Fine. She'll be home in a few days."

"A few days?"

"Yes, it was a very short cruise. Just a four-day trip, I think."

"More like the ship had to turn around and drop Maxine off for the sake of the other passengers," James cracks, with a wink at his wife. "Instead of motion sickness, they had Maxine sickness." He catches my eye. "Believe me, there's nothing you can take for that."

His face breaks into a sly smile, and I hear Millie's soft giggle. They're kind of cute like that. And so far it doesn't even nauseate me.

But other times I catch an undercurrent passing between them. Some sort of tension or something. I can't put my finger on it, but I feel like—I don't know. Like there are things Millie wants to say to James or vice versa, but they talk about other stuff instead—such as people at church, how dry the grass is, getting an oil change for the car, or blue-ribbon recipes. Okay, so I don't have it all figured out yet, and I can't really explain it, but I know I'm onto something here. It's not always giggles and jokes with Mr. and Mrs. Scott.

We begin to move to the living room when the phone rings. Millie heads for the phone as I zero in on my new favorite over-stuffed chair in front of the television. Maybe it's Mrs. Smartly calling for me. I can tell her about my first day.

"What do you want to watch, Katie? Are you a sports fan?"

I look at James like he's just asked me to kiss Rocky, and I'm about ready to fire off a comment about my distaste for all things sports when Millie's kitchen conversation interrupts.

"Hello? Hello? Are you there? Amy? Amy, can you hear me? It's Mom, Amy." And then a full minute of silence. "Amy, just tell me where you are. Can't you talk to me? Hello . . . ?"

Moments of nothing.

And Millie hangs up the phone.

James's eyes are glued on the TV, but he's not watching it, and he doesn't move a muscle. He doesn't go to Millie or make any effort to ask her about the call.

What is *this* about? Why would their daughter call and then not talk?

Maybe it's just one of those heavy-breather calls. Sometimes those are fun. Especially if you scream in the phone or blow a whistle like Coach Nelson's in the receiver. But clearly Millie didn't think that was a prank call. And from the way James and Millie reacted, this is not the first time this has happened—this phone call from Amy. Hmm, a mystery. What would those guys on CSI do?

"I'm going to take a bath and read upstairs." Millie calls from the kitchen, and I hear her make her way up the stairs.

Things are not all as they seem here in the Scott household, and I, Katie Parker, intend to get to the bottom of it.

Chapter sixteen

AH, ANOTHER GLORIOUS MORNING AT school. I survived my first biology class. It seems I got here just in time for pig dissection. Lucky me.

"Hey, Katie! Katie!"

Vincent's girlfriend and Angel are crossing the courtyard together. It's kind of nice having someone want to talk to you at school. Well, when that someone isn't hanging over the bathroom stall.

"What's up, Katie?" Angel high-fives me, and I nearly miss it. I didn't know we were at the high-fiving point in our relationship.

"Hey, the Scotts said I might be able to come over Friday night. They just wanted me to get the finer details." And they'll probably want to bug your house and run a surveillance operation while I'm there, if that's okay.

"The Scotts? Your foster parents?" Angel's friend stares at me.

"Yeah, James and Millie Scott."

"The preacher? Pastor Scott? You're living with a preacher?" Angel is totally unimpressed.

"Um, yeah." Why does her attitude bother me? "I requested Angelina Jolie, but she was all booked up."

It's like *I* can slam the Scotts, but they can't.

"Well, that is interesting." Angel looks at her friend, whose name I think might be Dawn or Donna or Destiny or something. "I'm having some girls over for a sleepover Friday night. Not much to say about it. It's all on the up and up. So, how about it?"

"Will your mom be home?" I know the Scotts will be checking. If Coach Freakazoid isn't going to be at home with us, I might as well not even ask to go.

"Well, yeah." Angel's snotty reply makes me feel stupid, but you never know. Not that I had friends over all the time back home, but if I had, there's a good chance Bobbie Ann Parker wouldn't have been home to greet them.

"So we're just going to hang out at your house?" I need information if I'm going to sell this to the Scotts. Those two will be like bloodhounds for the details.

"Sure. We do this all the time, don't we, Danielle?"

Danielle. I was so close.

"We're all about slumber parties, and we thought it would give you a chance to get to know the girls better." Danielle chimes in like a backup singer.

"Pizza, movies, gossip. You know, girl stuff."

Funny, I hadn't pegged Angel as the type to eat pizza and paint fingernails on a Friday night.

"Yeah, okay. I'll see what I can do. I'd better get to class." I don't tell them the class I'm nearly late for is band. They might take back their invitation.

"See you at lunch," Angel calls over her shoulder, and I head for my first band experience.

BAND IS A TOTAL flop. I can tell this is so not my thing. The band director stuck a trumpet in my hands and sent me out the door to learn the halftime show with the other Marching Chihuahuas. So far I've dropped the horn six times, stepped on the piccolo player, and I won't even go into what happened when I tried to get the spit out of my trumpet for the first time. Let's just say I haven't made any friends yet.

We are supposed to be doing this marching thing as we play. Since I can't play yet, I'm just holding my trumpet up and trying to get the routine down. It's really hard. Who knew band was so difficult? I'm really regretting making fun of these people.

The band plays their song, an old hit from the fifties, but the steps keep getting jumbled in my head. Maybe they could just let me freestyle? I can't seem to keep the beat. Maybe I'm beatless. Or beat illiterate. I mean, sure I can count to four, but my legs don't seem to be in sync with my brain. And then there's this fancy-schmancy turn thing we have to do. Okay, it's just a simple pivot to these professionals surrounding me, but I can't get it.

"Miss Parker! It's step two, three, and pivot and turn on four." The portly band director is trying with me, he really is. But every time he comes over and shows me the moves again, I get distracted by his bad comb-over. It would make Donald Trump jealous. Seriously. This man stands next to me, and I find myself mesmerized by the intricacies of his hair strands. Mr. Morton has really put some time and planning into his hair combing. Or hair arrangement, I should say. There are probably secret military strategies that don't attain the same level of difficulty as this guy's comb-over.

"Did you get that, Miss Parker?" Mr. Morton looks at me with a little less patience this time.

"Yes, sir. Pivot and turn on four."

"Right. Excellent. And make sure you keep your horn up, like you would if you were playing it." He smiles and returns to his post at the front of the band.

"One, two, ready, play!" And at the sweep of his arms, the band begins to play. I just kind of hum. Initially, Mr. Morton had me blowing into the trumpet, but when that only produced duck-calling noises, then later dying-moose noises, he politely asked me to stop trying.

"March, two, three, four! March, two, three, four!"

Oh, look, it's a grasshopper. I don't want to smash it. I'll just step over here a bit more to the left and—

"Oomph!"

Crash! Right into the trumpet player beside me, who falls backward into the percussion line behind him, who tumble over like dominos.

And I hadn't even gotten to the big turn yet.

"I'm sorry," I call out to the group around me. My face has to be flaming red.

Twenty marching Chihuahuas are staring at me. Hard.

Mr. Morton signals for the entire band to stop, and the rest of the group lower their horns and check out the ruckus. Oh, no.

"I'm so sorry. See, there was this grasshopper and . . . " From their expressions I can tell these band people are not going to be sympathetic to the plight of the insect life I just saved. "Okay, never mind. Sorry."

"Katie, maybe you should sit out today and just watch. Perhaps I threw you in too soon."

Oh, you think?

Mr. Morton sends me over to the sidelines. My career as a marching trumpet player is officially over.

"Hey, it's okay. It's your first day." Frances Vega, as in first-

chair-flute Frances, approaches me after class. I was so busy counting in my head and trying to stay upright I didn't notice her too
much in practice.

"Yeah, thanks. I think I'm not cut out for band."

"No, no! You don't know that! Don't give up yet, Katie. We
all have to start somewhere, and I think you did well for your first
day. Maybe you can get some private lessons when you decide for
sure what instrument you want, and you'll be marching and playing with us in no time!"

Frances looks so hopeful. Is there anything she's not positive
about? I just took out the entire drum line, and she's telling me she
thinks I had a successful first day?

"Hey, want to join me and my friends for lunch? We're heading to the caf right now."

You have to admire Frances for her persistence.

"No. But thanks, Frances." And I do mean it. I do appreciate
her trying. No one has ever made this much effort to make me feel
welcome at a school before. "I'm going to sit with Angel Nelson
today."

"Oh."

Just "oh."

I think I just found something Super Teen Frances isn't keen
on: Angel. These people around here are so shortsighted! Just
because someone looks like a troublemaker doesn't mean she is.
You don't see me breaking into the Piggly Wiggly in my spare
time, do you?

"Well, I'd better go. I'll see you later."

"Wait, Katie." Frances stops me. "Are you going to church
Wednesday night?" She pushes her shiny, model-quality hair out
of her face. "Pastor Scott may have already told you, but we have
something called Target Teen. There's a time of worship, the youth

pastor teaches, and then we just hang out."

"No."

"It's lots of fun."

For who? The people who call *that* fun are probably the same weirdos who would enjoy PE—Coach Nelson style.

"The Scotts haven't said anything about it, and it really doesn't sound like something I'd be into."

Things I'm currently not into: vacationing in the Middle East, being attacked by brain-sucking aliens, the planet blowing up in a fiery inferno, and spending a few hours at church with the local youth.

Frances opens her mouth, clearly not done with her pitch. Time to hustle out of here.

"See you later."

And I do a perfect pivot and turn on the count of four.

Chapter seventeen

"MOTHER, SIT DOWN. YOU'RE NOT having dessert first."

Maxine rolls her eyes like a thirteen-year-old and sits herself back down in the chair at the table. "Just admiring the broccoli," she mumbles.

My foster grandmother has returned from her cruise, tanned and with a suitcase full of stories and incredibly tacky souvenirs. Millie decided to celebrate her safe return (translation: the fact that they didn't throw her overboard) with a family dinner. Tonight's selection is shrimp and steak, compliments of James at the grill. I notice he's still out tending to the grill, even though he brought the food in about fifteen minutes ago. He must be cleaning that grill really good. Or he's afraid he'll have to try on his *Caribbean Cutie* T-shirt.

"We had shrimp on the cruise. It was simply marvelous. There's nothing like Caribbean shrimp, I always say."

Millie winks at me as she gets up and heads to the back patio, where her husband was last seen.

Wait a minute. Where does she think she's going? She can't

leave me alone with her mother. Is she mad? I can't talk to this woman. I accidentally got stuck on the phone with her right before she left for her cruise, and she went on for ten minutes straight about the importance of exfoliation before I threw the phone to Millie like a hot potato.

Maxine taps her long red nails on the table, beating out a rhythm that would make Mr. Morton proud. The clock in the kitchen ticks loudly. The refrigerator hums and whirs. I hear the answer and call of crickets outside. Bullfrogs croak, and a distant bird chirps.

Oh, for crying out loud, I can't take it!

Fine. I'll break the awkward silence!

"So . . . the Caribbean, huh?"

Maxine's eyes zero in on me, and she looks at me like she's just noticed I'm in the room—never mind the fact that I'm sitting right next to her.

"Who are your people, Katie Parker?" Her voice is raspy and reminds me of a jazz singer I learned about in Music Appreciation last year.

"My people? Um, the poor kind?"

"Don't try your sass on me, Sweet Pea."

I look around the room. No Millie in sight. I'd even settle for James. I'd really be up for some ESPN right about now.

"I meant where did you come from?"

"Didn't Millie tell you I'm from a girl's home upstate?" What does she want here, my social security number and prints for a background check?

"Where's your mama?"

Oh, I love this question. Well, who cares? I'm just gonna give her the truth. I'm sure she knows it anyway, and she's making me spill all this for torture purposes. I have a feeling she likes inflicting pain. Well, Maxine, you scab picker, you asked for it.

"My mama's in prison. Not jail, prison. She sold drugs and got busted by an undercover cop. It wasn't her first offense, so she'll be gone for a long, long time. She left me alone in our two bedroom trailer house most nights, so I learned to fend for myself. You learn a lot of stuff on your own." I give her a meaningful look that speaks volumes. Volumes of what, I don't know, but I hope it's intimidating.

Fear this, Grandma.

Maxine laughs, the sound rusty and deep in her throat. "Girl, let's get one thing straight right here and now. You're not so tough. If you can think it, I've done it. I lived a life before I married Mr. Simmons that would probably make your momma look like a choir girl. It's by the GOG I'm here, baby, the GOG." She nods once.

Do I even ask?

"The GOG?"

Maxine leans in close, our noses almost touching. "The grace of God. You know what I'm saying?"

Now I roll my eyes. "No, I don't." I cross my arms. I am sick of all this God talk.

"Sweet Pea, you can't outrun him, so you might as well not even try."

Oh, great. Now Grandma is going to talk in code. Perfect. I've read fortune cookies that made more sense. "I really don't intend to run anywhere, Mrs. Simmons." Except upstairs to my room—away from you.

"No, you're running. I know that look. I've lived it. He'll get your attention one way or another."

Oh, Millie. Where are you? Isn't our food getting cold?

"Look, Mrs. Simmons, I don't mean to be disrespectful—"

Maxine throws her yellow-blonde head back and laughs like I've just delivered the best punch line ever.

"I don't mean to be disrespectful, but I'm here and that's all I know. I'll admit, when I first got here, I did come up with a few ideas to blow this town, but right now, I'm staying. If you'd seen me in PE today you'd know I'm not exactly someone whose gift is running, so I plan to stick this out as long as I can . . . or until I'm sent back."

"Well, maybe I see someone who's out to prove something. You can't escape who you are, Katie Parker."

Maxine's eyes bore into mine. This woman is the queen of uncomfortable moments.

"Who I am? You think because my mom ended up in prison, it's just a matter of time before that's where I'll be? So that's who I am?" My voice punches with sarcasm, but the tears are building, pushing at my eyes. Who does this woman think she is? I'm getting life coaching from a nearly eighty-year-old woman wearing flip flops, a tank top, and a skirt that looks like a bunch of palm trees attacked it?

She sniffs. "Is that what I said?"

"Here we are! Who's hungry?" Millie and James Scott breeze in, and Mad Maxine quits her crazy talk. I inhale deeply and get up to refill my tea glass. And to put some space between me and Chief Speaks Riddles.

"I think everything's still warm. Fill your plates everyone."

While I'm not excited to dine with the Caribbean goddess, I am interested in the food. Steak wasn't a regular feature on the menu in the Parker house, and I've never even had shrimp before. What exactly is shrimp? And where are their heads?

"So Katie, you were telling us you found out more about Angel's sleepover?"

I smile at Millie, I'm so grateful for a new topic. One that doesn't make me feel like I'm a prime candidate for America's Most Wanted. "Yeah, so like I said, her mom is gonna be home."

"Yes, I called Audrey Nelson."

Did I see that one coming or what?

"You're going to spend the night with Audrey Nelson's girl?" This from the grandmother I never asked for.

Millie answers for me. "Yes, mother."

"That girl is trouble."

And I'm mad all over again. "Why? Because she looks different? Because of her hair?"

Maxine looks at me like I'm the one who's mental. "Who cares about her hair? Millie, are you sure about this?"

This woman better not blow it for me.

"Do you think Katie's been here long enough to let her go out with friends?"

"Maybe Millie and James have decided to trust me, Mrs. Simmons. And maybe they've decided not to pass judgment on Angel Nelson, too. What's wrong with that? You don't even know Angel."

"Oh, pipe down. I've known Angel since she was in bloomers in my Sunday school class, kicking shins and pulling hair. Believe me, I know that child."

"Forget it."

I throw down my napkin and charge up the stairs. Millie calls out for me, but I keep going until I reach my bedroom, slamming the door behind me. A little dramatic, yes, but as a teenager, it's my prerogative to slam doors. It's one of the few perks. I'd give it up for clear skin any day.

Knock. Knock.

Sigh. I'm betting it's not Maxine, ready to apologize.

And if I'm a sweet pea, what does that make her? Something in the prune family, I'm sure.

"Katie—"

The door opens and James and Millie walk in. Millie sits beside me on the bed, where I'm flipping through a *Teen Vogue* magazine with a lot of gusto. Page twenty-three, "Ten Things You Never Knew About Boys" . . .

"Katie, you just have to take Maxine in stride. You can't let her get to you."

"James is right. And he would know." Millie smiles.

"She preys on weakness," James says under his breath.

Millie clears her throat. "Katie, we've decided to let you spend the night with Angel and her friends."

Page twenty-four, "Sassy Skirts for Dreamy Dates." Page twenty-five—

Wait, what?

"I can go?" I drop the magazine.

"Yes. You can. But we're giving you my cell phone, and you are to call us if you need anything or if you want us to pick you up. Do you understand?" Millie's hand hesitates before she smooths the bangs from my face, like she's waiting for me to swat her hand away.

"I understand."

James has his serious face on. "The reality is, Katie, we haven't known you even a week yet. We are going to trust you to behave in a manner we would be proud of. And we hope Angel and her friends will do the same. But should something go wrong, you are to call. Got it?"

"Yes, sir." This is so awesome. My first sleepover! My first friends at In Between High! "There's not going to be any trouble. You'll see. This is going to be so great!"

Chapter eighteen

"PSSST! KATIE, WAKE UP."

I am rudely jostled awake by Angel, who apparently doesn't realize how much I value my beauty sleep. "What time is it?"

It's pitch black in the Nelson living room, where Angel, Danielle, and few other girls and I are camped out.

"It's 3:30. Come on, get up."

"We just went to bed." I roll over, desperate to get away from the little flashlight Angel is so rudely shining in my face.

"Come on, Vincent will be here any minute. We've got to get dressed."

What?

"Angel, what are you talking about?" I pull the sleeping bag over my head, give the zipper a yank, and cocoon myself in.

"Fun. That's what I'm talking about. We're gonna go out for a little bit. Come on, you don't want to miss this." Angel tugs on my sleeping bag.

"Yeah, actually I think I do."

"Look, if you're not mature enough to hang with us, then you shouldn't have come." This from Danielle.

"I'm not coming out of this sleeping bag until you tell me what we're doing." Or until I'm out of air. I think I'm in one of those sleeping bags you take with you when you're climbing Mount Everest or sleeping in an igloo.

"We're gonna visit a haunted theatre."

"A haunted theatre? You woke me up to see a ghost who's into show tunes?"

"What's the matter, are you scared?"

"I'm not breaking into any theatre, Angel."

"We wouldn't be breaking in. It's an abandoned building. Girls, I think she's scared."

"I am not scared."

"Really? Then maybe you're just too good for us then, huh? I thought you were one of us." I hear Angel stand up.

I unzip my sleeping bag and sit straight up. "Look, I don't think I'm too good for anybody, and I'm not scared." Scared of what my hair looks like, maybe. I have horrible bed head. I usually wake up looking like I slept in a wind tunnel.

"Then get dressed. We'll just be out an hour or so. We'll be back before our sleeping bags get cold." Angel, I notice, is already dressed. She's wearing jeans and a black T-shirt.

"Look, Angel, this doesn't sound good. I promised the Scotts I wouldn't get in any trouble." And nothing good can come from going out with the kind of bed head I get.

"There isn't going to be any trouble." Angel tosses my jacket at me. "Everyone in town visits the old haunted theatre. It's like a rite of passage. You should be grateful that we're showing it to you. But maybe you don't belong here. Maybe you don't belong with us."

"Everyone does this?"

"Everyone." Danielle pulls on her jeans. "I don't know what

you're afraid of. We'll go, we'll check it out, and we'll come back. No big deal."

I catch the sting in her voice, and it bothers me. No one has ever accused me of being a baby. "And you're sure this is a well-known thing to do in town? Nobody is gonna think anything of us being in the theatre?"

Angel hands me my jeans and shirt. "I can't believe you haven't heard of it yet, Katie. Everybody knows about it. Seriously. Just get dressed. It's totally cool."

"Well, if it's so cool then why are we sneaking out of your house at 3:30 in the morning to see it?"

"Because supposedly this ghost guy only comes out after dark, that's why. And my mom doesn't care if we go or not, as long as we leave her alone."

I believe Angel about the last part. Coach Nelson had been upstairs in her room during the entire sleepover. I saw her maybe once, and all she did was yell at us to turn down the TV during our horror movie marathon. She didn't seem too interested in anything Angel had going on.

"Katie, we're going. You can stay here or you can go with us. We thought you'd feel grateful we included you, but whatever." And with that, Angel, Danielle, and three other girls I had met that night file out the door, leaving me standing in the middle of the living room.

"I guess this is what we get for trying to be your friend," Danielle says in parting, pulling the door shut.

Well.

This is awkward.

Grabbing my shoes and the phone the Scotts gave me, I run out the door and race to the waiting car.

"Come on, Katie! Get in!" Vincent is holding open the

door to his Honda Civic. The spinners on the wheels reflect the streetlights.

Here goes nothing.

We drive for about five minutes. Five very uncomfortable minutes. Vincent is a smoker. A generous one—he shares his lit cigarette with nearly everyone in the car. I decline. There are a lot of ways I don't fit the poor-orphaned-girl stereotype, and this is definitely one of them. Don't these people ever listen in health class? Don't they know what's in those things? Ugh. I'm not inhaling asbestos and antifreeze, thank you very much. Well, actually right now, I am inhaling them, but not by choice.

Besides the air being contaminated in here, my rear end is asleep. The Civic is one small car, and somehow there are seven of us in here. We're all packed in like sardines, completely disregarding the seat-belt laws. In fact, I'm pretty sure one of the seat belts is wedged tightly in my backside. Ow.

The car slows and Vincent turns his headlights off. "We're here. Everybody out."

Vincent directs everyone out of the car and toward the structure I assume is the theatre. I'm already a little creeped out.

While everyone runs around to the back of the building, I stand still out front, rooted to the spot. I shine the flashlight I was given on the front, illuminating large wooden doors, a glass box office trimmed in brass, and an old-time marquis at the tip-top that says "Valiant" in Art Deco letters. I don't want to look away; it's so pretty. This isn't creepy; it's cool. I run my hands over the glass panes of the box office and imagine someone taking money from a flapper or a dude in a fancy hat. This theatre has seen a lot of years. I wonder if anybody famous has ever been here.

"Katie!"

Angel.

I heave a sigh. I guess I can admire the architecture later. Maybe in the daylight like a normal person.

"Come on, we don't have all night."

She grabs me by the jacket sleeve, and we run around the building to where the others disappeared. Angel points to a window above us. "Come on, give me a boost, then me and Vinnie'll pull you in."

"What? I thought we weren't breaking in? This doesn't seem right."

"Would you relax? You're being such a whiner you're embarrassing me. Quit making this a big deal. This is just the easiest way to get in. Now put your hands like this so you can lift me up." Angel interlocks her fingers and motions for me to do the same.

Fine. The sooner we do this, the sooner we can get back to the house.

Angel goes up and over with no problem. Now it's my turn. Vincent and Angel both appear in the window. I jump up, arms raised; they each grab an arm (a little roughly I might add), and I'm jerked through the window, my knees scraping and bumping the wall.

Inside, I see the glow of seven other flashlights as the others have already gotten to the business of looking for this legendary spirit. "So, how do we find this ghost?"

It's like I've stepped back in time. Old velvet curtains drape from the ceiling over the stage area. Accents of brass line the stage and the trim above it. There are seating boxes suspended off the far walls, a few on either side of the stage, and I imagine that's where the wealthy or the town dignitaries would have watched the performances. Old lights hang from the top of the stage, many of them rusty and broken.

Vincent comes to stand by me. "What are you talking about?

What ghost?"

I look at Vincent.

Vincent looks at Angel.

"I told Katie about how everyone comes to see the ghost who haunts this place. You know, it's like a tradition. And we didn't want Katie to miss out on it. I knew it would make her feel like she's really part of In Between."

Vincent and Angel continue to talk, their voices becoming inaudible as I walk toward center stage and discover the orchestra pit. A real orchestra pit. Like in *Phantom of the Opera*. This is so completely amazing.

"You can go down there, you know." Angel's voice startles me as I peer down into the pit.

"You scared me."

"I said you can go down there. There's a door off to the left of the stage. It will take you to some stairs that go underneath the stage to the pit. It's pretty cool."

"Want to go with me?"

"Nah, I've seen it hundreds of times. You should go check it out."

"Yeah, maybe later."

"Scared?" Angel's taunts are getting a little old.

"No, I'm not scared. I'll go down there. It's no big deal. You go find your ghost." I stomp off toward the stage and find the door that must lead to the orchestra pit.

The sign on it that said *Orchestra Pit* was a big help.

The door creaks open, and I shine my light down a set of stairs. I ease onto the first one and let go of the door, and the spring slams it shut. I check my pocket for the cell phone just in case Vincent's gang decides to get cute and lock me in here, then carefully make my way down the wooden steps. Turning a corner, I find the opening to the pit and go in.

There's not much down here. A few old chairs, some yellowed sheet music, dated 1946, and a couple of beat-up music stands.

I move in closer to see if I can find anything else when I hear it. A sound that doesn't belong. And it's definitely not a ghostly sound.

A hammer.

I yell out the pit opening. "Hey, what's going on?"

Nothing. Just more hammering. Then laughing.

Maybe they *did* find the ghost, and they're doing some arts and crafts projects with him.

At the sound of breaking glass, I'm alarmed. This is definitely not good. Now I hear a symphony above of breaking glass, curtains being ripped, the unmistakable hiss of spray paint, and the crash of unidentifiable things being thrown.

My heart pounding, I race up the steps and pull on the door. It won't budge.

Propping my foot on the door, I put my whole body weight into pushing on it. I bang and shove on the door, yelling for someone, anyone to let me out. A thought skitters through my brain: What would Frances Vega do? And then I remember the cell phone in my pocket. I'll call the Scotts.

It'll be okay. It'll be okay—*oomph!*

The door. It's open! I fly through the doorway and out into the theatre in time to see blue lights flashing outside and four police officers inside.

Staring right at me.

Chapter nineteen

FIND ME A BRIDGE. I will gladly dive off.

I am sitting in the back of the police car, handcuffed (hand-cuffed!) and shaking like a bobble-head. The police radio squawks commands and dispatches as we pass through the darkened town. I don't know when I'll get to make a phone call to the Scotts. I don't know when I'll get to go home or how long I'll be in the slammer (or pokey, as my mom calls it). And I don't know what happened to all my "friends."

I do know two things: The theatre has never been haunted, and I'm in deep doo-doo.

I tried explaining everything to the police, but they didn't want to hear any of it. They just grabbed me and threw me in the squad car, which stinks. Literally. I don't think whoever was in here before me made hygiene a top priority. At least I'm a clean prisoner. I even floss regularly. That ought to count for something.

My wrists ache from these stupid handcuffs. My pride is battered from being such an idiot. But my heart hurts for what I know is coming.

I can handle being sent back. It was just a matter of time. I never even took the tags off most of the clothes Millie bought for me. What is really gonna blow is the disappointment I'm going to see on the Scotts' faces. And their horrible look of "I told you so." They were right, and I was wrong. Wrong to the tenth power. Wrong times pi. Wrong to infinity.

And what if they don't believe me? What if they think I knew about this all along, and that's why I wanted to go over to Angel's? I can just hear Mad Maxine. "I knew that girl was a bad seed from the beginning." Maybe I am. Trouble does seem to follow me wherever I go. Was it inevitable I walked into this tonight?

I hope I never see Angel, Vince, Danielle, and those people again. Going to see a ghost? Hah. The ghost of breaking and entering? And then they run off and leave me to take the blame, which I'm not going to do. At one time I might have out of loyalty, but not anymore. I'm through taking the fall for people like Angel and Vincent.

I'm not like them.

I can't be like them.

I don't want to be like them.

Why wasn't I born with the instinct for right and wrong like other people? Why do I avoid all the good kids to hang out with and gravitate toward everyone I *shouldn't* be friends with?

I need Dr. Phil.

The cruiser comes to a halt in front of the In Between police station, and my gut clenches. I think I'm going to be sick; I've got butterflies slamdancing in my stomach. This is where I have to face it all—the Scotts, the theatre owners, and probably some fat guy policeman who'll want to interrogate me in a concrete room with a two-way mirror.

"Time to go." A man whose name tag reads *L. Brinkley* grabs my arm, and I duck out of the car.

The officer and a fellow deputy usher me into the police station, and I'm seated on a hard wooden chair in front of a desk. I read the name plate on it. Chief Harvey Hoover. Under different circumstances, I would comment on his unfortunate name, but tonight is not the time. Maybe in a few decades.

The station is deathly quiet, and I can tell this kind of excitement doesn't come along every night for the IBPD. Glad I could spice up their night.

A large man with a badge pinned on his rumpled polo slides into the desk and glares. What little hair he has is standing on end, so he hasn't been out of bed long.

"The owners of the theatre will be here shortly. I'll need to get some information first, then we'll be calling your parents."

I know they are referring to the Scotts, but I have a vision of them trying to contact my mother in the up-state pen. Wouldn't she be proud? Chip off the old block. My eyes cloud, and I blink away tears.

Chief Hoover paces and yells his questions at me. I answer him and try to include every detail. I am not going to the big house for those morons.

"So you're telling me they said there was a ghost"—he pauses for dramatic effect—"a ghost in the theatre, and you thought to yourself 'Sure, I'll go check that out.'" The last part he says in a girly falsetto, like it's supposed to sound like me—which it doesn't. Unless I sound like Barbie on helium.

"Yes, that's right. They told me everyone in town knew about this haunted theatre, and it was all shut down. But everybody visited it, like it was just the thing to do if you lived in this town." Okay, so now that I'm rehashing it for the policeman, it does sound far-fetched. This is exactly what I was talking about though—I seriously wasn't born with the kind of judgment and instinct everyone else was. Blame it on genetics.

"And this list of names here, these are the people who were with you?"

I check his list again, shifting in my uncomfortable seat. "Yes, those are the people who took me to the theatre. They are the ones who did the damage. I was in the orchestra pit the entire time."

"Who are your parents, girl?" The policeman scratches a stubbly cheek. "I know they are going to be so proud to get this early-morning phone call."

"James and Millie Scott." I am ashamed to even tell him, to sully their good name.

"As in Pastor Scott?"

Great. Let me guess — you go to his church?

"Yes, sir. You know him?"

"You're Pastor Scott's kid?"

"No . . . I'm their foster daughter. I've been with them for a week now."

"I'm a deacon at the In Between Community Church." The officer leans in closer. "That's *my* pastor," he hisses protectively.

I have clearly offended him. Yes, I know. I am the shame of the town.

Hey, where's my one phone call? I want to call Iola Smartly. Not that she could pick me up tonight. But if I have to stay in a cell tonight anyway, she could be here for tomorrow. I cannot believe I got handcuffed before Trina did. It's so unfair. She's probably moved on to packing foreign-made semi-automatic weapons, and I'm going to get arrested for stupid choice of friends.

"Well, we will be calling your — "

The chief is interrupted by another uniformed man who quietly relays a message, then points to something in a file. Chief Hoover frowns and looks at me.

"Well, get them on the phone." And with a "Yes, sir," the other man is gone.

"Now, where were we? Ah, yes, you were telling me about how you broke the law tonight and you are my pastor's foster daughter."

"Right. I mean, no. Yes, I am his foster daughter, but I did not break the law. I didn't do any of the vandalism. I told you it was the others. I didn't even know they were going to do it."

"You do realize this sounds completely unbelievable, don't you?"

"Yes." In a world that obviously just wants to chew me up and spit me out, why do I even try? If I ever did get a break in this life, I'd probably be in the bathroom and miss the call.

"So you didn't notice these other kids had brought spray paint with them?"

"No." I had noticed Vince looked a little bulked up, but with the way PE is handled around here, a person could double the size of his biceps overnight.

"And need I remind you that breaking into private property is against the law? Or did you not know that? Did you think it was okay to go into a locked building not belonging to you?"

"But they told me—"

"Do you own that property?"

"No."

"Did you have a key to the property?"

"No, but I—"

"Did you have the owners' permission to go onto that property?"

I shake my head.

"Then why in the world did you think—" The portly chief notices we're not alone. "Yes, Deputy Smith?"

"The owners of the theatre are here."

My back is to the office door, and I can't make myself turn around. I am frozen to the spot. My heart goes into rapid-fire mode, and I'm almost certain the chief can hear it pounding.

Chill bumps explode on my arms, and I fight back tears. I don't want to be the bad girl all the time. I want to be the girl who does something right, who doesn't find herself in these situations. How would it feel to just be someone else? A Frances? I would give anything to freeze this moment and step out of it, to disappear and avoid the anger and condemnation of the theatre owners forever. Their beautiful theatre is graffitied and shattered to pieces, and I was there when it happened.

"Miss Katie Parker, it's time you met the owners of the Valiant theatre. You can explain to them how you came to be on their property."

I swallow back bile, drop my head, and take a deep breath. God help me.

I turn around slowly and raise my eyes.

And meet the hollow stares of James and Millie Scott.

Chapter twenty

THE MOMENT I'VE BEEN DREADING is upon me. Millie is at the door. She knocks three times, then steps into my pink domain. I'm curled up in the window seat, which looks out onto the yard, and I hold a book, making a useless attempt to do some homework. Just as I can't focus on my literature assignment, I can't seem to do anything but worry and fight nausea. After we got home last night, I crawled in bed, clothes on, and just stared at the ceiling for hours, sleep being totally impossible. During this time with myself, I came to two conclusions: One, I am an idiot. And two: Things have got to change. Even if I'm on a Greyhound back to Sunny Haven today, I have *got* to get it together.

The ride home early this morning was torture. The police chief talked to James and Millie last night when they came in, James all rumpled and sleepy looking, and Millie, her makeup on and not a hair out of place. No matter the hour, Millie is ready for her close up, always made up, always poised and perfect. What she sees in me, I'll never know.

After signing some forms, the chief released me to the Scotts, and I followed them out to the car. No one said a word. James opened the door to the back seat for me, and I got in.

Silently.

James started the car and still nothing. I expected there to be yelling, finger pointing, condemnation. All I got was quiet. Eerie, heavy, make-me-want-to-hurl quiet.

We walked through the front door this morning around five thirty, and I had thought maybe that would be when the fireworks would start, when I'd see bared teeth and hear full-decibel yelling.

Nothing.

Millie hung her coat in the closet, then went directly to the kitchen and put on a kettle of tea. James looked at me briefly before addressing a spot near my feet and simply said, "Go to bed. We'll talk in the morning."

I stood there, my feet glued to the floor.

"That's it? That's all you have to say?" I couldn't let this go.

James shook his head slowly, in a way that was worse than any curse word, worse than any fist. "Go to bed, Katie." As in, *Leave my presence, I can't stand the sight of you.*

And now it's time to face the music. And time, no doubt, to pack my bags. I just hope Mrs. Smartly will take me back. But I'll have to worry about her when the time comes. Right now, I have my foster mother, whose property I broke into, standing in my room, waiting for my full attention.

Millie clears her throat. "I see you're awake."

I have got to play this cool. I want them to know I'm deeply sorry, but I have to leave with my dignity too.

Big inhale . . . and exhale. All right, here we go. To the point and dignified.

I launch myself into Millie's arms.

"Oh, Millie, I'm so sorry! I thought Angel was a friend—I thought they were all friends, but they weren't, Millie, they weren't! But I'm just so dumb about those things, and I don't want to be, but I am—and then they told me the theatre was just a cool place everyone in town goes to, and I should have been honored they were letting me in on something—like it would make me one of them and one of you, but it didn't—and when I was in the orchestra pit, they started tearing up the theatre—and I promise, Millie, I promise they never told me they were going to do that. I had no idea—you have to believe me! And then the police show up, and I'm all alone—and they left me—and then I was hand-cuffed—and then there was yelling—and then you two show up. And . . . I haven't slept a wink."

I am bawling. Full-on, snot-galore, puffy-eyed, splotchy-skin, wet-face bawling. Millie awkwardly pats me, then sets me away from her.

I wipe at my face and nose. She probably can't stand to touch me. Probably can't even stand to be in the same room as me.

"Katie, I've got some breakfast for you downstairs, and then James and I would like to talk to you."

"Millie, you have to know I—"

"You have five minutes, Katie. Then I want you dressed and downstairs." She turns on her small, fashionable heels and leaves my bedroom.

I have five minutes. Five minutes before I am told I'm a disap-pointing failure. Five minutes before I'm told to pack up my clothes—the ones I came in—and hit the door. Five minutes before my glimpse of a life I didn't even know was possible is over. No more steak dinners around a dinner table. No more shopping trips. No more pink, fluffy bedroom. No more parents, no home, no In Between.

James and Millie are seated in the breakfast nook, the morning sun shining on them and highlighting the signs of their own lack of sleep. Even Rocky looks worn out. Spotting me at the bottom of the stairs, Millie gets up and goes to the stove to deal with my breakfast.

"I'm not hungry." I couldn't possibly eat anything. Nothing that would stay down anyway. I wonder how my "friends" are doing. Do they even feel guilty? I probably have enough guilt and misery for all of us. Not that they care.

"You need to eat, Katie." Millie continues to fix my breakfast, taking some pancake batter and spooning it onto a hot skillet.

I look at the food. "Thanks, but I just can't eat."

My foster mother spoons out two more pancakes.

"Millie." James Scott's voice is razor sharp, and Millie's head snaps up. "She says she doesn't want any breakfast."

"And I said she needs to eat." Millie's eyes are fire, and I'm taken aback at her intensity.

"Millie, for crying out loud, would you just quit? Sit down."

So not only have I been a part of ruining the Scotts' theatre, but thanks to me, they're fighting. Town's favorite pastor and wife divorce. Cause? One week with me.

Millie stares at James, then goes back to her pancakes, at last flipping them onto a plate, which she leaves on the counter.

Setting a glass of juice in front of me, like an unspoken last word on the breakfast issue, Millie joins us at the table.

"Katie—"

"James, I wanted to tell you I—"

Millie holds up a hand. "Be quiet, Katie."

Words spin in my head, and I want to try them all, hoping some will be the right combination to make the Scotts magically forgive me.

"We need you to listen. Millie and I have not been to bed yet, and we have had a chance to discuss this situation thoroughly and come to some conclusions."

The waterworks start again, as shame sets my lip quivering and sends tears sliding down my cheeks. "I'm sorry. And I know I'm being sent back."

I blow my nose in a paper towel and dash away my tears on my sweatshirt. I can't even look at the two of them.

"You're not going anywhere, Katie." James's voice has my full attention. "And I mean that literally. You will not be allowed to do anything socially for a very long time. If it isn't school- or church-related, you more than likely will not be leaving this house."

"What?" Maybe Chief Hoover's yelling damaged my hearing. Surely James didn't say what I thought he just said. No walking papers?

"We've decided not to send you back." Millie looks at me like *What do you think about that, hot stuff?* I can tell I've broken her trust in me. I miss her fun face. This serious, cautious expression just isn't her.

"There are going to be a lot of changes around here for you, so you might as well get comfortable and listen." James rests an elbow on the table. "First of all, there will be no charges pressed against any of you. Your 'friends' and their parents were contacted early this morning, and we have full statements of guilt from all of them. Their stories matched yours. Instead of pressing charges and leaving them with criminal records, Millie and I have prayed about this and have come up with a reasonable punishment the police and the kids' parents have accepted. Since they did the vandalism, they will work in the community on behalf of the church for the next year. With their parents' supervision, they will take regular shifts at our community soup kitchen, do repair work on some of the local nursing homes, do errands and odd jobs for some of our elderly church members, and complete a whole list of useful tasks."

Whoa, they got off easy. I can't believe they weren't arrested. I don't know how they *didn't* get charged. I guess the pastor has some pull around here.

James rubs the bridge of his nose like he's trying to exorcise a headache (I think its name is Katie), then continues. "You, while you didn't participate in the destruction of the theatre, did break the law by being there. And you also blatantly disobeyed us by leaving Angel's home and running around in the middle of the night."

"But I—" An excuse is ready to fly off my tongue, but I swallow it. "Yes, sir."

"As I was saying, you, too, are guilty, though of lesser charges." James pauses to make sure he has my full attention. "Millie and I are very, very disappointed in you. We trusted you, and you have let us down." His voice is quiet, but his words are ringing in my ears. "First of all, you are not allowed to socialize with the group you were keeping company with last night. We can't stop you from seeing them at school, but we hope you realize a real friend doesn't pressure you into disobeying your parents. And a real friend doesn't lie to you or ask you to break the law."

"Yes, I know." Ah, the tears. Again. And the runny nose. I should just wad up some tissues and stick them in my nostrils to permanently stop the drip. It would be a lot easier. I'm way past the point of trying to hold onto any dignity here.

"And Millie and I have decided that, though we didn't make you go to church this past Wednesday night, you will be there every Wednesday evening from now on. This will give you a chance to interact with your peers and hopefully make some new, more—how shall I put it?—law-abiding friends."

"This is the easy stuff, Katie." Millie pushes my juice glass toward me with a pointed look. I obediently raise the glass and force some down. "James, get to the consequences part."

"Katie, here's what we've decided. You will take the school bus to the theatre after school and work there for a couple of hours every day with one of us. You will help us repair what your friends have destroyed and get us back on track with our renovation."

"Sure, sure. I'll definitely do that. But why me working in the theatre and not Angel and those guys?"

"We don't want them anywhere *near* our theatre." Millie's voice has ice in it, and her fierce protectiveness of the Valiant has me bristling.

"I, um . . . I never knew you had a theatre." I think there are more than a few things about the Scotts I don't know.

"James and I bought the Valiant about two years ago. It was the crowning jewel of the town once, but it had been abandoned for a few decades by the time we got to it. We have been refurbishing it in hopes of opening it back up to the community this fall." Millie glances at James. "In fact, we recently held auditions for *Romeo and Juliet*, and our grand opening and premiere was to be the last weekend of October."

A cannonball settles in my stomach. Their theatre. Now it won't be done in time for the grand opening. And I had a part in it.

One choice.

That's all it comes down to. One choice, one wrong choice, and I sit here eaten up with guilt and a hundred other horrible feelings I can't even begin to name. I have less than six weeks to do whatever I can to get the theatre ready. I will drive nails. I will paint walls like it's an Olympic event. I will spackle like I have never spackled before. And I will do . . . whatever it is you do with Sheetrock to the very best of my ability.

"Well, if it's meant to be, it will happen," James says gruffly. Millie nods, though she hardly looks like she agrees. She seems . . . heartbroken.

Great. Add dream-crusher to my list of crimes.

"So, continuing with your punishment, we come to the next part. Millie's mother, Maxine, needs someone to read to her, so you will be going to Shady Acres once a week to read to her." James takes a long drink of coffee, as if the idea of spending that kind of time with Maxine leaves a bad taste in his mouth. But I can do this. I'm not going to complain. Whatever they want me to do, I'll do it. I would shave that woman's armpits to make up for all of this.

Then an idea hits me. Does Maxine have a reading problem? Maybe she was so busy doing the cha-cha in her younger years she didn't take the time to brush up on her phonics. "Maxine can't read, can she?"

"Well, of course she can read, Katie. Don't be ridiculous," Millie sputters.

And now I've just insulted Millie's mother. I'm on a roll. Maybe for my big finish I'll kick her dog.

"Mother has yet to adjust to her new bifocals, and it makes it hard for her to see to read. She hasn't been able to read at all in the last few months, and even though I've gotten her some books on CD, it's not the same. She's a voracious reader of the classics."

James chokes on his coffee.

"James, you know how much she loves her Chaucer."

Millie's husband looks heavenward, like he's sending a quick SOS to God for patience. I don't think he and Millie think of the same person when they think of Maxine.

"So, as James was saying, you will go once a week and read to my mother. I know she will be grateful for the company and the books. I think Tuesdays will probably be a good day. Her afternoons are usually pretty full except for Tuesday. Mother has bridge on Monday, Bingo on Wednesdays, her knitting club on Thursday mornings, and salsa lessons on Fridays. What she does on Saturday and Sunday, I have no idea."

"Nor do we want to know," James mumbles to no one in particular. "And finally, we want to lay down some rules about school work. On the afternoon you went to Angel's, we got a call from your algebra teacher. Apparently in the week you have been in school, you have yet to turn in an assignment to Mr. Smith, and you have failed a quiz. Would you like to explain yourself?" James is through making cracks about Mad Maxine and back to being intimidating. I've noticed his forehead wrinkles when he's serious.

Right now he sort of resembles a Shar Pei.

"I don't know."

Millie and James exchange a look of anger-infused exasperation.

"You don't know? You don't know how you have a zero in algebra? You don't know how you forgot to do a week's worth of homework? You can't remember why you didn't study for the quiz?" Millie huffs, and I can see she is about to leave mad and move on to furious.

"I don't know." I drop my head and study my hands. What am I supposed to say?

"Look, young lady. I've had just about enough of—"

"No, Millie, wait." James halts his wife's oncoming rant. "Katie, what is it you don't know?"

I sit there in silence. I need to clip my fingernails. And some of that black fingernail polish is still on my pinky nail. Gross. I hate chipped polish.

"Katie, what is it you don't know? You don't know as in you don't care, or you don't know as in you don't understand math?" James's voice isn't so threatening now. In fact, it's borderline nice.

I nervously chew on my blackened pinky nail. "I . . . I, um." My shoulders rise in a shrug. It's hard to admit you're stupid. "I don't know because I don't get it." There. You happy? I'm stupid. "I don't know a trinomial from a polynomial, a variable from an exponent, and I sure don't know why sometimes a negative can magically turn into a positive. And FOIL? Well, that's what cheeseburgers come in."

"Okay. All right. Now we're getting somewhere." James nods.

"Yeah, we've gotten somewhere." I sniff. "We've gotten to the point where you realize I'm an idiot. I'm in the tenth grade, and I don't get even a little bit of what's going on in algebra. I'd put it into a percentage for you, but I don't know how!" Oh, math. My deep, dark secret. I've been able to skate by until now. Math . . . it haunts me and follows me—like bad BO.

"Millie wasn't sure, but I thought that might be the case."

"That I'm stupid?"

"No, no. Katie, you're very intelligent," James says in a rush. "We know that, and I would hope you do too. Not understanding something doesn't make you dumb. I'm sure you've been in and out of school enough to miss out on some important math lessons. Math is something that builds on itself. You have to be there daily so you don't miss out."

I'm not sure I'm going to like where this is heading.

James takes a drink of coffee. "Well, I had suspected as much. Thought, in fact, you might be behind on a few subjects, so I decided that what you need is a tutor. I put in a call to Frances Vega's parents this morning."

What! They called Frances? They told her about my criminal

weekend? They told her about my math handicap? Is this part of the punishment too?

James continues his explanation. "Frances is a bit of a math whiz, so she has offered to come over a few times a week to tutor you in algebra. I can help, too, of course, but I thought it might be better to have someone your own age who's been through the same class. Who knows, algebra might have changed since I saw it last."

Nope, I'm pretty sure it's the same. It's gross now, and it was probably gross back then. And I seriously do *not* want Frances's help with anything.

"But . . . but . . . couldn't we get someone else? Someone who's not Frances?" I am seconds away from begging.

"Katie, we like Frances, and more important, we trust Frances." These frosty words come from Millie, who is obviously going to need some time to get over being mad at me. "Also we will be paying Frances for the tutoring, so we hope you will take advantage of her offer of help and take it seriously. We will focus on the math, and then if we see other subjects that need attention, I'm sure she can help you with those too."

"Does Frances know what happened? What I did?" Humiliation on *so* many levels here.

James shakes his head. "No. But this is a small town. I can only do so much for you, Katie. People talking about the theatre break-in is just one of the consequences you are going to have to deal with."

Right. Well, it's not like I had a sterling reputation to protect anyway. And I wasn't planning on running for student-body president, so my nonexistent popularity plummeting into the negatives probably won't make much of a difference.

I guess I'll be returning to my toilet seat for lunch.

Time to break out the carrot sticks and reclaim my porcelain throne.

Chapter twenty-one

I SPENT THE REST OF Saturday in my room doing important things like arranging my eye shadows in their order on the color wheel, dusting my blinds four different times, counting the leaves on the crooked oak tree outside my window, timing how long I could hold my breath while standing on one leg, and avoiding the Scotts as much as possible.

I now know what an eon feels like.

The sun finally went down on that day, and I even managed to get a few hours of sleep. Which was a nice break from all the thinking I've been doing lately.

I awaken this morning to a sunshiny Sunday, and despite the fact that I desperately want to pull the covers over my head and stay hidden in my room for yet another day—if not forever—I sit up and place both feet on the cool hardwood floor. With a new resolve, within thirty minutes I am totally awake, showered, and dressed in a cute skirt and matching sweater Millie bought me last week. It's time for Sunday school and church.

Sunday school—the words alone send shivers down my spine.

I'm *so* not about church. And I feel certain anything with the word *school* tacked onto it can't be good.

But starting today, I am going to be perfect. I am going to make the Scotts trust me, proud to know me, and hopefully want to keep me long enough that I can wear everything in my closet at least once. The Scotts are not going to know what hit them. Good-bye, Katie, daughter of disaster, chaos, and bad decisions.

Now, if I only knew for sure how to make that happen. The first step in my Katie Parker makeover plan is to find and observe a role model. And since Miss Perfect herself, Frances Vega, will be in my home at least once a week, not to mention all the times I'll be around her at church now, she seems a likely candidate. I will watch and observe Frances like she's some rare bird on the Discovery channel. Notes will be taken, observations recorded. This might even call for some charts and graphs. Whatever it takes, I stand ready.

So today's goals are to get through breakfast without making anyone mad, suffer through church and watch Frances's every move, and hopefully get Millie to talk to me without growling.

The last one is pretty iffy.

I slink down the steps (pausing at step number ten to plaster a pleasant smile on my face and again at step number six to deal with a wedgie) and find Millie sitting at the table in the breakfast nook, drinking coffee. She stares out the window, lost in thought. And I don't think it's because she's counting oak leaves.

I clear my throat, and my nonMom turns her attention my direction.

"You look very nice. I knew that outfit would look good on you." Her kind words are spoken in a near monotone. "You're up kind of early."

"I'm ready for Sunday school," I proclaim, like I've just

announced my acceptance to Harvard or my discovery of the cure for cancer.

Call it a trick of the light, but I think I see Millie's mouth twitch ever so slightly, like she's thinking about being amused.

Millie stirs something into her coffee. "Sunday school, hmm? The youth service isn't really Sunday school as usual. But I'm glad you're so eager this morning. James has already left, of course." She blows on her java, then takes a sip. "Tell me, Katie, what do you know about Sunday school?"

I widen my giant, fake smile. "Not a thing."

Millie walks into the kitchen and starts her typical busy morning routine. "You'll be in there with kids your own age," she says, with her head in the fridge. "For the adults, Sunday school is just a time to really study the Bible and go a little bit deeper with God's Word and hopefully learn how it applies to your life. I think Pastor Mike makes it more of a worship service for our youth. But you'll still need that Bible we got you."

"Right." I bob my head. "Bring it on. Yay, Bible!"

Millie's head comes out of the refrigerator, checking to see if it's me who's talking.

What would Frances say? How would she respond? I try again. "I mean, an in-depth study of the Scriptures in pursuit of life connections would be quite stimulating."

Millie grabs the milk and sets it on the counter with a thud. "Katie, I . . . " Millie stops, her face contorted, I hope in deep thought and not pain. "I . . . oh, never mind. Look"—she sighs deeply and runs a well-manicured hand through her blonde bob—"while we are making you go to church every time we're there, we're not pushing any expectations on you. We can't make you trust in God any more than you can make us trust you right now. It has to be earned, not forced." Millie whips up her waffle batter, stirring fiercely. "I just want you to go with an open mind. That's all we ask. I'm not asking you to come back knowing how to quote some psalms, okay?"

My foster mother could easily get biceps Coach Nelson would be proud of if she keeps stirring that batter with such a vengeance.

"Millie, I just wanted to say I'm sorry and—"

"I know." She ladles batter into the waiting waffle iron. "I know. You've said you're sorry. You're just going to have to give me some time, Katie. I'm not quite ready to talk about all of this." Millie gives me a thin smile I can't quite decipher, but my heart senses a burden beyond any crime I've committed. I miss grinning, laughing, fashion-mag-reading Millie.

We eat our waffles in strained silence, punctuated by the occasional overly polite comment. I insist on doing the breakfast dishes before going up to my room to finish getting ready.

And faster than you can spell WWJD, nine thirty has arrived and it's time for church.

The parking lot is full of people—families, kids, old people. These are all James and Millie's people. Their flock, their posse. Even though most of them probably don't know about my night of crimes and misdemeanors yet, I feel like they are all staring at me, judging me. It's like I have *Shameful Loser* branded on my forehead.

Millie leads me into the church, hugging and helloing all the way (I luckily escape all the PDA, having to suffer through only one hug), and she takes me right to the large Sunday school classroom for teens.

Millie tells me good-bye at the door. "Okay, I'll see you after church. I'm sitting with the choir today, so sit with the other teens or Mother."

Wow. What a seating choice. I can sit with Mad Maxine or the teen churchies. That's like saying I can either swim with sharks or piranhas. I can eat worms or bugs. I can walk on broken glass or hot coals.

I push my way through the door and walk into a room full of teens.

Teens that immediately quit talking.

And stare at me.

Okay, their parents may not be up on the latest town news, but these kids obviously are. The silence transitions into whispers, and I don't have to hear a word to know what they are saying. My face is flaming hot, and I just want to turn around and run.

I look at the door behind me.

Then at the whispering teens.

And back at the door.

I can't do it. I can't stay here.

I've got to make it to the door before I start hyperventilating. I spin on my heel and all but sprint for the exit.

"Katie, wait!"

Nope, nope, gotta keep moving. Almost there.

"Katie, please. Hang on." It's Frances Vega. Frances, the girl I was going to watch and observe today, to learn from like she's my sensei.

A million thoughts zoom through my mind. Millie's broken-hearted looks, my goal of acting more normal, the way I felt when the Scotts told me they weren't sending me back. I close my eyes and try to muster strength. With forced determination, I face Frances, the wonder child.

"Hey, Frances. Funny meeting you here."

"You saw me here last week."

"Right." Okay, maybe I should've pursued the leaving idea a little more.

"Katie, I'm so glad you came. Come on back in. Please?"

I look over my shoulder. People are still staring and talking, but now they are at least pretending not to.

"Frances," I whisper. "Did you hear about Friday night? About the theatre?"

She probably was so busy doing her homework, practicing her marching band routines, and perfecting her chess moves that she hasn't heard about my crimes. Otherwise she wouldn't be so eager for me to join her.

"Well, duh. Who hasn't?" Frances looks at me like I'm from a different planet. "Now, come on. You can sit by me." She grabs my hand and drags me a few steps before I put on the brakes.

"No, wait, Frances." My face burns. My hands quiver. I look into the sea of my peers. "I can't stay here. Everyone knows, and they're talking about me. I'm blacklisted. I'm persona non grata. I'm an Olsen twin."

Frances leans in close. "We're not like that, really. People are gonna talk, sure. This is In Between. The last newsworthy thing to happen around here was when Mr. Spinks had a pig that could oink 'Yankee Doodle Dandy.'" Frances's ebony hair sways as she laughs. "Katie, here's the deal. You need friends—good friends. You might as well start making allies today, right? If people think badly of you, then prove them wrong. You can't do that hiding at home or in the church bathroom."

"I wasn't going to hide in the bathroom." Mostly because I hadn't thought of that yet.

"Come on, meet some of my friends."

I let Frances drag me around and introduce me to a few people. All of them are very polite, some of them even genuinely nice.

"Hi, you must be Katie. I'm Mike, the youth pastor here. Welcome." A giant of a man in a polo and khakis grabs my hand in a death grip and shakes it till my shoulder nearly disconnects. "Relax, you're among friends here." His grin is mischievous. Welcoming.

It's then I notice his earring, and when he high-fives a kid passing, I glimpse what looks like a *Mother* tattoo peeking out beneath his short-sleeve shirt.

He catches the direction of my stare. "Hey, we all make mistakes." Pastor Mike looks out at his youth group. "Every single one of us. Some of us are smart enough to move on, am I right?" His eyes sparkle with humor—and something else I can't identify.

I shoot him my most doubtful gaze. "I don't know."

He opens his mouth to deliver what I'm sure will be a theology-driven, pop-psychology-laden response (with sprinkles of judgment on top). "We have snacks."

Oh.

"I'll stay."

Chapter twenty~two

DRUMMING MY HANDS ON MY knees, I sit next to Frances in one of the cold metal folding chairs. And I thought pews were uncomfortable.

Pastor Mike opens the service by jumping on a makeshift stage and grabbing his acoustic guitar. He begins playing something everyone else instantly recognizes. Voices join, and an occasional hand is raised as the entire room sings.

Except for me.

Though the words are flashed on a screen in front, I've never heard these songs and don't want to participate. Their singing makes me feel uncomfortable, like an outsider. I wish I knew the songs, but in another way, I really don't. I'm more of a Beyoncé or Justin Timberlake type of girl. I can't say I'm into Pastor Mike unplugged. Still I can appreciate the sounds his guitar makes and the spontaneous harmonies that always happen when a group of people get together and sing.

After the music portion of the morning is over, we all sit down, and Pastor Mike gets his Bible out and rests it on a small music stand near him.

"Welcome everyone. It's a great day in the house of the Lord, and I'm glad to see you." The big guy is grinning from ear to ear like it's his birthday.

I barely contain an eye roll.

"If you're here, it's not by chance, but by purpose."

Yeah, it's called I got myself in big-o-trouble, and here I am.

"No matter where you're at in life, God meets you. Wherever you are."

I wish he'd meet me in the parking lot. Or maybe at IHOP. Anywhere but here.

"Today we're going to talk about a guy named Paul. Now this was a bad, bad dude."

I probably went out with him in junior high.

"I mean, he lived a horrible life. If you can think it, he did it."

If you can think it, he did it? Wasn't that something Mad Maxine said to me?

"He was despised. He ran with a tough crowd."

Well, preach on. You're telling my story now.

"Paul even murdered."

And this is where our similarities end. Even *I'm* not that bad. Aside from an incident I had in the first grade involving a goldfish and a toilet bowl, I have not achieved that kind of criminal status.

And then the oddest thing happens.

Pastor Mike gets my attention. As he dives into the details of his story, his face contorts into a hundred expressions, his voice changes like he's five or six different characters, and he's all over the stage. It's like I'm there, really there, witnessing the story of this rough guy, Paul.

When the story ends, I'm sitting straight in my seat, body

tense, like I'm watching an action movie.

Church or not, this dude can tell a good story. Somebody should write this stuff down.

"And the crazy thing is," Pastor Mike concludes, his voice a dramatic whisper. "The crazy thing is, Jesus said, 'You're forgiven. Your old life is gone. You're one of mine now . . . ' and Paul walked away a new man."

Like he got a life transplant. Sign me up for one of those.

"Where are you at today, guys?" The youth minister takes a long moment to meet the eyes of every person in the room.

When he gets to me, I look down.

"Are you ready to leave it all behind and pick up the new life Jesus is holding out for you—waiting for you to take?"

Jesus, if you're up there, I'd like a new life. Can I be one of those people on Laguna Beach?

"Let's pray."

Pastor Mike bows his head, along with everyone else in the room, and begins his prayer.

Deciding I've given this guy more attention than I intended to, I tune him out. With my head bowed, I raise my eyes and peek at Frances.

She's totally into this.

She's nodding in response to whatever the pastor is saying, her eyes shut, concentrating. Frances is so committed. I mean she's involved in everything, but she takes it all so seriously. She never lets up. How can I imitate that? She works hard at everything, is good at everything. Am I good at anything? Frances seems so comfortable with who she is and her place in this world. Last week, Mr. Morton gave up on me getting even a basic sound out of any instrument he had. When I couldn't even handle playing the triangle correctly, I was asked to consider another elective class.

I'm not even good at playing the stinkin' triangle!

Frances is a champion chess player, a student council leader, president of the science club, a trophy-winning flute player, blah, blah, blah. What am I? I'm just a non-triangle-playing girl.

I've got to find my talent. My strength. Maybe I'm a computer genius, and I don't even know it. Or what if I'm brilliant at cooking and sewing? Perhaps I'm an undiscovered vocal talent. When I get back to school it's time to investigate my options.

"Amen."

Amen. Oh, yes, the magic word, like "the end." Heads shoot up and a low chatter begins.

"Before you go, remember to come back Wednesday night when we kick it up a notch," Pastor Mike's booming voice carries over the rising noise.

Kick it up a notch? Oh, yeah, sure, let me guess, we add hand holding to our singing, and then you get really crazy with the lesson and bust out PowerPoint.

Frances turns in her seat to face me. "Hey, what did you think?"

It was uncomfortable, intense, occasionally entertaining, and not as bad as I thought. "S'okay. I mean I got some donuts out of it."

Her face falls a bit, but I can tell the fight is not out of her yet. "Come on, it's time for church. If we hurry, we can beat the senior citizens. They always try and steal our seats."

And like we're old friends, Frances reaches for my hand again and leads me out into the hallway and toward the worship center. "Hurry, we've got to get there before *she* does." Frances picks up her pace and begins to speed walk.

"Who? What are you talking about?" And do I really care? I just want a nice seat in the back, right under the exit sign.

Frances jerks me around a corner, her grip like a vice. "You don't understand, Katie. She does it just to spite us. I've heard she pays the bus driver to pick her and her friends up early. Well, not today. Today we are gonna beat her. We're claiming our pew."

We whip through the entry doors of the sanctuary, and Frances drops my hand like I'm suddenly plagued.

"Oh, no, she doesn't." Frances shoots down the left aisle. For a second, I think she's going to hurdle some pews and slide into one like it's home plate.

When I catch up to her, she's standing behind an occupied pew, shoulders slumped, hands shaking. What has gotten into her? Perfect Frances doesn't get angry, does she? What could possibly set her off like this?

"I *so* like to get here early." The voice comes from the woman occupying the pew in front of Frances.

"You . . . you . . . " Frances clenches her fists.

This is awesome.

"You couldn't have gotten here on the church bus. I checked its departure time, and it would have left exactly three minutes ago." Frances's voice cracks as she addresses the back of the woman's head.

The blonde-haired woman quits her inspection of her church bulletin, lays it in her lap, and slowly, ever so slowly, swivels all the way around to face her accuser. "Why, Frances, dear. It's such a lovely day. I rode my bike."

I gasp.

Mad Maxine.

Chapter twenty-three

"WELL, WELL, WELL. I SEE you have a new friend, Frances." Millie's mom clickity-clacks her long nails on the back of the wooden pew and eyes me like a tiger ready to pounce on its prey.

I gulp.

"You know we like to sit here, Mrs. Simmons." Frances is clearly not going to let this go.

"Now Frances, this church is plenty big enough for all of us. You and your little friends sit in that pew, and my companions and I will occupy this one." Maxine *tsk-tsks*. "This doesn't have to be difficult."

Beside me, Frances is radiating heat. "You know the youth group needs both pews if we all want to sit together. Can't you and your *companions* go sit over with the other"—Frances clears her throat—"*elderly* members of the congregation?"

Maxine's eyes flash wide, then shrink to narrow slits. "Look, Miss Vega, you and the other tiny tots will just have to find somewhere else to sit, because I'm sitting here, and as you can see from the church bulletins I've strewn about, the rest of the seats in this

row are saved. Now run along and leave me alone, if you please."
Maxine is now composed and cool as a cucumber. She turns back
to face the front. "I need some quiet alone time with the Lord."

Frances growls and stares at the back of Maxine's head for a
few tense seconds.

I'm all about Maxine's idea to go and sit somewhere else.
Getting as far away from her as possible seems like a smart move
to me. The last thing I want to do is put myself in Mad Maxine's
path so she can look down her long nose at me.

"Come on. Let's go sit somewhere else," I whisper to the
fuming Frances.

She shakes her head. "No way. We're staying here." Frances
plops herself down right behind Maxine.

Super.

With little choice, I too sit down. Of all the pews in this joint,
Frances has to pick this one. I consider choosing some random
stranger to sit next to just to get away from Maxine, but before I
can decide, other kids from Sunday school file in and fill up the
seats around me. Well, I'm not going to climb over them to get
out, so I guess this seat will have to do.

"Katie, there you are." Millie breezes in, her royal blue choir
robe billowing behind her. "I see you found a seat okay. Oh, hello,
Mother. Did you see Katie back here? And Frances?"

Maxine angles her head toward us, her face a mask of innocence. "Yes, dear. The girls and I have already exchanged greet-
ings, haven't we, ladies?" Maxine chuckles, like she's the angel of
good humor and congeniality. "Well, I didn't want to intrude on
the girls too much. I'll get plenty of time to chat with Katie this
afternoon when you drop her off at my house. No point in talking
her sweet little ear off now, is there?"

My mouth falls open. Did she just say I'd be seeing her

this afternoon? Isn't Sunday a day of rest? That's not restful. If Sunday were a day of torture, I'd say, sure, how about a visit with Maxine?

Millie eyes her mother, then me, then back to her mother. "Ah, well, I hadn't gotten a chance to talk to Katie about it yet." I don't miss Millie's slight grimace. "Katie, this afternoon James and I are going to get some things straightened out at the theatre. We thought we'd drop you off at Mother's, and you two could spend some time together."

Heavy dread settles in my gut.

"Uh, but I'd love to go to the theatre with you. I could get to work right away, you know? Do a little painting, a little cleaning . . . anything?" I desperately search for a task, but Millie shakes her head.

"We want to get some glass and other things cleaned up before we let anyone work on it. Mother can feed you lunch and you two can . . . oh, they're motioning for me to take my seat in the choir loft." Millie pats me on the shoulder.

It doesn't help.

"But Millie, I—"

"I'll see you after church. Good-bye, ladies." Millie rushes off and takes her seat on stage with the rest of the choir.

No! I'm not ready to spend time with her mother. She'll eat me alive.

In fact, I can't believe Maxine hasn't already taken the opportunity to publicly humiliate me, to rake me over the coals about Friday night. She must be sick. Because the woman has had ample opportunity to say something loud and catty about my run-in with the local law. Or maybe she's saving it. During the altar call, she'll probably stand on the pew and declare my disgrace for all to hear.

"See you about one o'clock, snookums." Maxine's sugarless voice drops a decibel. A chill dances up my spine.

Maxine's friends from the old folks home roll in (some literally), and she forgets all about Frances and me.

The service begins, and it goes on just like it did the previous week. The music director leads the congregation and the choir in a few songs, the words displayed on a screen for all of us to follow, much like in Sunday school. The songs are kind of lame, but the instrumentalists set up beside the choir do add some pizzazz. Granted, I've not had much church experience in my life, but who would expect a small town conservative church to have a guy rocking out on drums during a hymn? Okay, maybe not rocking out, but definitely getting with it.

The choir sings a final song, and James takes his place at the pulpit. He opens with prayer, asking for God to be present and to move among us. I bow my head, too, and use the time to ask God to let us out early. Hey, as long as we're offering up requests here.

James opens with a few humorous stories, which tear his congregation up, and then he moves into his sermon.

I look around at the good people of In Between Community Church. They are totally absorbing their pastor's message. Some are taking notes. A handful shout out *amens* or some other affirmation, while many are doing some serious head nodding.

Then I focus again on James. My foster father.

And I wonder how they don't see it.

How can his church not see how totally disconnected he is? With their heads nodding and pens scribbling, they are so into his message. How can they not see that their pastor isn't?

When I heard Pastor Mike today in Sunday school, I saw a guy lit up with excitement. He couldn't contain his enthusiasm. It was so real I could almost reach out and touch it.

Now, I'm no psychic, but I'm not getting the same vibes from James Scott. Sure, he's a good speaker. He's got it all—humor, good story-telling skills, intensity, a commanding presence. But then I look at those eyes behind his studious oval glasses, and I don't see the same fire and determination I saw in Pastor Mike. Or that I see in my English teacher when she's telling us about the power of poetry. Or even that I saw in Mrs. Smartly the day she left me and told me I was important in the world.

My brain searches for words and ideas to make sense of my theory, but I come up with nothing.

Oh, what do I know? Maybe James is just having an off day. It's not like he had a restful weekend. He's probably tired. A little bit of Katie does go a long way.

The service closes in prayer, and we're dismissed.

Thank goodness. I'm starving and my butt is numb from that pew.

"Katie, I'm so glad you came today." Frances's evil alter ego has apparently left her body, and she is back to being her normal, overly bubbly self.

"It's not like I had a choice."

"Well, anyway, it was good to see you in Sunday school. I hope you'll come back Wednesday night."

"I wouldn't miss it," I deadpan.

"Yeah?"

Frances beams, and I don't have the heart to tell her if I didn't show up Wednesday night the Scotts would throw me on the first bus back to the group home.

"The Scotts must be really great parents, but I'm really sorry about . . . " She juts her chin toward Mad Maxine, who is schmoozing and giggling it up with a few of her lady friends. "I'm here for you if you need someone, you know, to talk to."

I'm oddly touched by Frances's concern. There's no reason she should even be talking to me, let alone offering me a comforting shoulder. If the roles were reversed, I would probably think suffering Mad Maxine was poetic justice for the crimes of Friday night.

"Thanks, but I think I'll be okay." I run a hand down my new skirt, smoothing it out and trying to appear cool and confident. Inside, I'm already quaking over the thought of spending an afternoon with the old battle-ax. I'm seconds away from wrapping myself around Frances's ankles and pleading for her to take me home with her.

"Maxine and I are cool."

Cool like the iceberg that sank the Titanic.

Frances raises a single eyebrow. "Well, okay. I guess I'll see you Monday at school."

"Yeah, sure." If I live through lunch with one psychotic senior citizen. "See you Monday."

Frances smiles her megawatt smile and leaves the pew.

"Frances—" I stop her.

"Yeah?"

"Thanks. You know, for sitting with me and all." Okay, insert awkward silence here. "And, um . . . yeah, see you on Monday."

And I bolt out of the pew.

Chapter twenty-four

"NOW WE'LL ONLY BE GONE a couple of hours, okay?"

I sit in the backseat on the way to Maxine's. The drive of doom. Millie has been giving me random dos and don'ts for my afternoon. I can't keep it all straight in my head, so I stare out the window at the passing landscape and occasionally nod like I'm absorbing her every word. Something about if Maxine asks to play rummy, watch out for an ace card with a bent corner. And how she likes to talk about her Vegas showgirl days, but don't let her try on her old costumes or I'll be picking up feathers for hours. Then there was some detail about if Maxine asks if I want to see her latest tap-dance routine, I'm to say no because there's a flaming baton involved.

"Here we are." James catches my eye in the rearview mirror. He gives me a hearty wink, like he's trying to bolster my courage. Or maybe it's just a parting sign of affection in case I'm never heard from again.

The three of us walk up to Mad Maxine's door, where we find her watering a pitiful looking mum. She wears mud-caked work gloves, and a small gardening spade hangs in the canvas tool belt tied around her waist. Pushing the brim of her massive sun hat up with two fingers, Millie's mother stops her task and sets her gaze on me.

Much like a cobra would before spewing poisonous venom.

"Hey, Mom." Millie approaches her mother, kissing her on the cheek, but avoiding a muddy embrace.

Maxine holds her arms out wide to James for a hug. Brown sludge drips off her gloves. "Come here, you big lug."

James shakes his head and laughs. There's probably nothing she could pull out of her bag of tricks that he hasn't already seen.

Maxine peels off her nasty gloves. "Just tending to my botanical garden here."

We all take a moment to survey the single mum and the skeletal remains of what might have been a fern.

Millie gets down to business. "Okay, now you're going to feed Katie, right?"

"Well"—Maxine's predatory eyes meet mine—"sure. I thought I'd rustle us up some burgers and fries. You like burgers, dontcha?"

"Yes, ma'am." With my eyes, I'm pleading with James and Millie not to leave me. I would scrub their toilets for the rest of my life if they would scratch the Maxine visits off my punishment list.

James smiles and pats my shoulder. "We'd better go, Katie. You have my cell phone number if you need anything." He leans in closer and whispers near my ear. "If she offers you any fruitcake, just say no. Learn from my mistakes; don't repeat them."

With a look that conveys "May the force be with you," James takes his wife by the elbow, and off they go.

Leaving me alone. With Maxine.

"Well, come on." She opens the door for me to follow her inside. "Let's get you something to eat. You're surely starving. I know I am, and I had a bag of Cheetos and some Twizzlers during church."

Maxine leaves me in her little living room area, then walks back into the hall that leads to her bedroom. She comes back with a pair of high-top tennis shoes in hand. Plopping herself on her couch, she props one foot at a time on the coffee table and laces each high-top up tightly.

I stand in helpless confusion as Maxine grabs a giant silver purse, something more closely related to luggage than a handbag, and digs around until she finds a tube of lipstick and a compact. Powder flies everywhere as she fluffs the stuff on her nose, then making a pouty face, artfully applies her lipstick until her mouth is a bold, glossy red.

With a smack of her lips and a snap of the compact, she throws it all back in her bag, jumps up from the couch like an explosion and barks, "What are you waiting for? Let's go!"

I've only been here a few times, but anytime I'm in Maxine's senior apartment, I step into an alternate universe where things only make sense to her and her kind.

"Where are we going?" I dare to ask.

She reaches under the couch, her tail end straight in the air, and pulls out a pink helmet.

"We're going to get something to eat."

My eyes widen.

"You didn't think I was going to cook for you, did you?" Maxine laughs.

I shrug.

"Girlie, I haven't cooked for anyone since 1978, and I'm sure not going to give it a whirl today." She shoves the pink helmet down over her head and fumbles with the chin strap.

What in the world? I don't know what's going on, but it reeks of wrong, and I *cannot* afford to get in any more trouble. "Mrs. Simmons, I think this might be a bad idea—"

"Well, fine!" Maxine huffs.

Whew. Close one.

"Then *you* wear the helmet." And before I know what hits me, the helmet is crammed on top of my head and Maxine is strapping me in.

"No, Mrs. Simmons, I was saying we shouldn't—"

"Look, I'm in the mood for burgers and fries, and I'm in charge here." She yanks the apartment door open.

"Mrs. Simmons, what are we doing?"

I'm talking to myself.

Maxine is already outside, leaving me standing in the middle of her living room.

I cautiously walk to the doorway and peer out to see where the crazy lady has gone to.

"Get on."

Maxine sits on her bicycle built for two, grinning like she's the queen on her royal throne. Balancing on one toe, she throws the kickstand with her other foot, then pats the seat behind her.

I close my eyes and count to five. (I know I'll never make it to ten.) "Now, Mrs. Simmons—"

"Call me Maxine and get on this bicycle, girl. That's an order."

"Mrs. Simmons—"

"*Maxine*! Don't address me like I'm so old I drool and need to be spoon fed."

My mouth snaps shut.

I cannot get on that bicycle. This woman hates me. She would not think twice about finding another chicken truck to run into with me riding shotgun.

"Look, here, Sweet Pea, you have until the count of five to get your backside on this seat. You are at my house; you will obey my rules. And I say get your tushie on my ride, or I'm leaving without you."

I look at Maxine—an odd mix of trendy and tragic in biking gloves, high tops, and a Nike reflective running jacket. Her teeth are clenched, and her lips form a single glossy line.

I do not trust this woman.

"Five."

She's insane.

"Four."

My life is at stake here.

"Three."

She knows what I've done. She didn't like me before, and there probably aren't words for what she feels for me now.

"Two."

My picture will probably be on the back of a milk carton. *Katie Parker, last seen in the Shady Acres Retirement Community wearing a biking helmet the color of Pepto-Bismol.*

"One!"

Maxine puts the black high-tops to work and pedals her bike down her sidewalk. As soon as she hits the parking lot, I begin chasing her.

"W-a-a-a-a-a-i-t!"

I catch up enough to grab the back seat, close my eyes, leap frog onto the back of her bicycle, and hold on for dear life.

"Where are we going?"

She hollers back, but I can't hear her over the flapping of the plastic ribbons coming out of her handlebars and the constant honking of her bike horn.

"What?"

"The Burger Barn."

I catch my breath and begin to help her pedal. Maxine veers off Central Avenue, and when we hit Olive Lane, she leads us onto the sidewalk. Along the way, we meet a few joggers, two speed walkers, and the occasional mother pushing a stroller. But Maxine owns the sidewalk, and she lets it be known by standing up on her pedals as we fly by, honking her obnoxious horn all the way.

We hang a mean right and two more lefts, coming out on First Street. I'm thoroughly out of breath, but Maxine maintains her frantic pace. From First Street we turn on Maple, then Persimmon; we cross through someone's well-kept yard, ducking under a string of unmentionables on a clothesline, shoot out onto Main Street, and upon Maxine's shouted command, we lean into a right curve before sailing into the Burger Barn parking lot, coming to a stop so abruptly my face slams into her back.

"Oomph!" I remove her Nike jacket from my mouth and arise to see we are in the drive-thru.

Maxine taps on the drive-thru window.

"Helewww! Maxine Simmons come a calling. Open up!"

She slaps her palm on the glass a few more times before a teenager, an upperclassman I recognize from In Between High, opens the window and takes in the sight before him.

"Well, Ms. Maxine, how's it going today? Don't you look extra fine?"

Chapter twenty~five

"HELLO, YOURSELF, BRYANT," MAXINE COOS, and if I'm not mistaken, she's batting her eyelashes at him.

I'm going to be sick.

"You sure look lovely today, Ms. Maxine." The guy in the drive-thru window winks at Maxine like she has prom-queen potential or something.

I want to say, "Hey, Burger Boy, drop the routine. She has bunions older than you."

Maxine flips her wild hair. "Oh, my . . . really? The wind is up a little today, so I'm sure I'm just a mess after our leisurely bike ride through town."

Leisurely bike ride? I've seen Hell's Angels bike slower than Maxine.

"Looks like you have company today. And it's not Mr. Sam either."

"Mr. Sam?" I lean in closer so I can get in view of Bryant. "Who's Sam?"

Maxine turns around quickly, shoots me a withering look,

and shoves me out of her way with a pointy elbow. "Never mind, Señorita Nosy."

Maxine returns her attention to Bryant, her face instantly a vision of sweetness. "Bryant, this is Katie Parker. She goes to In Between High too. Maybe you've seen her around?"

Bryant leans out of the window and gives me the once-over. "Nope, don't believe we've met. Are you new?"

I nod, thoroughly humiliated to be on a bicycle built for two in the drive-thru lane of Burger Barn, wearing a stupid pink helmet.

"Well, she's a cutie, our Katie. Dontcha think, Bryant? Now you and Katie here can chitty chat all you like at school, but right now we are in some serious need for cheeseburgers."

"Coming right up, Maxine. You just tell me what you want."

This guy is falling all over himself trying to kiss up to Maxine. It's enough to make a girl lose her appetite.

"You're the sweetest, Bryant." Maxine reaches out and play-fully slaps his hand resting on the window. "Okay, I will take a number two, a number seven, an extra cheeseburger, hold the pickles, and two chocolate shakes."

Bryant scribbles her massive order. Are we feeding just the two of us, or is the rest of Shady Acres going to join us too?

"Okay, Mrs. Simmons. That's a number two, number seven, extra cheeseburger, and two chocolate shakes," Bryant from Burger Barn repeats. "And for Katie?"

"Well, tell him what you want," Maxine says impatiently.

"Uh . . . um . . . " I hadn't even looked at the menu. "I guess a cheeseburger."

Maxine chortles like I've just committed a Burger Barn faux pas. "You're such an amateur. She'll take a number three, extra cheese, and throw in two more chocolate shakes, and don't be stingy with the chocolate."

Bryant and Maxine swap a few more pleasantries before he shuts the window, leaving us to wait for our order. An order that could feed a small nation.

Maxine rotates on her mammoth bike seat, and we are uncomfortably face to face. Great. Here it comes. Our big talk. This is where she tells me I am a disgrace, she knew it all along, and she wants me to leave her family alone forever.

"You mention anything about Sam to Millie, and I will be all over you like stink on a dog. Are we clear?"

What? Who? I don't even know this Sam person, for crying out loud. "Um, yes, ma'am."

Isn't she going to say anything about my crimes? My misdemeanors? My outlaw ways?

"Sam is . . . well, it doesn't matter. Just keep your yapper shut, and we'll get along like peas and carrots, you follow?" Maxine moves in closer. We are forehead to helmet.

I swallow. "Yeah, sure, whatever you say, Mrs. Simm—"

"*Maxine*," she barks, her breath hot on my wind-burned face.

"Maxine," I amend.

Bryant flings open the window, putting an end to yet another painfully weird moment with Maxine.

"Here you go." He holds out our food in a sack nearly as big as a trash bag.

Maxine hands Bryant the money before setting the food, with much maneuvering and readjusting, in the giant basket on the front of her bike.

"Thanks so much, Bryant. A pleasure doing business with you, as always. Tell your momma I said hi, and here's a little something for all your hard work."

Maxine puts a five dollar bill in Bryant's hand, and suddenly all his pathetic fussing over her makes sense. That rascal.

"Thanks, Maxine. See you Tuesday for half-price night."

Millie waves bye-bye at Bryant like she's fresh out of junior high, then pedals us out of the parking lot. I look back and see Bryant still waving. And a trail of at least five cars in line, waiting to be served. How embarrassing.

The ride back to Maxine's is much easier, as I now know when to lean, when to pedal harder, and when to duck in time to avoid hanging brassieres.

Exactly seven point two minutes later, we climb off the bike. I barely resist the temptation to kiss the pavement. Maxine grabs the food, and I meekly follow her into her apartment. Her lair.

"Put the helmet under the couch, would you? I don't like to risk someone stealing it." Maxine points toward her scarlet couch, and I peel the headwear off and obediently place it underneath, where it joins a baseball bat, a giant box of beef jerky, a yoga mat, two wigs, a signed and framed picture of Orlando Bloom, and a neon hula hoop.

Of course. She wouldn't have dust bunnies under her furniture like normal people.

Maxine motions for me to follow her into the kitchen, where she hands me plates to set on the table in her little dining area. She unpacks the carryout sack, burger by burger, with one eye on her task and one eye on me. A little chill dances up my spine. There is no denying it: I'm scared of this woman. With the way she's looking at me, this could very well be my last meal.

"So . . . " She tosses two cheeseburgers and a bag of fries on my plate.

My eyes reluctantly meet hers. It's time we get to it and address the elephant in the room.

"So"—Maxine's voice is low and dangerous like one of those cops on TV—"I'm quite ashamed of you, you know that, right?"

I nod. "Yes, ma'am." I have shamed her and her family, and she no doubt does not want me living under the same roof as her daughter and son-in-law.

"Yes, indeed. I could not believe it." Maxine shakes her head dramatically, then tears into her first cheeseburger.

I roll a pickle around on my plate, my head hanging low.

"I know I let you down. I know you think I'm no good."

Mad Maxine slurps her shake. "Yeah" — she smacks — "you did let me down. Let me down in a big, big way."

"Yes, ma'am." I'm ready with the offense. "I know it was a mistake, but I'm through making those kinds of bad choices. And I just want to point out, although I was there, I wasn't the one who did the real damage."

Maxine's eyes narrow to slits. "If you're with the guilty, then you *are* guilty, little missy."

My eyes are on my plate. "Yes, Mrs. Simmons . . . er, Maxine."

Maxine grabs her shake and punches it in the air. "And to think you would be a party to Frances Vega trying to kick a woman of my seasoning out of her pew. What were you *thinking*? But no, here you go and side up with Frances, whose sole mission in this life is to write her name on my seat in church."

I raise my head. My eyes fly to Maxine, who is sucking on her straw so hard her cheeks are caving in.

"What?"

"Yeah, here we are, practically family," she spits, like the words *we* and *family* leave a bad taste in her mouth. "And you have the nerve to stand by Frances as she tries to boot me out of my pew. You didn't even take up for me. Did nothing to defend me. What kind of foster granddaughter are you, anyway?"

Um, a really confused one.

I broke into her daughter's theatre, it got totally trashed, and *this* is what she has to say to me?

"Maxine, I think you've been wearing your helmet a little too tight," I mutter under my breath.

"I heard that sass." Maxine talks around a mouthful of fries.

I'm just going to go for it. Address the real issue. "Look, I know you know about the—"

"Pass the ketchup—"

"—break in. I guess everyone in town knows about—"

"And the salt." She reaches across the table, totally ignoring my efforts at a real conversation.

"What I'm trying to say is I—"

"Oops, I'm going to need your napkin there." Maxine grabs my last napkin and dabs at a spot on her jacket.

"Maxine, I'm trying to tell you—"

"They never get the right mustard to ketchup ratio on here." Maxine does an intense study of her bun.

I try again. "I know I wasn't supposed to be—"

She lifts up my cup for inspection. "Your shake's melting."

"If you would just hear me out for a—"

"Where is the other cheeseburger?" Maxine rifles through discarded bags, wrappers, and napkins with a focused urgency.

"Maxine, are you listening to me at all?"

"Girl, if you know the whereabouts of my other cheeseburger you'd better speak up now."

Oh, that's it.

I slam my shake down and spill my guts in a single breath. "I broke into the Valiant Theatre. It was a stupid thing, but I had no idea they were going to vandalize it, and I'm sorry. I'm sorry if I've embarrassed you and hurt your family, and I'm sorry you were right about me." And inhale.

Maxine raises a quizzical brow.

"You think I'm a total loser. You've thought that since you first laid eyes on me. You think I'm trash, I come from trash, and I will always be—"

"Now hold on just a hairy pickled minute there!" Maxine points her manicured finger my way. "You're trash, huh? Tell me, do *I* think this, or do you?"

I swallow. "You do."

"Really." She holds my gaze for a few painful seconds. "Have I ever told you that you were trash?"

"No, but you might as well by the way you act." Millie is going to kill me for talking to her mom like this.

"Look, you little spring chicken, if I thought you belonged in the compost heap, I would tell you." Maxine nods her head once. Like case closed. Enough said. End of story.

A weird silence settles over the little kitchen, magnifying every noise. The clock ticking, a car passing by, the ice settling in the freezer.

Maxine meditates on her meal, but I break into her deep burger thoughts anyway. "Um, Maxine . . . I don't understand. Aren't you mad? Don't you want to tell me off?"

The cheeseburger is dropped, and Maxine focuses on me. "Yeah, I'll tell you off." Smack, smack, swallow. "You let that shake melt, tootsie, and you're going to see me go from zero to ugly in a matter of seconds. Now drink your shake, and eat those fries. I can't stand to see a girl who doesn't appreciate her trans fats."

"Maxine . . . " Why can't I let this go? Am I *still* talking? "What those others did—Angel and them—I'm not like that."

"That's between you and God, sister." Maxine attends to some mustard on her upper lip. "Not you and me."

"I am sorry." And I am. I want her to know that—no matter what she thinks of me.

"Yeah, yeah, that's what Nixon told me. Are you gonna eat those onion rings or play with them?"

I push all the onion rings and fries her way.

"So you believe me?" I brave a smile.

She takes another bite. "I'm thinking about it."

"And you trust me?"

Maxine swats my elbows off the table. "Girl, I keep my ATM card in my bra." She pats her ample chest. "I've got a very short list of people I trust . . . I'll let you know when you make the cut."

Chapter twenty~six

RRRRR! RRRRR! RRRRR! RRRRR!

Alarm clocks are evil. Evil, I tell you. I'd hit snooze again, but I've already done that six times.

I do not want to go to school. I think I'd rather face a hundred Mad Maxines than everyone at school. There will be people pointing and staring and talking about me. That will be all sorts of zip-a-dee-doo-dah fun. Then there will be Angel and her crew. Ugh, the thought makes my stomach hurt. What's that going to be like? Will they be mad at me for turning them in? Will they be groveling at my feet for bailing on me and leaving me to deal with the police? I just want them to stay away from me. Angel's mom will probably take it out on me in PE today too. I can't imagine how that class could get worse, though. What's she gonna do, make me bench press her SUV? Do a thousand push-ups—with the Chihuahua football team on my back?

Knock. Knock.

"Katie?" Millie peeks her head in. "Katie, aren't you up yet?"

I pull the covers over my head. "I don't feel good." Well, it's mostly true. I don't feel at all good about going to school today.

"What?" Millie stands next to my bed and gives the blankets a tug. She places her hand on my forehead. "You don't seem to have a fever."

I cough. Twice. "Are you sure? We should probably check."

"What are your symptoms?" Millie runs a hand over my hair.

"My symptoms?" Let's see, fear, embarrassment, regret, and the strong desire to morph into someone else.

"Yes, tell me how you don't feel good."

I cough again. "Millie, the symptoms . . . um, they're just too many to name."

My Florence Nightingale of a foster mom sits down on the bed. "Well, enlighten me."

I make a pained face. "Millie, it's not good. You might want to sit down for this . . . oh, you are. Sorry, my eyes are so blurry I can barely make out what's what." My hands strike out, searching. "Where are you, Millie? Millie, are you there?" I flail my arms some more.

Millie grabs my hands and rests them in her lap. "Ah, yes. I'm right here, Katie. You were telling me about your symptoms?"

Do I hear sarcasm in her voice? In my time of need?

Sniff. "I think my system might be shutting down. I feel terrible. Millie, I hate to break this to you, but I have . . . " I have the what? A virus? No, it has to be something serious. Ebola? Oh, what about that bird flu? Millie's studying me closely, waiting for an answer. Think, Katie! "I, uh, have the Ebola bird flu virus." *Cough. Cough.*

"You have the Ebola—"

"Yes, I have the Ebola bird flu virus. I know, it's probably fatal. There's not much modern science can do for me." I swipe at my eyes, hoping I'm creating a tender moment. "Try to carry on without me. You can have my T-shirt collection." Through my squinted eyes I see Millie's face drawn into a sincere frown.

"Oh, Katie, I could never take your favorite T-shirts."

Aw, how sweet. Millie does care.

"You can leave those to Rocky. I never told you, but he usually likes to sleep on your clothes after I've taken them out of the dryer."

Ew. Sick. Tender moment over.

"Well, remember me fondly, Millie. Tell James thanks for the memories." My voice is all despair and tragedy—but tastefully so. "Just a pine box, if you please. Nothing fancy. I am just an orphan, after all."

Millie shakes her head solemnly. "I guess if this is it, then I could just go ahead and take the iPod you got last week. You won't be needing it now. Your ears will probably be the next thing to go—with this Ebola bird flu virus."

What?

"No, no. That's okay. I want to go out with the gift of music in my ears."

"Oh, no, you'll probably be comatose in the very end." Millie's tone is sadness personified as she tucks the quilt around my shoulders. "I'll just keep the iPod. You know, in fact, I should probably take your computer, too. You'll be too busy being quarantined when the Center for Disease Control gets here. I should probably go call them. And how do you feel about spending your last days in a plastic bubble?"

"No! Er, I mean, no, stay with me just a little bit longer. I'm cold . . . so, so cold. Like death has its very hand upon me. Oh, look at the pretty white light. . . . " My voice trails off, and I close my eyes.

"Oh, speaking of light, Katie, I should probably get your TV."

Millie stands up. "Yes, I want to make your room as peaceful and relaxing as possible for you. I know, I'll go get Rocky. He's been waiting a very long time for the opportunity to snuggle with you."

I open an eye. Millie has left my bed and is at the door.

"Well, look who's right here, sitting in the hall. Come here, boy," she coos. "You've been waiting for this moment, and now your big day is here. Rocky, jump on the bed with Katie. She needs a big, sloppy kiss."

Oh, my gosh. Oh, my— *no*! Before I can yank the covers back over my head, Rocky the Wonder Dog—all five hundred pounds of him—jumps on me, his nose digging around for my face, which I try in vain to cover with my hands.

"No! Rocky, off. Ew, no, gross, stop! Stop it, Rocky. I said get off! Ew, not on my face. That is *so* sick!"

Rocky sniffs and snorts and licks, his nose and tongue everywhere at once. He paws at the hands sheltering my face. Can't . . . take . . . this . . . much . . . more.

"Get off of me, you freak!" In one swift motion, I grab a quilt and bound off the bed, landing on the other side of the room.

Millie adjusts her earring, her face bland. "Wow, that was an amazing recovery from the . . . what was it you said you had again?"

Rocky leaps off the bed and heads my way, clearly thinking this is some grand new game.

"The . . . the . . . " I'm unable to form any thought besides *gross*.

"Oh, yes, the Ebola bird flu virus." Millie's voice is dry as toast, but she's biting her lip like she's trying not to smile. Of all the nerve.

Rocky noses around, searching for my hands under the quilt I have wrapped around me. The stupid dog thinks the only function of hands is to pet, to feed, or to throw a ball.

"Call him off, Millie." I clench my teeth and refuse to make eye contact with the mutt.

"Oh, I will," Millie says slowly, like she's got all the time in the world. She takes a leisurely seat on my bed. "But first you have to tell me what you'd hoped to achieve with this sick routine—and a very bad one at that."

Rocky finds my hand and starts to bathe it with his big, nasty dog tongue.

"I'm waiting, Katie."

Lick, lick.

"Okay, okay! Just call him off."

"Rocky, come here." Millie snaps her fingers, and the dog is by her side in an instant.

I sigh. "You know what this is about. I don't want to go to school."

Millie nods, petting her dog. "Uh-huh. And . . . "

"And I've been thinking homeschooling would be a great option for me."

"No."

"Come on! One-on-one time with me. Think how close we'd become. Don't you want to build our relationship?" I give Millie a cherubic smile. I've got innocence and charm coming out my pores (and doggy germs, too, no doubt).

"Yes, I do. And I also want you to build your education, and that is going to happen at In Between High."

"Millie, I don't want to go to school. Please, just let me have today off."

"You faced church okay. Now it's time to deal with everyone at school. You have to face the consequences—all of them." Millie holds her arm out, and I find myself gravitating toward her, sitting on the bed, and letting her put her arm around me.

"I know this is tough, kiddo, but you gotta do it." She rests her head on mine. "You're going to go to school, hold your head up high, and go about your day."

"And what if Angel or Vincent or those guys approach me?"

"Then you turn around and walk the other way. You have nothing to say to them."

I inhale a big gulp of air then let it out. "Can't I stay home just one day? I could help you out at the theatre."

"Nope. Your job is to go to school. Besides, I'm going in to do some work at the church. I'll be at the theatre this afternoon when you get there."

"But, Millie, what if I just—"

"No."

"Okay, but maybe I could—"

"No."

"Oh, I know, what about—"

"No, no, and no." Millie laughs, then playfully shoves me away from her. "Get up, get dressed, and meet me downstairs in twenty minutes. We're running late."

"You're going to send me to school on an empty stomach?"

"I've got a bagel downstairs with your name on it, Katie, but if you're tardy, I'm leaving you to face the counselor all on your own."

"Oh, now that's just cruel." I toss a pillow at Millie as she heads out the door.

Her head pops back into view. "Well, you can just tell her all about your Ebola bird flu virus."

Millie's laugh travels all the way to my room as she marches downstairs.

Woof!

Oh, no. No way. "Millie! You forgot your dog!"

More laughter from the stairway. "No, I didn't!"

Chapter twenty~seven

DEAR MRS. SMARTLY,

Hey, long time no see. Or hear. Thanks for your last letter, even though it was very short. It was so newsy. I was just riveted by the news that you got a new goldfish for your desk. And yes, I do think Stan is a fine name for your new gilled friend.

Today was my first day back at school since "the incident." I like to say that out loud so I can do quotey fingers. I find it kind of odd you didn't call me to bawl me out about "the incident." I pulled a Trina, and you have nothing to say to me? No yelling? No threats? I guess you're too busy with your new pet goldfish to work up a good lecture.

What a day. Longest day of my life. (Well, maybe except for the time the electricity went out at Sunny for twenty-four hours, and we were without air conditioning and television, and you made us play I-Spy for like twelve hours straight.)

So after a bit of a slow start this morning, Millie took me to school. When she pulled into the school parking lot, put the car in park, and just sat there, I had a flashback to the first time I sat in the parking lot with her — my stomach in knots, my palms sweaty, and my deodorant sending signals that it was off duty for the day.

The weatherman had predicted clear, sunny skies for this morning and a crisp fall temperature of fifty-nine degrees. The thermometer on Millie's rearview mirror said forty degrees, and the rain spitting down had me wishing I hadn't bothered with the straightening iron. My own forecast? How about stressful with a hundred percent chance of freaking out.

English class started out fine. I really like that class. We've just started reading a play out loud. It's *Julius Caesar*. I haven't read much from ol' Bill Shakespeare, but he's still kinda cool. Ms. Dillon, my teacher, says it's about this dude who thinks he has all these friends, but then they turn on him and stab him. I so relate. Well, minus the death part.

But about twenty minutes into the class, in walk Angel and Vincent — you know, the stabbers. They handed Ms. Dillon a note, like they had been in the principal's office, and then took their seats. Close to me. Vincent didn't even acknowledge me, but Angel watched me from the time she gave the teacher the note to the moment she sat down in her seat. She looked at me like I was some sort of parasite. Definitely not in a "Hey let's do another sleepover really soon, okay?" way. I just stared right back, like "Don't even think you can intimidate me, Angel, Miss I-Have-the-Most-Ironic-Name-in-the-World."

It's like our staring needed a soundtrack and subtitles.

So after class I go to my locker, put my books away, and slam the locker shut.

And there was Angel.

"You better have a good reason why you ratted on us this weekend," she hissed.

Oh, no she didn't. No way I was letting her put this on me.
"Oh, right, I should've taken up for you? Why? To thank you for the
cool way you left me there with the cops? Or maybe because you
have been *such* a good friend to me? I don't think so."

"We didn't mean for you to take the fall."

"Really? My mistake then. I guess I got the wrong idea when
I walked out of the orchestra pit and I was surrounded by graffiti,
broken glass, and the police! And you guys were nowhere to
be found!" I stepped closer to her. "I must've gotten a little bit
mixed up when the police pointed their cute little flashlights and
guns at *me*. And the moment when the police put the handcuffs
on me — only me — might have given me the idea that I was
supposed to take the blame — alone. But now that you're here to
explain it all, Angel, it makes so much sense."

Angel could see I wasn't backing down, and some of her
bravado slipped. "Look, Katie, it's just — "

"No, *you* look. That was my foster parents' theatre. And you
knew it. You took me to the Valiant expecting me to help you
guys destroy the place. And then you left me there to take the
blame and deal with the police all by myself."

"We took you in. When no one else would hang out with you
here, we let you be a part of our group. We thought you could
handle it. We thought you were one of us. But obviously you're
not. Real friends stick together, Katie. So before you go pointing
fingers, you think about that."

I laughed in her face. "I was seconds away from getting my
first mug shot. A mug shot with bed head, to top it off. Wow,
Angel, I've never had friends as good as you. I know it's my loss.
I may never have the opportunity for such friendship again. And
five years from now when I'm watching the evening news, and I
see you and your 'friends' (and I did the quotey fingers here) on

TV being arrested for jewelry heists or grand theft auto, I'll say, 'oh, if only I could have stuck by them and been lucky enough to be their "friend."'"

Angel opened her mouth to counterstrike, but I hugged my books to my chest and nudged past her (and in the spirit of Trina, I might have purposefully bumped into her shoulder just for drama's sake).

After English, I went to World History. The man who teaches that class probably knew your great-great-great-great-great-great-great-great-great-great-great grandfather. He's that old. And the whine of his hearing aid always makes me think there's a cat being tortured somewhere in the room. But aside from Mr. Patton falling asleep twice during his own lecture, history came and went without a problem.

Ditto for algebra.

But next . . . was lunch.

I grabbed my lunch bag and went in search of a seat. In a different bathroom where Frances Vega wouldn't find me. I vaguely remembered a bathroom in the gym wing and took off in that direction.

I turned down the corridor and hit bathroom pay dirt. Taking a deep breath (because you never know what the air quality will be like), I opened the door and claimed my stall. Digging into the lunch bag Millie packed for me, I pulled out two homemade chocolate chip cookies. This day called for dessert first.

I decided I would take a bite every time I had a pitiful thought, every time I felt sorry for myself.

The cookies were gone in five seconds.

Do you know what it's like to want more, Mrs. Smartly? Or to be so totally out of your element and all lonely? That's my life here, you know? I don't *want* to sit on an old broken toilet in a stall with

"Lisa loves ~~Ben~~ ~~Dustin~~ ~~Mark~~ ~~Shawn~~ Devon" written all over it. But Angel and those guys were the only people I knew, and I sure can't go hang out with them now. What's a girl to do?

So back to my lunch…I half-heartedly reached for my turkey sandwich, and there on the sandwich bag was a sticky note. It said:

Katie, have a great day! Remember, keep your chin up and go make some new friends. (Ones who don't carry spray paint on them.) I'm praying for you.

Love,
Millie

So what did I do? I stuffed my lunch back in the bag. I squared my shoulders. I lifted my chin. And walked out of that bathroom.

With toilet paper on my shoe.

Some kid pointed it out on my way down the hall. Real cool.

Okay, so I was off in pursuit of friends. No problem. I mean, should've been easy, right? Simply walk into the cafeteria, pick a table, sit down next to someone, and say, "Hey, I'll bet you want to be my friend. Well, today just happens to be your lucky day." Mrs. Smartly, I know you think you have it rough being the director of Sunny Haven, but this teenage business — it makes your job look like a day at the pool.

I opened the cafeteria doors. Two hundred heads swiveled in my direction. All eyes were on me. (Okay, maybe five or six people stopped eating their burritos long enough to look my way, but it felt like two hundred.)

I spied Frances and her gang of non-troublemakers over in a far corner. Nope, I wasn't gonna sit there. I knew Frances would let me eat lunch with her, but I don't think I'm ready to go from wannabe cons like Angel to Frances and her squeaky-clean group of valedictorians.

I scanned the cafeteria, aware of how incredibly awkward it was to be alone in the cafeteria, searching for a single friendly face to connect to. Being a dork is quite uncomfortable. I know you can relate, Mrs. Smartly.

I surveyed the room. There were the computer and techie kids. The gamers (they show up to school wearing big hoodie sweatshirts every day and pull their gaming devices out of their pockets when they think no one is looking). The cheerleaders (can you even imagine me approaching them?). The jocks (seated right next to the cheerleaders, of course). There was the table of agri students (the farm kids), the preps, another table of goths, the band people (easy to spot because there is usually someone among them tapping out the latest marching song with a pair of spoons). I could go on and on (and I should just to get you back for the six-line letter you sent me last week), but I finally decided to pick the table the farthest away from both Frances and Angel.

I approached the table and stood there. Totally awkward.

An upperclassman wearing a T-shirt emblazoned with some unknown symbol noticed me first. "Dude, is there something you want?" Sir Righteous talks like the turtle off of *Finding Nemo*.

Here goes, I thought to myself. "Um, yeah, I'm kind of new here. Do you mind if I sit with you guys?"

The table was full of guys and girls, none of which I would label preps, but not exactly on the goth side either. Their clothes were a bit rough, but in a very deliberate way.

The group looked to one another, a few shrugged, a few nodded, and finally their spokesperson nodded. "Yeah, I guess. The more the merrier, I suppose."

We exchanged a few pleasantries, such as where I'm from,

what my name is (which raised a few eyebrows — clearly they'd heard about my little jaunt to the theatre), and briefly discussed the neutral topic of our feelings on cafeteria food. Then the group returned to the conversation I had interrupted.

"Okay, so dude, I was at my dad's last night, and I did this 360 pop shovit into a backside 50-50 grind." This from a tenth grader who dared to wear a hat in the cafeteria.

A girl sitting next to me spoke up in a heavy Texan drawl. "Oh, dude, I've totally been working on that too. But check it, yesterday I tried a nollie boneless on my new board and landed on my hand. Today I'm gonna try an inverted handplant."

I picked at my sandwich, wondering what alternate universe I had stepped into. When we were discussing cafeteria food, the pros and cons of the school pizza, the value in checking milk expiration dates, and the importance of avoiding school meat loaf at all costs, things had seemed so normal. But pop shovits? Handplants? Three-sixties? If this was gang lingo, I was in so much trouble.

"So I did a wall ride, right, and I'm on the vert, then I totally run into Principal Wayman. I was so busted." This from a guy who introduced himself as Jeff.

"No way." I don't know whether to act shocked or impressed. I attempt an expression somewhere in between.

"Totally."

"Hey, Katie, do you skate goofy or regular?"

Mrs. Smartly, I had just about decided these people were making illicit drug references when Frances Vega appeared at the table.

"Hey, dudes," she threw out, like she was down with their slang.

"Frances! What up, yo? How's that manual coming?"

At this point my head was about to explode.

"Totally killer, Jason. Thanks for helping me with it. I'm definitely getting better."

Frances turned a very definite shade of pink. Our little Frances Vega was blushing!

"As soon as you're ready to hit the skate park, you let me know, okay?" Jason's eyes never left Frances.

"Yeah, well, you know, it will be a while. I'm still not very stable on the board, and my parents aren't too big on the skate park." Frances shuffled from one foot to the other. Very interesting.

Skaters. These people were skaters — not drug dealers, not gang members. Still, I was totally out of my element. I don't know a wallie from a wheel.

I stayed at the table long enough to finish my lunch, and it actually helped that Frances ended up sitting down by me and joining in the conversation. The skaters moved on to different topics which I could contribute to, thanks to Frances and her brilliant conversation skills.

When the bell rang signaling lunch had ended, Frances followed me out the door.

"Were the bathroom stalls all taken today?"

"I'm not a total chicken, Frances." No, I didn't bother to tell her I had begun my lunch on a toilet seat again. What she doesn't know can't hurt her. And there's a very short list of things Frances Vega doesn't know.

"You could have sat with me and my friends, you know. I looked for you, but couldn't find you."

"Yeah, well, thanks. I made it fine. Look, I've got to go. I have PE next." Just couldn't wait to get to PE, you know?

Now, Mrs. Smartly, I will tell you about my day in physical education.

Oh, wait, here's Millie. I'm writing this letter at the Valiant, waiting on her. This letter writing is for the birds. If we were e-mailing right now, I'd tell you something funny. And then you would e-mail back and say something like my e-mail had you ROTFL. And I would e-mail back and say LOL! Wouldn't that be GR8?

Okay, it's time for me to get to work. But you owe me a letter — a good one. I don't want to hear about how you cleaned out the dryer lint screen again, okay? CUL8R!

LUV,
KT

Chapter twenty~eight

AS PER INSTRUCTIONS, I TOOK the school bus to the theatre after school.

The *public* school bus.

It's something everyone should experience at least once. Today on my ride, a first-grader shared my seat. She proudly showed me her artwork, a blob of red paint she said was a pony, and then talked herself into a sleepy coma. When she fell asleep, her head bobbed until it landed on my shoulder and her paste-crusted hands rested on my jeans. The kid in seat number twenty picked his nose when he thought no one was looking. Spit wads sailed overhead. The gnome sitting behind me kicked my seat to the beat of the bus driver's George Strait CD the entire ride. If that brat does it again tomorrow, I'm going to have to show him who's boss—and it ain't him. Across the aisle, a group of middle schoolers gathered, trying to burp out "All My Ex's Live in Texas."

Now, standing in the foyer of the Valiant, I shudder at the memory.

From here I can see Millie sitting in her car in the parking lot. She appears to be in a serious conversation on her cell phone, and she doesn't look happy. After a few more minutes, she snaps the phone shut, runs a hand through her hair, brushes on some lip gloss, and makes her way to the theatre. She looks stressed, but I decide not to mention it as she breezes into the foyer where I'm waiting.

"Hey, Millie." I proceed with care. Not only is Millie worked up over something, but I'm anxious too. My first day on the job at the Valiant. Who knows what awaits me inside. Like a scaredy-cat, I've been standing in the entryway, putting off going into the theatre for as long as possible. It's not easy to return to the scene of the crime. And now I have to look at it with Millie, see it through her eyes.

"Hey, kiddo, how was your day?" Millie puts a smile on her face and gives me a quick hug. She knows the hugging thing still doesn't have the total Katie Parker seal of approval. But if anybody can get away with it, it's Millie.

"Oh, you know, the usual." Ugh. I eye the giant double doors leading into the theatre lobby. Don't feel so good.

"No, seriously, how did it go?" Millie stops and gives me her full attention.

I sigh and make a figure eight on the floor with the toe of a new, but vintage-looking Nike. "Well, I went to English, faced off with Angel."

Millie's eyebrows rise.

"But no blood was shed. No WMDs were fired." I wave it off. "It was a fairly peaceful meeting."

"Okay." Millie nods. "Go on."

It's kind of odd to have an adult listen to you. I mean really listen.

"So then I went to history."

"And Mr. Patton fell asleep," Millie finishes.

"Right, and Mr. Patton fell asleep. Oh, and on the second time he fell asleep, this guy named Steven went up to him and tapped him on the shoulder to wake him up. That didn't work, so Steven dropped a history book on the floor right next to him."

"And he slept right through it?" Apparently everyone in town is familiar with Mr. Patton's teaching style.

"No, he shot out of his chair, yelling, 'Give me liberty or give me death!'"

Millie's face softens, and her warm laughter fills the foyer.

And my face falls as she swings the giant doors open, leading the way into the lobby.

I stand horrified at the sight. Graffiti everywhere. Antique counters smashed. An old popcorn machine, probably an original, in pieces. Lights broken. Carpet ripped. Scarlet fabric, which had been artfully draped here and there, now torn and strewn about the floor.

And this is just the lobby.

They accomplished so much destruction in so little time. I guess that night I was so lost in my own little world, so in awe of the theatre and exploring the orchestra pit that I didn't hear most of their noise.

Either that or I need to borrow Mr. Patton's hearing aids.

I reach my hand out to Millie. "I—I don't know what to say." I shake my head in disbelief. In disgust. There is nothing I can say to make this any better. "I promise I didn't know. I just didn't know."

My stomach rolls. I'm *not* like Angel and Vincent. I may have a questionable past and, undeniably, a questionable future, but I could never do something like this. Unlike my former "friends," I'm not into criminal activities, and I would never purposefully hurt someone.

Looking at Millie's face, though she's trying to wear a smile, I can tell she's hurt.

"Millie, I—"

"I know." Again, the plastic smile. "I know, Katie. Look, we have a lot to do today, so let's get started, okay?"

She moves away from me and opens the theatre's black lacquered doors.

I gulp.

"Sam!" Millie hollers into the theatre. "Sam, we're here!"

Sam?

"Sam's a caretaker of sorts here. And now that—well, all of this happened, he's overseeing the repairs." Millie props the door with her foot and scans the theatre for the missing Sam. I remain far enough behind the door that I don't have to see inside—yet.

"Ah, here he is. Come here! I want you to meet Katie."

I'll just bet this Sam is on the edge of his seat, filled with excitement to meet me. Me, the girl who was with the kids who did all of this. If this guy yells at me or uses some choice expletives, I will probably start crying on the spot.

"Come on." Millie pulls me through the doorway; I hesitate, but when Millie shoots me a warning look, I step forward into the theatre.

The inside of the theatre looks even worse than the lobby. Some of the old seats, which look like they had just been redone, are ripped, cushioning hanging out, material shredded. Images and words I can't even bear to look at cover various places on the Art Deco tile. Curtains hang in tatters, and broken windows are boarded up. Sawhorses are set up in random spots, as people I don't recognize deal with the repairs needed on all the wood in the theatre.

"Sam got a crew of volunteers from the church to help us out."

Millie points to a group of men measuring and conferring over something on the balcony.

A man who looks to be in his seventies walks our way up the center aisle. He's dressed in blue-and-white striped overalls, and his heavy brown work boots are flecked with mint-green paint.

Wiping his hands on his bibs, he smiles at Millie, then me. His face crinkles in multiple places, and his white, bushy eyebrows lift with his grin. "Hello, there, ladies. I've just brewed a hot pot of coffee. Can I get you some?"

Millie politely declines. "None for me thanks."

I do not. "One cup, two sugars, and three shakes of cream, thanks." A fresh cup of Joe. Perfect for the nerves or whatever ails you.

Millie rolls her eyes. "Katie will have a water, but I'll get it. I'm going back to the theatre office to get her a snack. Sam, this is Katie. You've probably met her at church."

Sam sticks a gold-splattered hand out, and I shake it. So far this man hasn't shown a single sign of wanting to stone me for my misdeeds and poor choice of friends, so what's a little paint on my hand?

"Nice to meet you, Katie. I don't believe I was there the day you were introduced in church. I was in Kansas visiting my sister."

Millie checks her watch and takes a few steps away from us. "Sam, I'll leave you with Katie. Start showing her around and maybe get her started on the project we talked about. Katie, I'll be back with some snacks."

"No carrot sticks!"

Sam chuckles. "Yesterday she fed me celery. I'm seventy-five years old, most of my own teeth are long gone, and she forces celery sticks on me."

"Millie's pretty serious about her veggies." I like this man already.

"Serious? Girl, she's on a one-woman mission to promote the food pyramid."

Girl. Just like Maxine called me—

Sam. Maxine. Oh, hold on.

Looks like you have company today. And it's not Mr. Sam either. That's what Burger Barn boy said to Maxine last Sunday. Well, my, my.

"Are you friends with Maxine Simmons—Millie's mom?"

Sam's eyes bulge at my question. Bull's-eye!

Looking to his left, his right, and behind him, Sam leans in close. "What do you know?"

I know I just received confirmation of a secret love affair between Sam and Mad Maxine! Oh, my day just got *so* much better.

"Are you her boyfr—"

A hand clamped over my mouth halts my sentence. Sam puts his nose to mine. "Don't even say that word out loud. Whatever you want, I'll give you, but you cannot tell Millie anything."

I lower my voice to a whisper. "Are you Maxine's boyfriend?"

Sam nearly does a 360, looking behind him for anyone near enough to hear. "I said not to say that out loud!"

"Okay, how about are you Maxine's special friend?" I wiggle my eyebrows for effect.

Sam takes his old cap off, wipes his brow, and begins to wring the hat in his hands. "Look, I don't know what you heard, girl, but Maxine Simmons and I are just friends. Friends, that's all. But if Millie even suspects there's more to it, my goose is cooked. So you just name your price, whatever it takes to buy your silence."

I consider this for a moment. "That cup of coffee would taste really good right now."

The old man snorts. "I meant like a five spot. Not something guaranteed to get me in even more trouble with Millie. You heard her tell you no." He shoves his cap back on top of his bald head.

Sam scans the room again, then rubs a rag over the black lacquer door, pretending to polish it. "Now, you want to tell me what you know?"

I shrug. "I don't really know anything. Sunday, when I went to get lunch with Maxine, the guy at the Burger Barn asked where you were, like you and Maxine were regulars, and when I asked Maxine who Sam was, she shushed me." I narrow my eyes. "Anytime there is shushing involved, you know something is up."

Sam takes a deep, ragged breath and exhales slowly, and I'm pleased to note he doesn't have nasty old-man breath but a pleasant wintergreen smell.

"Do you want to tell me what's going on and why you're acting like you're protecting a national secret here?"

Sam is about to wear the door out with his polishing. "It's nothing. Forget it."

I lower my voice. "Are you and Maxine . . . terrorists?"

"No!" Alarmed at his own volume, Sam grabs a handkerchief out of his back pocket and again swabs his forehead.

"Here you go"—Millie appears out of nowhere, carrying a tray—"two waters and a plate of homemade oatmeal cookies."

Sam and I both jump, the two of us looking guilty as thieves. Though I have no idea why *I'm* looking guilty. I have enough trouble of my own without taking on anyone else's.

Millie sets the tray down. I thank her, but my strange new friend stands there with his mouth hanging open like he's waiting for a cookie to come in for a landing.

"Sam, I'm going to run a quick errand in town. Can you get Katie started here?" Millie digs in her purse for her car keys, her earlier stress still apparent. A package is under her arm, but the only writing on it I can make out is *Priority Mail*.

"Uh, sure thing, Millie. You take your time." Sam's voice is a little high pitched. This man really needs to work on his poker face.

"Okay. Katie, are you going to be all right here?"

I nod.

"You just follow Sam's orders. Oh, and Sam, if James calls, tell him I've stepped out for a bit, and I'll be right back." She calls out a good-bye and disappears behind the extremely shiny doors.

"What was that about? She acted all nervous." I'm talking mostly to myself.

Sam scowls. "Let's get to work."

"Wait a minute. You haven't told me why you and Maxine are all hush-hush."

"There's nothing to tell. Maxine and I are friends. We both live at Shady Acres, and occasionally she honors me with her company." Sam's face explodes in pink to the top of his ears.

"You're sweet on her."

"Friends. No more." Sam chews his cookie. "But Maxine would devise cruel and creative punishments for me if she found out her daughter knew we'd been spending time together."

Cruel and creative punishments designed by Maxine. Images skitter across my brain, and I shudder. This woman would not bother with a simple tar and feathering. No yard forking for her. Egging Sam's little porch at Shady Acres—baby stuff.

"If you're just friends, then what's the problem?"

"Come on," Sam says gruffly. "We have work to do."

I cross my arms and lean on the doorway. "No information, no work."

"Little missy, if you don't work, then I will report you to James and Millie, and you will be in a heap of trouble."

"If I don't get information, then I'm telling James and Millie I caught you and Maxine making out in the back pew last Wednesday night."

A girlie gasp escapes from Sam's mouth. "You wouldn't!"

I lean in. "I would."

"Fine!" Sam's Adam's apple bobbles. "I've been courting Maxine for the last year. She won't hardly go out in public with me, and when she does, it's when she knows James and Millie are out of town. We can't be anything more than friends because Maxine feels it would upset Millie, and she says now is not a good time."

That's the most ridiculous thing I've ever heard. Sam and Maxine are even more messed up than a couple of junior high kids. I've seen couples on Jerry Springer make more sense than they do.

"What do you mean, not a good time? Because I'm here? Because I got in trouble last weekend?"

Sam shakes his head. "No, of course not. It's not that. It's . . . it's . . . "

"Yes?"

"It's . . . "

He's on the verge of telling me. Come on, Sam. You can do it.

"It's none of your business, that's what it is. Now let's get to work."

Chapter twenty~nine

"SO HOW WAS YOUR DAY today, Katie?"

James pours milk in each of our glasses, then waits for my answer.

Tonight's dinner theme is breakfast. Millie is whipping up more of her mean waffles, from scratch of course. Next she's gonna tell me she tapped a maple tree to get the syrup. Actually tonight's meal is surprising — not a vegetable in sight. Millie must not be feeling well.

Even though I was exhausted after my long afternoon at the theatre (okay, it was only two hours), I set the table myself and even made little origami swans out of the napkins. I am quite artistic, I must say. I didn't even know it, either, until I got out of band and into Art I.

"My day was okay. School went better than expected, and then the afternoon at the Valiant flew by."

James is inspecting his napkin d'art.

"This is a great turtle, Katie."

"James." Millie brings the waffles to the table, "Are you blind?"

Yeah, you tell him, Millie. Some people just can't appreciate good art.

Millie holds her folded napkin up proudly. "It's a frog."

True artists (like Picasso or me) are always misunderstood.

"Millie told me about your day at school. How did the theatre go? Did you meet Sam?" James passes a bowl of fruit.

"Yeah, met Sam. Nice guy." I steal a glance at Millie.

"Sam's very nice, Katie. Not only is he going to help you, but you'll probably learn a lot from him too."

"Sure," James agrees. "Sam can teach you all sorts of things."

Oh, I'm learning a lot from Sam, all right. He has a wealth of knowledge.

As if there's some silent signal I still don't quite get, James and Millie simultaneously reach for my hands, and James begins to pray for our food.

"Dear Heavenly Father, we thank you for this day. We—"

Ring! Ring!

The sound of the phone rudely interrupts our prayer time. I don't move. I've learned when you live in a preacher's house, the phone calls are pretty much constant, but when these people pray, there's no stopping.

James doesn't miss a beat. "We thank you for this time together, and—"

"I'm going to get that." Millie pushes her chair away from the table, and James and I raise our bowed heads in disbelief.

I'm instantly uncomfortable. I think Millie is probably breaking a cardinal rule in this house. No one has ever left the table during pre-dinner prayer. I ought to know, it took me five different attempts before I caught on. (Sometimes a girl just *has* to go to the bathroom . . . or catch the last five minutes of *Wheel of Fortune*.)

"Millie?" There's a slight edge to James's voice.

My foster mom wears a deer-in-the-headlights look. "I . . . I, um. Well, it could be an emergency. Then wouldn't we feel badly if we didn't answer it?"

Ring! Ring!

"Let the machine pick it up."

"James, I'm just going to get it. I'll be right back."

Ring! Ring!

James throws his napkin on the table and follows Millie into the kitchen. Rocky, who had been resting at James's feet, jumps up and darts out of his way.

Well, okay. Awkward moment.

"Millie, come on, we're praying. What is going on with you today?"

James is whispering, but I want to say, *Hello! I'm right here. Ten feet away.*

Ring! Ring!

Millie turns around to answer her husband. "Nothing. I just thought we should be courteous and answer the—"

Silence.

No more ringing.

Millie looks toward the phone. And frowns.

"Well . . . " Millie wraps her necklace around a finger, then lets it unwind only to coil it up again. "I guess they'll call back if they want anything."

My foster parents stand between the kitchen and breakfast nook for a few uncomfortable seconds. They simply watch one another.

"After *amen* we eat, right?" I had to break the silence.

The Scotts look my way.

"What? I just wanted to make sure before I committed a big Christian faux pas." I lift up my fork like *I will eat this waffle. I ain't scared.*

The two return to the table. Millie smiles as if we didn't just have a soap-opera moment, and Rocky once again lies at James's feet.

James restarts his prayer, and at his "Amen," I tear into my waffles.

And they are all I could've hoped for. If James is right, and there is a heaven, waffles will surely be on the menu there. Hopefully the fruit and vegetables Millie is always pushing will not. I mean, it can't be heaven if you still have to eat your broccoli, right?

"So Katie, you were telling us about the theatre." James stabs a sausage. "Did Sam introduce you to everyone?"

"Yeah, I met the crew. They said they've been enjoying the homemade cookies Millie's been bringing them everyday."

"Were they practicing for the play while you were there?" Millie frowns at the untouched fruit on my plate.

I dutifully eat a few bites of strawberries and bananas. "Uh-huh. *Romeo and Juliet*, right? I recognize it from last year. We read it in English class."

I remember Ashley Buckingham, the captain of the junior-high-cheerleading team, was Juliet; but during the week she was out with the flu, I was picked to read her part. I acted like I didn't want to read, but secretly I did. Ashley read her part without any expression at all. I mean, the scene in which Juliet thinks Romeo, the love of her life, is dead should not be read in the same tone of voice you would use to read your science book. So when my chance came, I read the part of Juliet like I meant it. I *was* Juliet.

I still remember a few of the lines and like to quote them at totally inappropriate times.

"Right. *Romeo and Juliet*. Millie and I thought we would

open the theatre with a classic everyone knew. How were the actors doing? Were they able to rehearse around all the noise and workers?"

I shrug. "It seemed like they were doing okay." At least the lead roles, played by two In Between High seniors, said their lines with some enthusiasm. The guy who played Romeo, Chase Fitzpatrick, kept flubbing up his lines. But I think it's only so his Juliet would continue to step close to him to point out his error in the script.

James and Millie continue the conversation about the play. I use this opportunity to slip Rocky some sausage links under the table. Rocky sits by James's chair, but I've figured out it's just because it gives him the best access to my secret handouts. He can have all the sausage he wants. I'm more of a bacon girl myself.

"Bev called me today." James helps himself to another waffle and douses it in syrup.

"Oh? What did she have to say?" Millie takes a drink of milk.

Bev is the director of the play. That's one of the many things I learned from Sam today.

"She wanted to discuss postponing the opening of the theatre and *Romeo and Juliet*."

Millie drops her fork. "No! I mean, we can't. They've all worked so hard. We're working so hard. We'll get it done."

"Millie, I don't think the theatre is going to be ready. You don't want to have the opening night if we're not ready. It's not fair to the actors and it's not fair to all we've worked for."

I pick up my milk to wash down some guilt. The Valiant is pretty messed up. I don't know how it can possibly be done on time.

Millie pushes her hair behind her ears, then her hands return to her lap to grip her napkin. "No, we set the date and we have to stick with it. It's important, James. The theatre will be finished. It has to be."

I'm so engrossed in their exchange I fail to notice Rocky has been licking my hands, cleaning off all traces of sausage. Ew.

My dog-breath hands fly back to the table.

"I just don't see how we can work any faster than we are. I want the community to see the Valiant in pristine condition. I want the opening to be perfect." James pushes his glasses up on his nose.

"So do I, James. But the opening has to be on the thirtieth. There can't be any delay in—"

Millie's rebuttal is interrupted by the door bell. Frazzled, she looks at the clock, running a hand through her hair. "It's Frances. I forgot she was coming by tonight."

I choke on my waffle, my fifth for the night. "What?"

Millie opens the door. "Frances, remember? She's going to tutor you a few nights a week in algebra."

Oh, yeah. How could I forget?

"Hi!" Frances calls out an ubercheery greeting. A major contrast to the negative vibes we had going on at the dinner table.

The Scotts surround Frances, taking her books, her coat, her purse, getting her a drink. She's like the foster daughter they wish they had.

"Okay! Ready to hit the books?" Frances just radiates enthusiasm.

It makes me want to hurl.

There is no need for that level of excitement over mathematics. The grin she's wearing right now would be the grin I would have if I won the lottery. Or if a driver's license magically appeared in my hand. Or if I met Josh Hartnett.

I lead Frances and her smiling face up the stairs to my room. Rocky follows us.

"Aw, hey, little guy. Aren't you the cutest thing?"

"Frances, Rocky is neither cute nor little. Are you sure you've got the smarts to help me with algebra?"

Frances flops on my bed and looks around. Tonight my tutor and fellow *Chihuahua* is wearing a T-shirt promoting "Peace, love, and trees," a zippered hoodie, and some worn out jeans with a cool-looking belt. If I wear that kind of stuff it looks like I'm a hobo. But on Frances, it looks like it's straight out of *Teen Vogue*.

"Your room is really awesome, Katie. You did a good job decorating."

I dig my algebra book out of my backpack. "Oh, I didn't do any of the decorating. It was like this when I got here. Millie did it all." I love my room. I never get tired of looking at it.

"I guess this probably was Amy's room."

"What?" I nearly drop my book.

"Yeah, Amy. The Scotts' daughter."

In one leap I'm sitting right next to Frances. "What do you know about Amy?" I never thought of Frances as a source for info on the subject of the Scotts' daughter.

Frances flips through my algebra book. Her eyes light up as if she's reading something interesting—like a romance novel.

"Frances, focus." I snatch the book out of her hands. "What do you know about her?"

"Not much. Just that she doesn't live around here."

"Where does she live?"

"I don't know." Frances shrugs like this is no big deal.

"Did she go to In Between?" Maybe I could search for her picture in an old yearbook in the school library.

"Yeah, I remember she was homecoming queen a long time ago. She was really big in sports, choir, and track. Oh, and the theatre."

"In the theatre? Like in drama and stuff?" My mind races at light speed.

"Yup. If you go in the school theatre, there're all those pictures of the plays that have been done since the school started a million years ago. Pastor and Millie's daughter is in quite a few of the pictures. Why are you asking me this?"

Why? Because things are totally weird around here. Because I think if I find out the story about Amy it will explain a lot.

And because I think Amy is the reason the Scotts are reopening the Valiant.

Chapter thirty

TODAY WAS ANOTHER FINE DAY of educational enrichment. The other kids aren't glaring at me or anything anymore, and so far Angel and her groupies have stayed out of my way. Lunch was just as awkward as ever, though. I declined an invitation to sit with the skateboarders again, and instead sat with a group I thought looked pretty harmless. Turns out I sat down with the poetry club. It went a little something like this:

"Hey, guys . . . um, mind if I sit here?"

They looked friendly enough. A little oddly dressed, like they were expecting Woodstock III to be announced any time now, but they seemed nice.

"Sure. We're just discussing our poetry selections for the next issue of *The Soulful Chihuahua*."

I did a double take. "*The Soulful Chihuahua*?"

"Yes, it's the monthly poetry mag we put out."

A dude hiding behind his hair spoke up. "And we're the soulful Chihuahuas."

"Well . . . soulful Chihuahuas, pleased to meet you. I'm

Katie. Katie Parker."

"Katie, are you into poetry?"

I am *so* not into poetry. I thoroughly dislike the stuff. You read a poem, and it speaks to you. You write a stupid essay on it, and the teacher tells you your interpretation is wrong, and the author is really saying something else entirely. Oh, really? Did you talk to the author yourself? No, I didn't think so.

"I've read my share."

"For this lunch meeting, we are discussing Emily Dickinson," a girl named Liv said.

"Oh, yeah." I remembered some Dickinson. "She's kind of a downer."

Gasps erupted. French fries fell. Pizza dropped to plates.

"You don't think so?" I asked, too aware of their predatory stares.

Okay, while I don't know a lot of Emily Dickinson, I don't remember her writing any poems about giggles and ponies. But I wasn't going to argue with these poetry die-hards. They meant business. I was afraid if I pushed the issue, they would resort to fisticuffs (that's old English talk for a fight. I'm reading Shakespeare, remember?). Can you imagine explaining *that* to Millie?

Katie, what on earth did those kids beat you up over?

Poetry, Millie. Poetry.

"Emily Dickinson did write about death. But she celebrated it." A guy threw his hands in the air for dramatic effect. "Maybe you wouldn't understand. We artists carry the burden of being misunderstood."

"Oh, no! I totally relate." Finally we had found some common ground. "Like last night I made these swans when I was setting the dinner table. Except they weren't swans, they were napkins, you know? And I'm like . . . "

Blank stares all around me.

Yeah, so that was lunch. Good times. I'm not sure where my place is with the In Between student body, but it's definitely not with the soulful Chihuahuas.

And that was pretty much the highlight of my day.

Waiting here for the school bus, which will take me to Mad Maxine's, I believe I'm about to face the low point of my day. Today I start the final phase of my punishment—reading to Maxine. Can't wait.

I scan the crowd of people rushing out and leaving the campus. You have the kids who hang out in the parking lot. Then there's the type who squeal and peel out because they think it's really cool (it's not). There are the bus riders like me who stand outside waiting, impatient and resigned to our fate—a noisy, stinky, bumpy ride. Don't forget the kids whose mothers pick them up at the carpool line, and—

Oh, no.

No, she couldn't.

She wouldn't. I have done nothing to deserve this level of public humiliation.

Honk! Honk!

"Outta my way!" *Honk! Honk!*

"Sweet Pea!" *Honk! Honk!*

Mad Maxine.

Swerving in and out between cars and kids, Maxine is pedaling her hardest to reach me. Today's frock of choice is an *I Love Elvis* sparkly tank, black capris, and black patent leather heels. Yeah, I said heels. Because who doesn't ride a bicycle in two-inch heels?

"Yoo hoo! Katie! Katie Parker! I see you!"

I turn my back to her, hoping in vain that if I can't see her, then I'm invisible.

"Don't you get on that bus!" *Honk! Honk! Honk!*

Maxine's bike squeals to a stop right behind me. "Hey, I'm here to pick you up. Me and Ginger Rogers."

I am forced to turn and acknowledge Maxine. If the principal knew she was here, the school would probably have to go into lockdown. I'm sure he knows her.

"Ginger Rogers?"

With love in her eyes, Maxine pats her bicycle seat. "My bike."

"You named your bike?"

Maxine scoffs. "Who doesn't?"

"I think you're confusing bicycles with yachts, Maxine."

My foster grandma waves the idea away with a hand. "Look, are you going to get on or not? We've got stuff to do."

People are staring and pointing, and I am extremely uncomfortable. Like, right now I'm looking for some poets to hang out with.

"Get on. Come on!"

I step closer to Mad Maxine so at least one of us won't be yelling. "No. I am not getting on that bike."

"Ginger Rogers."

"Fine, Ginger Rogers. But I don't care if you call it Jake Gyllenhaal, I'm not getting on."

Everyone loads onto the buses. Maxine blocks my way. With Ginger.

"Move, Maxine. I need to get on the bus."

"Look, girl, as soon as school is out on Tuesdays you are on my time. And I say get yourself on this bicycle. We'll be home quicker. If you ride the bus you won't get to Shady Acres until after four. I can have you at the apartment in five minutes."

The bus takes off.

Without me.

Sighing deeply, I begin to walk. And yes, at this point I know it's ridiculous. I am walking to her apartment, and she will follow me on her bicycle built for two. But I'm embarrassed, and I'm a little mad. I mean, I'm trying to make some friends at this school. I don't think I earned any cool points today by having my lunatic foster grandmother honking at every minivan in her path and running over students not smart enough to feel threatened by the senior citizen in the hot-pink helmet and matching knee pads.

"You've got a long walk ahead of you."

"Yes, I'm aware of that." This backpack is getting heavy.

"And you know I'm going to follow you the whole way."

"Never would've guessed."

"Aw, come on, Katie Parker. Get on the bike. We've got things to talk about."

Maxine rides in swooping figure eights around me. I start humming just to annoy her.

"I heard you met Sam Dayberry yesterday." *Swoop, swoop.*

I come to a dead stop.

Maxine slows. "What?"

"That's what this is about."

Maxine wears an innocent schoolgirl expression. "I have no idea what you are talking about, young lady."

"Yes, you do. You came here to pick me up because you wanted the scoop on Sam. And I would bet my Abercrombie jeans you have been waiting all day for three o'clock, dying to get to me as soon as you could to hear what I have to say about meeting your boyfriend."

Maxine's mouth falls open. "He is *not* my boyfriend! Don't you ever say that out loud. I will wash your mouth out with soap! I will get a switch from a tree and tan your hide! I will make you scrub my toilet with your own toothbrush! I will . . ."

Maxine can tell I'm not buying it.

"Just get on the bike."

I stand my ground.

"I have ice cream and hot fudge at the apartment."

And five minutes later we're home.

I TAKE A SEAT on the red overstuffed couch in Maxine's living room. Maxine's heels clip-clop in the kitchen as she whips up our hot fudge sundaes.

Maxine pokes her head around the corner. "Do you want whipped cream on yours?" She wipes her hands on the gingham apron she's put on, like she's preparing a ten-course meal instead of a single dish of ice cream with some store-bought chocolate sauce on top.

"Yes, of course." Approval shines in her eyes.

I can hear the whipped cream being squirted into one bowl, then another, then one long, hollow *whoosh*.

"Maxine, I know you're spraying that stuff in your mouth. That is so gross."

From the kitchen I hear coughing and a can being set back on the counter.

"Do you want a cherry on top?"

"Yes, please." I do love cherries. In fact, I can tie two cherry stems with my tongue at the same time. No wonder somebody snatched me up to be their foster child. I've got skills.

Maxine slinks around the corner again, a telltale blob of whipped cream on her upper lip.

"Nuts?"

You certainly are.

"Okay, here we are. Two bowls of hot fudge sundae—Maxine style."

Maxine places the bowls on the coffee table in front of me. They are the size of serving bowls, not your nice little cereal dishes. Bananas are sticking out in every direction from the ice cream, and chocolate sauce fills the bowls like soup. The whipped cream piled high on top of each sundae stands at least six inches tall. Cherries are stuck here and there to finish it off.

It's the most beautiful thing I've ever seen.

"Dig in." Maxine hands me a big spoon, and the two of us go to work on the masterpieces before us.

"Okay" — Maxine says around a mouthful of chocolate — "So what's new?"

I set my bowl down, careful not to let any of the chocolate sauce spill over onto the coffee table. Not that I think Maxine would be upset over the mess on her furniture, but I have a feeling that, like me, she would hate to see good chocolate go to waste.

I reach for my backpack and dig around until I find a book. "Here, Millie sent this for you. She said you've been waiting on it."

Maxine grabs the book. "*The Scarlet Letter?*" She chucks the book onto the table.

"Yes, it's what she said you'd want me to read to you."

Maxine snorts. "If I wanted to hear stories from another dead white guy, I'd go hang out in the recreation hall."

"But Millie said you loved your classics."

Maxine picks up the book again, laughing to herself. "Hester has an illegitimate child, the old guy she's married to is mean to her, the town turns on her, and she gets her dresses custom monogrammed, blah, blah, blah. Next!"

"Next? What do you mean? That's all I brought for you. Millie said you two have spent hours discussing classic novels."

Maxine reaches for her ice cream. "Let's just say you kids didn't corner the market on Cliffs Notes, you know what I'm saying?"

"So you don't like books?" Maybe I won't have to read to her after all.

"Of course I like books. Just not the old musty ones. Millie likes the stinky books. I just try to keep up to please her. She loves to talk about *li-tra-chure* and the *classics*."

I nearly choke on a cherry stem. "Is that your British accent?"

Maxine huffs. "Oh, never mind."

"Australian?"

"I said be quiet."

"Kind of cockney with a touch of Jamaican."

Maxine clears her throat. "What else do you have?"

"I don't have anything. Millie sent only one book. I guess I'll tell her to send over a copy of *Green Eggs and Ham* next time." I take a one last bite of my sundae, then with much regret and sadness, put it down on the table. As much as it pains me, I just can't eat anymore.

"Well, what are *you* reading?" Maxine asks, still going strong with her own dessert and, like a trouper, showing no signs of slowing down.

"Nothing you'd be interested in. It's from our school library."

"Perfect. Read it."

I retrieve it from my bag and show her the pretty pink cover. "Maxine, it's written for a sixteen-year-old." I toss the book on the cushion beside me.

"Uh-huh . . . and?"

"And . . . " I take a deep breath and lean back on the couch to relax my stomach muscles from all that eating. "It's about a teenage girl. She finds out she's a princess, goes to live in a foreign country, endures rigorous training to become royalty, wins the heart of everyone in the land, hooks up with a boy, and finds out she is to one day be queen of an entire nation."

Maxine claps her hands together. "Finally! Something I can relate to." She grabs the novel and flips through it.

The book is thrust into my hands, opened to page one.

Maxine leans in closer. "You may begin."

And so I do. I read chapter after chapter, stopping after the main character meets her grandmother, the queen, for the first time.

"Oh, keep going. Do your queen voice again." Maxine's eyes are wide and sparkly, and her hand is over her heart like I'm reading a suspenseful thriller. And every time I talk like the aristocratic grandmother in the novel, Maxine closes her eyes and smiles, like she's there.

I mark the page with my bookmark and shut the book. "Enough for today. It's nearly five o'clock. Millie will be here anytime, don't you think?"

Maxine checks her watch and frowns.

"Now *that's* a book." Maxine stands up and carries our melted ice cream creations into the kitchen. (Well, what's left of mine. Hers was eaten and the bowl licked clean. And I mean literally.)

"You're a pretty good reader."

My back straightens and my cheeks warm. "Thank you."

"I mean, I wasn't even sure if you were literate."

I grab a discarded pink kneepad and throw it in her direction, and Maxine's deep laugh fills the tiny apartment.

On her return, my foster grandmother brings me a glass of lemonade and puts it on the coffee table. Right next to a coaster.

"*Sooo.* You were telling me about meeting Sam Dayberry at the theatre." Maxine throws herself back onto the couch. She grabs a pillow and fluffs it.

"No, I wasn't." I keep my voice neutral, like this isn't more interesting than *Days of Our Lives.*

"Oh, I thought you said something about him. I'm old. I don't hear very well." She flicks a piece of lint off the couch.

"Maxine, the FBI doesn't have equipment that picks up sound as well as you do. You know I didn't say a word about Sam. *You* did."

Maxine adjusts a ring on her finger, then studies her nails.

We sit in silence, and I begin to count in my head how many seconds it will be before she cracks.

One Mississippi.

Two Mississippi.

Three Mississippi.

Four Mississippi.

Five—

"Okay! Fine! Just tell me what you know!"

I pretend to consider this for a moment. Maxine drums her fingers on the arm. She crosses then uncrosses her legs.

"Tell you what . . . "

"Yes?" She moves in closer, and her hot-fudge breath wafts over me.

"You tell me what you know about Amy, and I'll tell you what I know about Sam."

Maxine leans back, straightens her posture—on alert. "What did you say?"

I know I'm pushing it, but I need information here. This woman knows everything. "I said I will give you Sam information, if you tell me about your granddaughter."

The climate in the room has changed now. Gone is the silliness. The fun of the sundaes has melted, and the dreaminess of the book has disappeared. Maxine is serious. Her face is unreadable.

"What is it you think you need to know?"

I glance out the living room window, expecting Millie to drive up anytime. "Why is she such a secret?"

Maxine looks at the floor for a few seconds then returns her eyes to mine. "Every family has their heartaches, girl. Ours is no different. Amy is my granddaughter, and wherever she is, I love her." Maxine nods her head, her peroxide blonde waves swaying across her shoulders. "I love that child." She sips her lemonade. "But that story is Millie's to tell."

"Why? Why is it Millie's to tell? Her daughter shouldn't be a secret."

"She's not a secret."

"Oh, no? Well, then explain the phone calls no one will talk about or the packages Millie takes to the post office every week or the weird tension between James and Millie sometimes."

Maxine's mouth stretches into a slight smile. "Sometimes you let things simmer for a long time without even realizing it. And we all need someone to come along and remind us to stir the pot. You know what I'm saying?"

"Stir the pot? Simmering? No. I don't have the slightest clue as to what you are saying." I need information. Not a spaghetti recipe.

"Well . . . " Maxine breathes in deeply, considering her words. "All I have to say is the Lord knows what he's doing." Maxine considers me for a brief moment then nods her head again. "Yes, I do believe the Lord knows what he's doing."

Chapter thirty~one

WE SHOULD NAME OUR PIG.

Frances turns her notebook around so I can see her scribbled message.

I scrunch up my face and whisper a very strong "No."

Due to some evil plotting on the counselor's part, today's schedule is mixed up to accommodate torturous standardized testing for the juniors. So it's Thursday classes on a Wednesday schedule. It's taken me the entire three weeks I've been here to learn my schedule, and then they play today's cruel trick. I've been confused all day. And the smell of this class isn't helping to clear my head.

Next time, I'm bringing nose plugs to biology class. It reeks like pickled pork and formaldehyde in this room. Mr. Hughes partnered us up today for our first foray into pig dissection. I was lucky enough to get Frances. And I'm serious. She can be a bit overenthusiastic for me sometimes, but I'm not so dumb I don't know the value of a good lab partner. Besides, Frances is growing on me.

"You may begin cutting. . . ."

I block out the rest of the teacher's instructions and focus on a *Star Trek* poster on the wall. What is it with *Star Trek* and science teachers?

"Katie, are you listening?" Frances taps her pencil on the metal tray the pig is in.

I pull my shirt up over my mouth and nose. I will also be finding a face mask to bring with me to biology. I know dead pig vapors are seeping into my mouth. I'm eating pig air.

"Frances." I inhale deeply through my shirt. "Do you realize we are going to smell like dead pigs when we leave this class? In fact, we will smell like dead pigs for the next three weeks." I shudder in my seat.

"What are you talking about?" Frances hands me the dissecting knife. Like she thinks *I'm* gonna cut into that thing?

"You know, like when you go to a Mexican restaurant and you come out smelling like fajitas?" An occurrence that has never bothered me personally.

"Yeah . . . ?"

I lean across the science lab table. "You smell like a dead pig right now."

Understanding dawns on her olive-toned face. Then acceptance. "Oh well."

I slide the knife back her way. "I'm not ready to hurt this pig yet, Frances."

Frances giggles. "You can't hurt it, Katie." She moves in closer, pushing the blade back onto my side of the table. "It's already dead," she whispers like she's letting me in on a big secret. "Now let's name him!"

"How do you know it's a him?"

"Well, if you pick up his tiny leg and look to the—"

"Never mind! Okay, okay, let's just get this over with."

Frances sighs. "Tell you what. Rock, paper, scissors—best two out of three, and loser cuts into Sir Oinks-a-Lot here."

I think it's an established fact I don't have good luck. Her rock smashed my scissors, and her paper covered my rock. Done deal.

I pick up the knife and approach the pig. Closer, closer, zeroing in on my target. Here I go—

"Frances, this seems ungodly." I throw out the sentence I heard in church last Sunday.

She adjusts her safety goggles with the back of her gloved hand. "What?"

"Um, yeah. Last night when I was flipping through the Bible Millie gave me, I think I saw something in there about this."

"Really? Let me guess, it's in the book of Sausage?"

"Well, no." There's not a book of Sausage, right? "I think it's in there with all the commandments. Like with the Ten Commandments." I get another strong whiff of the animal, and my eyes cross.

Frances nods. "Oh, so thou shall honor thy father and mother. Thou shall not kill. Thou shall not commit adultery. Thou shall not—"

"Slice open a pig if you don't want to, yes. Exactly. Chapter 12, verse 19, page one hundred?" I hold up my hand and add an amen. Because I am here to testify that I am not cutting into this animal.

Frances laughs and her whole face lights up. Even in a lab coat and surrounded by pig stench, she is beyond pretty. People like her should live on their own continent. That way the rest of us wouldn't have to suffer.

"Katie, I won rock, paper, scissors fair and square; so get to it."

This girl isn't budging. I would offer her a cash bribe, but (a) I don't have any money, and (b) she wouldn't take it.

Okay, deep breath. Oh, ew, not that deep.

All right. Here we go. And . . . cut.

"Katie, are you okay?" Frances's voice echoes in my head.

"Yeah, I'm okay." I wore too many layers today. It's an oven in here. "Did someone just turn the heat up?"

"Here, sit down." Frances pulls out my lab stool.

"No, really, I'm fine." Seriously, did I forget my deodorant today because I am sweating like a—well, never mind.

"I'm going to work a little bit while you catch your breath, and then you can help me out." Frances picks up the knife and goes to work, checking our lab manual every few minutes. "So . . . are you going to church tonight?"

"Bacon Bits."

Frances looks around the room like she's searching for a translator.

"What are you talking about?"

"Our pig." The room spirals around me. "That's his name."

And my world goes black.

"KATIE! KATIE, CAN YOU hear me?"

Oh, no. I did *not* pass out. I have never passed out in my entire sixteen years.

"Katie, how many fingers am I holding up?"

I peel open my left eye and see Frances's face inches away from mine.

"Frances, if you administer CPR you will totally destroy any future chances of either one of us ever having prom dates."

Frances sits back on her heels. "She's come to, Mr. Hughes. She's okay."

Okay? I'm totally humiliated.

"You were only out a few seconds." Frances checks her watch, then grabs my wrist, searching for a pulse.

I jerk my hand out of her grip. "Do you mind?"

Slowly I sit up, but only to find I am surrounded by twenty-five biology classmates gawking at me like I'm a new species. I stifle a groan, and with the help of an overly attentive Frances, I stand on my own two feet.

Mr. Hughes breaks through the masses. "Katie! Are you okay? Oh, you gave me such a scare."

I rub the back of my head where a bump is starting to protrude. "Thanks, Mr. Hughes, but I'm okay." Nice of him to care.

"Well, that could have been a disaster!" The teacher puts a hand to his chest, like he's having heart palpitations. "It's a good thing you didn't knock the pig off the table, because those things cost over two hundred dollars." With an exaggerated smile, my teacher runs a hand across his forehead. "Whew!"

"Mr. Hughes . . . I . . . you . . . oh . . . I'm taking Katie to the nurse." Frances grabs my arm and begins to lead me out of the classroom.

"Oh, yes, by all means, take her to the nurse. I was going to suggest that myself." Mr. Hughes takes one last survey of the pig and hands Frances the hall pass.

I follow Frances out into the hall. She is grumbling to herself and stomping at quite a good pace.

"I mean, the *nerve* of that man!"

"Hey, Frances—"

"All he cares about is science and his precious equipment." She throws her hands in the air and continues to storm away from me.

"Hello, injured here. Slow down." My head is really starting to hurt.

"I should've let him have it last year during the science fair when Billy O'Rourke's volcano experiment blew up, and Mr. Hughes made a mad dash and knocked Billy out of the way to save the beakers."

"Frances . . . "

"I love science. I do. But I will not be one of those scientists who is disconnected from the world and everything around me." Frances turns a corner and continues her conversation with herself.

I stop in front of the water fountain and get a drink, comforted by the cool of the water (but totally grossed out by what's always in the water fountain). I wonder how long it will take before Frances realizes I'm not with her.

"Oh!"

Six seconds.

I hear Frances running down the hall. She skids to a stop beside me. "Katie, I'm sorry. Are you okay? Do you need help walking?"

I begin to laugh, but it jars my head. "No, I'm fine. I just wanted to let you have some alone time with yourself. You seemed to be in a pretty deep conversation. I didn't want to interrupt."

Frances returns my smile, and it hits me that our status has changed. Does she think of me as her friend? Do I consider her a friend?

"Are you sure you're all right?"

"Seriously. I'm fine. I would like to get some aspirin though." We continue our walk, slowly this time, toward the nurse's office. "So . . . I was going to check out the drama department at lunch. Get a look at those cast pictures you were telling me about."

"The pictures of Amy Scott?"

"Yeah. Um, do you want to come with me?" Maybe seeing the pictures would jar Frances's memory about anything she might know about Amy.

"I have a student council meeting during the last fifteen minutes of lunch—"

"Oh, okay, yeah, no problem. I don't need help or anything. I was just being polite and—"

"We could go during the beginning of lunch."

My mouth opens. Then closes. "Really?"

"The bell is going to ring any second now. If we go as soon as the nurse is done with you, it will give us a good fifteen minutes to check out Amy's pictures."

"Thanks, Frances. I really appreciate it." I'm touched that Frances, who's a member of nearly every club and organization in this school, and who carries a BlackBerry to keep up with it all, would pencil me into her schedule.

The bell rings when I'm in the nurse's office, and after five minutes of assuring Frances and the school RN I'm fine, I am released with a couple of aspirin and a baggie of ice to put on the bump.

"Okay, on to the theatre department. Have you met Mrs. Hall yet?" Frances keeps up a steady pace while I walk behind her, leaving a trail of water from the leaking ice pack.

"Um, no, haven't met her."

"Mrs. Hall is the head drama teacher. Maybe you've seen her. She has long, red hair and wears a different colored scarf over her head every day. She usually dresses in black. Wears a lot of jewelry. She's cool though."

We enter the school theatre, and I toss my ice pack in the trash.

I pause in the doorway for a moment and just take in the theatre. Like the Valiant, this place just kind of speaks to me. It's like it has an attitude of its own. I love the quiet. And the history. That old beat-up stage has seen a lot of plays, I would imagine

Lots of Chihuahua thespians. Heavy black curtains frame the stage. What would it feel like to be on the other side of those curtains when they rise? What would it be like to be in the spotlight, getting a standing ovation, being in an auditorium full of people who can't stop clapping for you?

"Ladies, can I help you? The sign up sheet for auditions is out in the hall."

A petite woman with bright auburn hair floats down the side ramp of the stage, her fuchsia and gold skirt billowing around her, and she stops in front of us.

"Hi, Mrs. Hall. We're not here to sign up for the play." Frances puts her hand on my shoulder. "This is Katie Parker. She's new to In Between High, and she wanted to take a look at your theatre."

Mrs. Hall's eyes sparkle, matching her bejeweled ears. "Oh, a theatre lover, are we?"

I realize she's speaking to me. "Oh, um, well . . . yes, ma'am." Am I?

"What have you done?" Mrs. Hall's face is all intense.

I shoot a look at Frances. What have I done? "Well, ma'am, I guess a few weeks ago I got in some trouble and — "

Frances elbows me in the ribs. "She means what plays have you performed."

Oh. Right.

"Um, well, none. Oh, except I was Mrs. Claus in my third-grade play. Did a little singing, a little dancing. You know, rocked around the Christmas tree, jingled a bell or two."

I remember singing my heart out, saying my memorized lines flawlessly, and nobody was even there to see me. My mom had dropped me off with some lame excuse about running an errand and returning in time to see my performance, but she never showed up. The school had to call some distant cousin to pick me up after the program. I just remember the entire night I watched for her. Even when I was onstage and saying my lines. I never took my eyes off the audience.

Reason number 498 of why I have yet to write the woman a single letter since I've been in In Between. Not that I'm bitter.

"We're having auditions for our yearly musical. Sign up if you're interested." Mrs. Hall's hands move at her every word. Everything about her is flowing, moving, and overly expressive.

"I think I'd like to look around here if that's okay." I take a step in the direction of some cast photos hanging on the wall.

Mrs. Hall follows me. "Ah, yes, do check out the pictures. These are all the plays we've done since 1989. Taking the cast's picture on opening night is a tradition I started when I began working here many moons ago." She waves her hands Vanna-White style over a row of black-and-white photos hung in frames.

The three of us inch our way down the wall, and Mrs. Hall is only too happy to share her play production memories with me. Every single one of them. And there have been a lot of plays since 1989.

I tap Frances's shoulder and shoot her my SOS look. We aren't getting anywhere. I've been looking at these pictures for ten minutes and have yet to see Amy.

"And then for our spring show in 1992, we decided to try some-thing more cutting edge, so we did a series of mime one acts."

Frances steps behind Mrs. Hall's back and points to the oppo-site wall. *Over there,* she mouths.

"Well why didn't you say so?" I ask.

Mrs. Hall turns to me. "What?"

Whoa, good acoustics in here. "Um, I said, swell, way to go!"

"Oh, well, thank you. Where was I? Yes, I recall. Now in the fall of 1993 —"

"Mrs. Hall, Katie is staying with James and Millie Scott. She was really interested in the cast pictures with their daughter Amy."

A bittersweet smile spreads across the teacher's face. "Ah, yes. I remember Amy Scott well. Amazingly talented. So much potential." Mrs. Hall shakes her head. "She would be over there with the photos from the last decade. I think her last play with us was about seven years ago, her senior year."

Her ankle bracelets chiming, Mrs. Hall leads us across the auditorium to the far wall. These pictures are also in black and white, but I can tell they are more recent.

"Amy Scott, Amy Scott, Amy Scott . . . Ah, yes, here we are. I believe we have six different photos of plays that starred Amy."

Pointing out each one, Mrs. Hall lists every production and gives information on each one.

I study each cast shot. Amy was no wallflower. She's front-and-center in every image. Despite various costumes and varying degrees of stage makeup, Amy looks happy and . . . I don't know, normal. She looks like a student who's excited and into what she's doing—just like the rest of the cast. What did I really expect to learn?

I sigh and run my hand over the knot at the back of my head. It feels like an egg is trying to sprout out of my skull. Stupid pigs.

"You have a great theatre, Mrs. Hall." I'm ready to call this what it is: a failure. "Thanks for letting me look around."

"Sure. You girls come back anytime. And don't forget auditions next week! Tell your friends!"

As Frances and I make our way to the door, Mrs. Hall calls after us, "You know, I don't hear from Amy much anymore."

We stop.

"She used to send me a postcard or an e-mail from time to

time, updating me on all of her auditions, but I haven't heard from her in about two years."

"Amy's a professional actress?" *Now* we're getting somewhere.

Mrs. Hall chuckles to herself. "Well, I don't know about that. Last I heard she was in Los Angeles trying to get a walk-on part in a horror movie. And the year before she had been in New York auditioning for some off-Broadway plays." Mrs. Hall shakes her head. "It's a cruel business, acting. It will take the strongest person and eat them alive. And if you're not very strong to begin with . . . well, let's just say it's hard to keep going on years' worth of rejections. And it sure doesn't pay the bills."

I try not to show my excitement at this wealth of information. "Mrs. Hall, I was wondering what you meant when you said—"

"Mrs. Hall you have a call on line four, Mrs. Hall a call on line four."

At the overhead speaker's announcement, my moment is lost.

"That will be the costume store I've been trying to reach all week. It's about time they called me back. Our productions keep those people in business, and I can't even get a simple phone call returned."

The teacher flounces off in a mismatched cloud, bemoaning her costume woes.

"Well, we learned something today. Didn't we?" Frances studies me.

"Yeah, sure. I learned Amy is somewhere trying to be an actress and . . . that's about it."

"Mrs. Hall didn't sound like she thought Amy's Hollywood pursuits had a happy ending, did she?" Frances checks her watch.

"No, she didn't. The plot thickens."

"You could just ask Millie about it, you know."

"Frances, would Sherlock Holmes take the easy way out?"

"It's not the easy way out, and you know it. If Millie and James haven't told you the whole story about Amy, then maybe they don't ever intend to."

"Yeah, but I don't feel comfortable coming right out and asking them why their daughter is such a big secret. I thought I was going to hyperventilate last week when I had to ask Millie to buy me some tampons. And the topic of their daughter is even more personal." I shove open the theatre doors, and we walk back the way we came.

"Oh, hey, it's time for my meeting. I gotta run, but I'll see you later." Frances throws her apple core into the trash can and readjusts her backpack. "See you at church tonight, right? Wednesday nights are the best."

"Yeah, I'll be there. Can't wait."

"Better watch out. It grows on you. Like mold." Frances walks backwards, her grinning face pointed in my direction. "Yep, you'll be counting the minutes 'til Wednesday night church. I can see it now."

"Go to your meeting, Frances. And watch out for that janitor there."

Frances turns around in time to narrowly miss a collision with an extra-large custodian.

"Oh, and Katie?" Frances calls over her shoulder.

"Yeah?"

"You smell like Bacon Bits."

Chapter thirty~two

"SO TODAY YOU'RE GOING TO be re-covering some of the theatre seats. It's pretty simple. I'll show you how to do a few, and then you and this mighty staple gun can take it from there."

Sam Dayberry kneels on the floor of the Valiant with one of Millie's homemade cookies in one hand and a piece of fabric in the other. I hadn't anymore than walked through the door, and he was firing off instructions and waving tools at me.

"Okay, you take this fabric here, which I've already cut out for you, and you are going to cover, fold, tuck, and staple. Got it?" Sam demonstrates the process again. "Easy. Cover, fold, tuck, and staple. Once we get these covered, I'll screw them into the seats. Now you pick up your staple gun and try it."

I grab a cushion and lay my upholstery over it.

"I don't hear you."

I bite my lip to control a smile. "Cover . . . fold . . . tuck . . . and staple." I hold the finished product up for his inspection.

Sam studies my handiwork and whistles his approval. "Very nice."

"Thanks," I mumble, like it's no big deal. But it is.

The two of us work in a comfortable silence for a few minutes. The theatre smells like sawdust today—a group of guys are here again working on some of the wood repairs. The smell stings my nose, but I like it. It smells like progress, and progress keeps Millie happy.

I also like watching the play practice on stage. The director, Bev, a slender woman about Millie's age, is sitting in the front row, watching her cast of *Romeo and Juliet* rehearse. Every few minutes, she calls out corrections and suggestions, and the cast stops and begins again. Like Romeo, Juliet is a senior at In Between High, and she's playing her part like she's Sorority Girl Juliet. If you ask me, she's not miserable enough and is way too enthusiastic about her every line. I mean, when she gets to the part where she says, "Deny thy father, refuse thy name," the girl is smiling. A big, fake smile. Like she's waiting for her photo op. Now that's just not right. From what I remember of the story, and from what I've picked up from watching rehearsals, Juliet is pretty miserable over not being able to be with Romeo. So a little less grin would be in order.

Sam leans over to survey my work. "Doing good, doing good. So anything new at In Between High?"

"Um, no." Tuck and staple. "Oh, wait, yeah. Dissected a pig today. Passed out. Bumped my head. Have a major knot."

Sam laughs. "Maybe it will get you out of school tomorrow."

"I can only hope. I don't want this head injury to be in vain." I send Sam a slanted grin. "So . . . " I lay out my material on the next cushion. "I saw Maxine yesterday. Tuesdays are my day to read to her, you know."

Sam keeps his head low. "Oh, did you?" He continues to work, his movements becoming more pronounced.

"She asked about you."

Sam stops. He looks at me for a moment. Then returns to his task, muttering, "These things don't affect me. I'm a grown man. Seasoned." Staple. "Mature." Staple. "Completely unaffected." Staple, staple.

"Sam?"

He sighs. "Yes?"

"You just attached your shirt to the seat."

"Blast it!"

My senior-citizen friend reaches for a screwdriver to pry his shirttail from the seat. His flustered hands fumble.

"Look, you two like each other, so what is the deal?" I watch his progress. Or lack of it.

"Did she say that? Did she say she liked me?" Hope replaces his previous expression of aggravation.

"Well, no."

"Then forget it." He pulls the staple, and a piece of his shirt comes with it.

"Hey, I'm no expert on romance or anything, especially of the retirement home variety, but you just need to make a move. Tell her how you feel."

Sam lays his screwdriver down and gives me his full attention.

"Say, 'Maxine, I like you. And I want more than secret runs through the Burger Barn drive-thru. I deserve the real deal.'"

"I deserve the real deal." Sam tries it out, his eyes focusing on something beyond me, like he can visualize his heart-to-heart with Maxine. "I deserve the real deal."

"There you go." I pat him on the back.

Sam nods. "Yeah, there I go. *Go*?" He jumps up, his shirt catching on one final staple and giving with a short rip. "I forgot . . . I gotta . . . uh, I gotta go. What time is it?"

Where did our bonding moment go? "It's four thirty."

"Oh, no. I'm late. I need to leave." He dusts off his knees, readjusts his hat, and scrambles away from me.

"Wait! Where are you going?"

Sam yanks open the exit doors. "I'm, uh . . . uh, I'll see you later. Carry on. You're doing great. Keep it up. Bye." And he shoots out the door.

Pretty impressive speed for an old guy. Why wouldn't someone of Maxine's biking skills be attracted to him? Clearly he can keep up with her.

I pick up the seat bottom and continue the re-covering process, my attention drawn again to the actors.

"Deny thy father! Refuse thy name!"

Bev bolts out of her seat and approaches the stage. "Okay, stop, stop. Stephanie, maybe a little less enthusiasm this time? Remember, you wish Romeo would stand up to his family and fight for you. You wish nothing else would matter but the two of you. All right? You shouldn't be happy. This is not a happy time."

Not a happy time? Has Stephanie even read beyond her kissing scene? Hey, Stephanie, you take a dagger to the heart in the end. Nothing Juliet can smile her way out of.

"Hello there. How is it going?" Millie comes up behind me, snapping her cell phone shut and taking in my progress.

"Oh, hey, Millie. Not so great. Bev's yelling at Stephanie to quit smiling. Stephanie keeps doing her Juliet-as-played-by-Cheerleader-Barbie routine. It's not going well."

"No, Katie, I meant with you. How are you doing? I see Sam has you reupholstering some of the seats." Millie picks up a cushion. "Looks like you're doing a wonderful job. This looks great."

I can't help but smile. I am kind of proud of my work.

"Where's Sam?" Millie checks her watch and looks around for her right-hand man.

"Yeah, I don't know. He took out of here like his overalls were on fire. Said he had to go somewhere."

"Oh. Okay." Millie shrugs it off. "Well, are you ready to go?"

I gather the materials and set them in Sam's toolbox. "Sure, let me grab my backpack." I retrieve it from a nearby corner and sling it over my back, carrying the bulk on one shoulder. "Home, then church, right?"

"Well, change of plans. I'm going to drop you off at Frances Vega's house. James and I have to be at church early for a deacons' meeting I completely forgot about." Millie walks toward the lobby, and I fall into step beside her. "So you'll eat dinner with Frances and her family, then go to church with them." Millie pauses to read my expression. "Mr. and Mrs. Vega are very excited to have you."

Her attempt at encouragement reminds me of Stephanie.

I give her a slight smile. Hanging out at Frances's? Part of me is nervous, worried I won't be polished enough for her family, and part of me thinks it's kind of cool.

On the way to the Vegas' house, I check my hair three different times in the car mirror, making sure I have shaken out all the stray sawdust.

"You look beautiful. Oh, I forgot to tell you, I brought a change of clothes in case you needed them." Millie points to a bag in the backseat. "I grabbed the pink shirt and some jeans. Church on Wednesday nights is very casual. And I packed your toothbrush."

I'm impressed. "Cleanliness is next to godliness?"

"Yeah, that and I don't want *my* foster kid going around with bad breath." She grabs my cheek and gives it a playful squeeze.

The sedan zips into Frances's driveway, and Millie shifts the car into park.

"Okay, so I'll see you tonight after church. Make sure you girls do your homework."

"Millie, this is Frances Vega's house. They probably won't feed me until I've finished my homework."

Millie grabs my bag of clothes behind the seat. "Have fun. Hey, and Katie . . . just relax. Be you. Well, not totally you. Don't show them how you can play 'Jesus Loves Me' with armpit noises."

"Maxine taught me that."

"Yes, I know." Millie rolls her eyes. "I'm beginning to wonder at the wisdom of forcing you two together every week."

I climb out of the car, just as Frances steps onto the porch, waving.

"See ya, Millie."

She wheels out of the driveway, waving goodbye.

"Katie! I'm so glad you could come over!" Frances radiates excitement, and I can only laugh and shake my head.

"I thought I should warn you." Frances takes a deep breath. "My mom is from China, and my dad is from Mexico."

My mouth flies open in mock shock. "How could you *keep* this from me?" I take a step away from her, as if to leave. But then I notice Frances looks so serious. "Hey, I was kidding."

No response.

"Frances, what's wrong with you?"

She shakes her head. "Well, I just mean . . . Oh, nothing. Don't say I didn't warn you. Come on in."

I follow Frances into the house. And my head spins for the second time today. Total sensory overload. I'm surrounded by multicultural artwork, photography, flags, and knickknacks. It's like China and Mexico went to war here—and I'm not sure who won.

"Bienvenidos! Welcome! I'm Cesar Vega." Mr. Vega enters the

foyer and grabs my hand in a tight grip, shaking it until my teeth rattle. "We are so glad you are joining us tonight. We have heard much about Zhen Mei's friend, Katie."

"Zhen Mei?" I whisper to Frances, who is right by my side.

"Remember? It's my name. Duh. We covered this on day one."

"Yeah, well, we also covered where the bathrooms were, but that doesn't mean I didn't try to tinkle in the janitor's closet."

"Yes, yes, so good to meet you. I'm Ling, Zhen Mei's mother." A tiny Asian woman wiping her hands on a kitchen towel comes to stand beside her husband. "We've been looking forward to meeting you, haven't we, Cesar?" Her long black hair sways as she nods in answer to her own question.

Mr. Vega laughs beneath his black mustache and puts an arm around his slight wife. "Oh, si, we see you in church, of course, and we are so proud to have you in our home." The two smile at me, and I don't know whether to laugh or run. This definitely explains where Frances gets her enthusiasm.

"Um, thank you. Thanks for having me?" It comes out more like a question, and I try to channel Stephanie's Juliet and plant a smile on my face. I suddenly notice the smell traveling from the kitchen and take an appreciative whiff. "That smells awesome."

Mr. Vega's smile gets even wider, and he looks like he's considering hugging me. I take a step back just in case.

And bump into a statue of a dragon.

"Oh, tonight you are in for a special treat, Katie. Is she not, Zhen Mei?"

"Sure, Dad." Frances is totally unimpressed.

"Tonight, Chef Cesar is in the kitchen, and I am whipping up a lovely menu of enchiladas de camarones. You will love it. All of Zhen Mei's friends love it, do they not?"

"They do!" Frances's mother nods vigorously.

I hear a *humph!* from Frances.

"Zhen Mei, you are a lucky girl to have such fine fare this evening," her father scolds. "Some kids' dinner comes out of a box."

Frances grabs my arm and drags me out of the living room and down the hall. "Can't we just have pizza for once—like normal people?"

"Dinner will be ready in twenty minutes!"

I follow a steaming Frances into the third room down the overly decorated hallway. Frances's room is like entering another world. It's so different from the rest of the house. Her walls are a funky green, with white-and-black accents in random places, like art.

"Luis, get off my computer. I am not messing around. I have homework to do, and I have a guest." Frances approaches the intruder in her room and points her finger in the direction of the door.

Frances's brother puffs his chest out and sticks out his hand for me to shake. "Hi, I'm Luis, and I'm five. I'm the man of the family in case you need anything." His big brown eyes watch me behind large round Harry-Potter glasses sitting crooked on his face.

"You can't even spell *man*. Now out, Luis. Go play games on Ming Yu's computer."

Luis crosses his arms and pokes his lower lip out. "You are interfering in my educational enrichment, Frances."

She checks the computer. "You were playing tic-tac-toe. Now scram, brat." Frances takes her little brother by the shoulders and gives him a gentle push out of the room. She shuts the door on a sigh. "Take a seat."

"So your brother calls you Frances, but your parents don't?" I settle myself into a black director's chair.

"Yeah." Frances flops onto her bed, rummaging through her backpack. "I have been called Frances since the first day of kindergarten. The teacher couldn't pronounce my name, so I told her to call me Frances, my middle name. My brothers and sister call me Frances too. I'm the oldest, so they have to, or I'll beat them up." She grins.

"But your parents don't call you that?"

Frances's face clouds. "No way. They say I should be proud of my culture and embrace who I really am."

I don't follow. "Who you really are? What does that mean?"

"I don't know if you picked up on this, but my parents are both really proud of their heritage. They are both first-generation Americans, which they're proud of, but they are really big on making sure we kids know where our family comes from, the culture, traditions, holidays, blah, blah, blah." Frances shakes her head and flips her science book open.

"I think it's cool. What's the problem?" I've never seen this girl negative about anything.

"Cool? You think it's cool to celebrate every American, Chinese, and Mexican holiday? I can't keep them all straight. I wake up to a new holiday every day. I'm surprised they remember my birthday for all the other celebrating we do. And then my mom and dad are always in this competition over whose culture is the most important, and whose culture we'll recognize today, and it just never ends." Frances takes a deep breath. "I just want to be Frances. Not Zhen Mei Frances Vega. I don't want to be torn between two cultures. I just want to be me." She grabs her notebook to begin on our science review. "My parents drive me nuts."

Oh, to have parents to drive you nuts (and not in a "I'm in jail again, feed the cats" sort of way). I'd love to have two parents who love me, who want to cook for me, who give me some cool name and care that I know where I come from. I don't even know my dad's mother's name. How's *that* for not knowing your heritage? What if I need something from her one day, like a biscuit recipe? Or a kidney?

I open my science book and together, Frances and I finish our review questions just in time to get called to the dining room.

The Vega dining room is wall-to-wall family portraits and watercolor renderings of historical events. As I sit down next to Frances, I wonder if eating next to a painting of a man being gored by a bull is all that good for the digestion. Dinner time is a bit chaotic. Mr. Vega brings in the food as his wife corrals the younger three Vegas.

"Zhen Mei, take the knife away from your brother."

"Maria, we sit down in our high chair."

"You put the frog back outside, didn't you, Ming Yu?"

"Luis, put the plate down. It does not belong on your head."

"Ming Yu, no reading at the table."

"Luis, get the napkin out of your ear."

"Maria's poking me with her fork, Mom."

Frances grabs the fork out of the baby's chubby hand and looks at me like *Can you* believe *I have to live with these people?*

I smile.

Mr. Vega clears his throat and all the chatter magically stops. "Let us pray."

I put down my water glass and bow my head, totally used to the drill.

"Dear Heavenly Father, we thank you for this day. Lord, we thank you for our guest, Katie, and pray for your blessing upon her. Lord, we ask you to be with the pastor tonight as he brings the message and with the youth pastor, as well. Bless this food to our nourishment. In Jesus' name we pray, Amen."

And the tornado begins. The noise level jumps a few hundred decibels as the food is passed around. All the Vega children tell about their day, and Frances tells her parents about my passing out. Before the end of the story, she is out of her seat, imitating my final moments of consciousness. "Bacon Bits! Bacon Bits!" The table erupts into laughter, and Mr. Vega is wiping his eyes with his napkin. Little Luis tries to top the story by telling about a kid in his kindergarten class who stuck a crayon up his nose. Everyone at the table looks at one another—and then they burst into laughter again.

I have really learned to enjoy my mealtimes with the Scotts, but dinnertime with the Vegas is totally different. With the Scotts it's just the three of us, and it's kind of quiet. But here? Platters clanging, little kids yelling, glasses spilling, loud voices talking over one another, obnoxious laughter, and—joy. These people are happy.

They're a little kooky, but they're happy.

I don't know if I would call the Scotts' home joyful. Do I make them unhappy? Does the fact that Amy's gone make them unhappy? Sure, on the surface everything is fine. But tonight I got a taste of what happiness really is. Tonight, as I eat this weird shrimp dish, I can feel their joy just as much as I can taste the hot spices.

Something's missing at the Scotts. And whatever the Vegas have, I want James and Millie to have it too.

Chapter thirty~three

"LUIS, IF YOU DON'T MOVE over, I *will* sit on you."

I duck into the Vegas' minivan after Frances clears her brother out of the way.

"I want to sit by Katie." Luis bats his eyes at me, then sticks his tongue out at his sister.

"Luis has a girlfriend!"

"Stop it, Ming Yu!" Luis yells to his older brother. He leans in close as he climbs into his seat. "Do you *want* to be my girlfriend?"

I take a good look at his chocolate-milk mustache. "Um. Not today, but thanks." Finally a boy who will ask me out. And he plays with Power Rangers.

We all buckle up, and Mr. Vega closes everyone's door and steers the van onto the road. Mrs. Smartly would love this vehicle. I think the seats are real leather, not wannabe leather.

Mrs. Vega pops in a worship CD, and soon the entire family is belting it out like they're on *American Idol*. Little Luis, like me, doesn't know the words, but he's making them up as he goes. At least, I don't think "Jesus loves peanut butter, and so do I" is really a line in the song.

Four tunes later, Mr. Vega slides his minivan into a parking spot at the church, and the seven of us pile out.

"Zhen Mei, do me a favor and take your little sister to the nursery." Mrs. Vega hands over a drooling Maria and her diaper bag, and the little girl clutches her big sister, making a quick grab for Frances's hair.

"Ow. Okay, let's go take Maria to the nursery, and then we'll go to Target Teen." Frances transfers the baby to her other hip and consults her watch. "We're a little early."

Church is still a little overwhelming to me, especially now, on my first night of the teen ministry. I hate getting somewhere early. It's all awkward. "I'll catch up with you in a little bit. I'm going to go say hi to James and Millie before church."

Frances and I take off in different directions, and I hustle toward the office, excited to tell my foster parents about Frances's not-so-tame family. I round the corner leading to James's office, wondering if the Scotts know Mr. Vega's grandfather was a famous matador in Mexico. And Mrs. Vega's parents still live in China, and her father is a—

"You *knew* she was coming."

I freeze in my tracks, hearing James's raised voice.

"Yes, I did." Millie's answer is cool.

"You've known she was coming this whole time, and you didn't think to tell your husband? She's my daughter too, Millie."

"I know that, James. I just thought—"

"This is why you don't want the opening date moved back. Because you told Amy about it and think she's going to be there." James laughs. But there's nothing funny about it.

I move a little closer to the office door, keeping one eye on the hallway in case someone walks by.

"I think she's coming this time. I really do." Millie's voice catches a little.

"When are you going to get it? She's not coming. She might *never* come back."

"She's our daughter. How can you say that? And you wonder why I didn't tell you."

"Millie, I love Amy. I want our daughter back, too. But we've been fighting this battle for too long. I'm tired of it—tired of it all. I'm fed up with my wife sneaking off to the post office to mail care packages and wire money like I don't know what she's doing. I'm tired of getting Amy's two-sentence postcards from a different town every few months." James lowers his voice, and I can hear him walk across the carpet.

I ease back a few steps.

When James goes on, his voice sounds so . . . tired. "Don't you think I'm sick of you being upset all the time? Tensing up every time the phone rings?"

"I can't change the opening night." Millie blows her nose. "I won't change it."

"This theatre is about the town, too, Millie. And it's about us . . . and all our hard work. Do you really want to open when we're not even close to being ready?"

"Do you want to take the chance of our daughter being there and the theatre being closed? I'm not willing to risk that."

I hear the faraway sound of the choir practicing. The sounds of their up-tempo praise song seep through the walls.

"Millie, when is it time to stop chasing her? We've done all we can. Sending her more money isn't going to make a difference. Writing one more letter isn't going to make a difference. And reno-vating that theatre isn't going to make a—"

"Forget it. You're not even listening. I have to get to choir."

I plaster myself to the wall and slink back around the corner. *Please go straight down the hall, Millie.* Maybe she'll be so distracted she won't notice me out of her peripheral vision.

"Millie, I think we need to talk about this. You — "

I hear the door slam, and Millie escapes out of the office. She's racing my way.

Think of an excuse. Why would I be standing here? I'll just tell her I was looking for her. It's the truth. Granted, I'm flattened to the wall like Spider-Man, but that's of no matter.

Here she comes. Her heels catch on the carpet with every step. Closer. And closer.

In a haze of beige silk, Millie sails right past the hallway I'm cowering in, not slowing for a second. I hear her sniffing and digging in her purse, but she continues her march down the corridor and exits the office wing.

My breath escapes in a *whooosh.*

Wow. Majorly intense. I've never seen those two fight like that. Didn't know they had it in them. I have got to do something. What if they get a divorce? Can preachers divorce? If they split up, I'm back in Sunny Haven for sure.

There must be a way to get the theatre open on time. They need money and they need more workers. Maybe Sam would know some more people to recruit.

I speed walk out of the office area, and with my mind spinning with ideas and what-ifs, I quickly navigate my way around the halls until I find the youth wing.

Sigh.

I guess I'd rather be here, my first night of Target Teen, than eavesdropping on another argument between my foster parents. I open the doors and find the Sunday school room has been transformed. I do a frantic search for Frances, afraid I've stumbled into the wrong room. The lights are slightly dimmed and candles and lamps are everywhere, like I'm no longer at church, but at a coffee house. The room vibrates with talking and laughter. Music blasts out of speakers on the stage, and I have to stop for a second and listen in appreciation. Ah, who doesn't love the hard banging of a drum and the steely whine of a few guitars?

I catch a few words of the lyrics and realize this is Christian music. I shake my head and smile. What will these people come up with next?

"Hey, welcome! Come on in. Katie, right?"

I'm high-fived by the youth pastor, who tonight is even more casual in jeans, worn and faded in a hip way, and a brown T-shirt that says *I Love Disco*. Only a man with a pirate's face and biceps bigger than baby Maria could get away with that shirt.

"We are so glad you decided to join us tonight. It's gonna be a great night." He pats me on the back with his tire-sized hands, and my breath hitches. "You won't be sorry."

Judging from the gleam in his eye, I suspect he knows Wednesday night church was definitely not my idea.

"Katie, meet my wife." Pastor Mike calls for his wife over the pounding of the music. "Laura, this is Katie."

A slender blonde woman wearing a ponytail and a generous smile grabs Pastor Mike's outstretched hand and joins us. "Katie, so good to meet you again! We met the Sunday you were introduced to the church, but you were shaking so many hands you probably don't remember."

No, I don't remember. I think I was too traumatized by all the hugging that went down that day. "Nice to meet you again—"

"Laura." She laughs, her blue eyes glowing. "Call me Laura."

Like Pastor Mike, she must be in her late twenties, but there is something about the two of them that makes you think they could be your friends. Like they might *get* you — a highly unusual quality to find in adults.

"Have you been to Target Teen before?" Laura has to practically yell above the noise.

"No. This is the first Wednesday night I've been at church." Ever.

"You're gonna love it. As you can tell it's very relaxed. Very contemporary. We'll have some music and then Mike will talk."

"Katie! Over here!"

Frances waves me over to where she's standing among a group of other kids our age. Some I recognize from school. They all wear smiles and look friendly, but you never know. I'm still very much aware of how different I am from everyone here. They're, like, from another civilization. I still don't know their ways, their songs, their jokes, their lingo. And their Bible? Until Nicholas Sparks puts out a version, I don't know that I'll ever get through that thing.

Laura waves at Frances and her group. "Looks like your friends are waiting for you."

Are they? I take a brief scan of the room. Are these the type of people I could ever be friends with?

"Katie, come on. I like to be close to the front." Frances reaches for my arm and pulls me alongside her and her friends, who are walking toward the stage.

"Oh, hey, Frances . . . I don't know. Isn't this kind of close? I don't want to be looking up the pastor's nose or anything."

Frances ignores me and introduces me to some of her friends; some I've already met, and some I recognize from school.

"Great sweater, Katie." Jessica, a girl in my history class, smiles warmly.

"Thanks." I wrack my brain for something to say with a few more syllables.

"I love pink. Don't you? Last year everything in my closet was totally black, but this year, I think almost everything I own is pink." This from Belinda, a girl I met last Sunday during church.

Soon the conversation revolves around the topics of clothing, shoes, and boys. I even add a comment or two myself and find it's not so bad talking to them. Almost normal. Like I'm just one of the girls. I look over at Frances and she's smiling at me. I smile back, knowing I wouldn't have made it through the doors of this room had she not been here tonight.

"All right, welcome! I'm Pastor Mike, and I am glad you're here tonight."

Conversations stop and the churchies break out into yelling and applause.

"If you're here for the first time tonight, you don't know what you've been missing. But you're about to find out. We are here to praise the living God. We don't take that lightly . . . but sometimes we do take that loudly."

Cheers erupt again. Frances and her friends yell and clap like they're at a Cowboys game.

"As the band takes the stage, find a comfortable spot. And get ready to worship like you mean it."

And the crowd goes wild.

Everyone in the room moves closer to the front, remaining standing, eyes fixed on the teenage band members strapping on guitars and adjusting microphones. Well, this is interesting. Don't tell me the churchies are gonna rock out.

The room darkens even more, and stage lights, hanging suspended above the band, begin to glow as the musicians rip into their opening chords, electric guitars and percussion exploding into sounds that I have never heard in a church, never thought would be allowed in a church. My mouth involuntarily forms an *O*, and out of the corner of my eye, I catch Pastor Mike watching me. I turn my head in his direction, and he grins his pirate grin and gives me a double thumbs-up. Okay, so the music is totally hot. I'll give him that. Definitely not what I expected.

The band, fellow students at In Between High, transitions into another number, more acoustical, but still loud and pulsating. I love that feeling, when music rumbles in your chest and soaks all the way through, like it's a part of you. I don't know the lyrics, but Frances and her friends do, and a few of them raise their hands up in the air. Whoa, if this turns into a mosh pit, I am so telling James. But the girls close their eyes, as do others across the room, and continue singing, hands reaching toward the ceiling. Frances, I can tell, is praying, and I feel foreign and awkward with their displays. Maybe a mosh pit wouldn't be so bad. At least I get the general concept of that.

I make myself quit staring and force my attention back to the band. They, too, have their eyes closed as they begin singing a quieter, slower song consisting of two acoustic guitars and the lead singer. The words jump out at me, and I take in their lyrics of sacrifice and hope. I can totally relate to the lines about searching for hope. Yeah, send me some of that. Does God even know I'm here? Does he see me, surrounded by his people — literally — totally uncertain of my future, even of where I'll be next month?

How can I buy into all of this when I've never seen him? Where was he when I had to put myself to bed most nights? Where was he when I got hauled off to Sunny Haven? How do you dig out of that and come out with hope?

The final notes of the song evaporate, and Pastor Mike takes center stage, his worn-out Bible in hand. The room transitions into a hushed silence.

"Guys, let's pray. Dear Heavenly Father, we love you and we praise you. We sing out to you tonight, acknowledging we do have hope in you. Without you, we are empty and lost, and . . . "

Empty and lost. Okay, I kind of relate there. So is this guy saying if I don't believe in God, then things are never going to get better? I mean, I don't know that I'm empty really. Do these people think I'm empty? Because I'm not empty. *So* not empty.

Partially drained perhaps . . .

"Father, we ask you to open our hearts and ears tonight. Let us be sensitive to what you have to say to us . . . "

And how am I going to know when God is talking to me? What if I don't hear him? Mr. Morton, the band director, had to yell at me through a bullhorn to get my attention, and that still didn't work. What if God's talking to me now? Um, God . . . are you talking to me now?

Nope. Not getting anything.

Well, maybe he only talks to people like Frances, who make straight *A*s and run around with the right people and concentrate really hard when they sing in church.

"Lord, we thank you for sending your son to die on the cross for our sins . . . "

And what does *that* mean? I need a glossary here. Are some people just born getting this stuff? Is there a remedial class I should be taking? Yes, that's probably what I need — remedial algebra *and* remedial church. Church for Dummies.

I should check Amazon.com.

"We ask that your Spirit be in this place . . . "

Your *what*?

"And we pray you would speak through me as I bring the message . . . "

What would happen if he prayed for Justin Timberlake to speak through him during the message?

"We surrender this time to you and come to you with seeking hearts. In Jesus' name we pray, Amen."

As if on cue, everyone sits down and reaches for their Bibles. I pull mine out of the backpack I had to bring in with me, and seeing the smooth leather cover with my name on it gives me a happy little charge.

"Turn in your Bibles to Jeremiah, chapter 29," Pastor Mike says, breaking the silence. The room fills with the sound of the thin pages turning.

Jeremiah . . . Jeremiah . . . Jeremiah. I flip through my Bible like I know what I'm doing. Why can't this thing be alphabetized? The books starting with *J* should be together, and they should come before the ones that start with *K*. Okay, scanning my table of contents (at least someone thought to include that), there aren't any books beginning with the letter *K*, but I'm still on to something. Maybe I could tell James and Millie my idea; they could invent these new, easier to use Bibles and make tons of money and be able to open the theatre on time.

In his booming voice, Pastor Mike begins his story about this prophet dude named Jeremiah. With his enthusiasm and facial expressions, the guy once again brings his tale to life, his words wrapping around me and involuntarily drawing me in.

"So Jeremiah was this really smart guy. And God spoke to him."

Because unlike me, Jeremiah didn't need remedial church, right?

"And Jeremiah had a lot to say because the people in the land were not acting right. They weren't following God's orders. They weren't obeying Scripture. And Jeremiah would say, 'Hey, something big is about to go down. You guys are gonna be *so* sorry you're living this way.' But no one would listen to him . . . no one would obey God."

Across the room, guys and girls are scribbling notes, copying down bits and pieces of the message. I consider reaching for a notebook and pen, but decide to let the words empty into my head and not on paper.

"And Jeremiah warned them and warned them. And you know, eventually it wore on him. He got sick of being around people not living right. He got fed up with the people who didn't care about him, didn't care about God. He was disgusted with life as it was, and he tried to tell everyone, 'Hey, there's more out there. There's more to life than this. If you'd just surrender to it, life could be so much better.'"

Pastor Mike pauses to let his words sink in, and his gaze travels across every one of us in the room. And when his eyes meet mine, I feel a slight tug. Like he's watching me closer — reading my thoughts, like everything I'm thinking is scrolling across my forehead.

Holding up his Bible, Pastor Mike moves about the stage. "Because who could create a better life for you than the Creator of life, God? Guys, tonight God wants the chance to get his hands on your life. He wants you to hand the keys over and let him drive." The preacher holds his Bible to his chest. "I haven't even gotten to the most important verse in this chapter tonight. And you know what? I'm not going to. Your homework, your assignment from me — from God — is to read Jeremiah 29, verses 11 through 13. It's God's personal message to you tonight, and I don't want to give it to you. He does."

I shut my Bible. But not before wedging the attached piece of ribbon in Jeremiah twenty-nine.

Pastor Mike's voice softens. "I challenge you. Maybe not tonight, maybe not tomorrow, but soon, read that passage. Imprint it on your heart. Tattoo it on your brain. This is God's road map for your life, his promise of hope for you. He wants to pull you up from the pit you're in and give you so much more. Let's pray. Dear Heavenly Father . . . "

Kind of deep tonight. I don't know. I just don't know about any of this.

God, if you are out there, I just want to put in my request for things to be okay between Millie and James. I'll probably survive if I have to go to another foster home, but frankly, the thought turns my stomach. So, yeah. That's all I wanted to say.

"Amen."

Amen.

Chapter thirty-four

"ALL RIGHTIE, I'M GOING TO partner you up. It says here you are to do the weighted ball toss until . . . let me get my glasses . . . hmm, is that right? Yes, that's what it says . . . it says do the weighted ball toss until your little pansy arms fall off." The PE substitute tugs up a droopy knee high and begins to number us off.

Coach Nelson is blissfully absent today. And even though she left a list of horrendous activities no human being could physically accomplish, it's a relief the Queen of Mean and Lean is gone. If only she had taken her daughter with her.

"Now, if your number is fourteen, raise your hand. Good. You two ladies will be together." The sub pushes up her bifocals. "Fifteen?"

I raise my hand.

And so does Angel.

"Congratulations, you're partners. Sixteen . . . "

I have successfully avoided Angel and her friends for sixteen days, five hours, and nine minutes. Her militant mom has had some sort of twisted mercy on me ever since the "incident" and made sure we were never anywhere near each other in PE.

How sad is it that I'm missing Coach Nelson right now?

I chance a look Angel's way.

She sneaks a peek in my direction.

Do I walk over there? Or does she walk over here? Do I suck it up and be the mature one?

Maturity's kind of overrated, you know?

Oh, okay. I stretch one foot out and plant it on the hardwood floor. I drag my other foot to meet it. Look there, a whole step. I'm reeking of maturity.

Ah, forget it. I close the space between the two of us, grabbing a weighted ball as I go.

I'm going to think of something profound and life changing to say to her.

"Hey." Simple is good too. I like simple.

"Hey." Angel's eyes flit to me then return to focus on her scuffed Nikes.

I hold the ball in my arms and think of what I'd really like to do with it.

Tweeeet! Our sub, Mrs. Droopy Stockings, blows on the whistle so hard something drops. Off her shirt? Was it a necklace maybe? Her hair clip?

She bends over to retrieve her lost possession and her glasses fall. I watch as the older woman helplessly feels around on the gym floor for her lost possessions.

I squat and settle the ball on the floor. "Let's go help the poor lady." I sigh and wave a reluctant Angel to follow me. "Come on."

Angel and I approach the befuddled PE replacement and swoop in to retrieve the objects of her search. We resurface, holding our treasure.

Angel presents the sub with her glasses.

I open my hand, only to realize my fingers had been tightly wrapped around . . .

Dentures.

Ew! I throw the teeth at the woman like they're a hand grenade.

Angel bites on her lip, but her giggles explode. Watching her face, I lose any ground I've gained on maturity and give in to bubbling laughter.

"Totally sick." Angel catches her breath as we walk back to our spot.

"I held that woman's teeth in my hand." I suppress a shiver.

The whistle trills again, and Angel and I share another laugh as we heave the weighted ball back and forth.

"I'm not even looking over there to see if she dropped her teeth this time." Angel hurls the ball my way.

"If she did, it's your turn to pick up the dentures. I get the glasses." I smile hesitantly, bending deeper to take the weight.

Except for our labored breathing, the next few minutes pass by in semi-comfortable silence as Angel and I focus on staying upright and keeping the million pound ball going—without dislocating anything important.

"I see you found new—*oomph*—friends." Angel wipes her sweaty face with her T-shirt.

I'm dying here.

Want.

Water.

And a stretcher.

"Yeah—*ow*—I guess." I gasp in air, grateful for the seconds the torture device is not in my arms.

"Those people . . . think they're better . . . than everyone else."

My noodle-like arms barely secure the ball. "No . . . they don't . . . Been really nice to me." I have to stop and catch my breath. I hold out my hand for her to give me a moment. Oxygen. I need oxygen.

Afraid of the whistle, I risk a look at our substitute, and see her slumped over in a seat, mouth wide open, snoozing away. I point her out to Angel, then crawl my way to the nearest bleacher, gasping for breath.

"I just think . . . you're out of your league, that's all." Angel spills onto the seat next to me.

I take a few moments to let my heart rate slow. "What's my league then, Angel?" I push my dripping hair out of my eyes. "You guys are on the wrong track, and I can't get pulled down in all that."

"Whatever."

My face burns but not so much from the workout. "'Whatever'? Angel, wake up. We were an inch away from wearing stripes and posing for mug shots. Hanging out with you nearly got me arrested. Do you even *get* that?"

"It was a mistake, okay?" Angel swears, and it sounds wrong to my ears, ears that have grown accustomed to the G-rated life at the Scotts.

"You know" — I drag in a breath — "I've learned a lot since I've been here. And I'm finally getting it. There are mistakes, and then there are choices. Tearing up the Valiant — that was a choice." I shake my head, seeing the destruction in my mind, recalling Millie's hurt.

"Oh, so I guess your new friends are perfect?"

"Look, I don't know what you're so angry about. I don't know if I'll be having sleepover and pedicure nights with these people anytime soon, but I do know, so far, Frances and her friends aren't out to spray paint the town or do things that result in a police escort." It's like I'm talking to a wall.

"Katie, I actually feel sorry for you." Angel's disdainful laugh sounds forced. "If you think you have anything in common with Frances and her type, you are so totally blind. They don't care about you. And when they get up close and catch a glimpse of where you really come from, they'll drop you faster than a pair of false teeth. But don't come crying to us."

I digest her words and find I can't completely discount them. I've never hung out with the "good" kids before. Never been in the "in" crowd. I *am* way out of my league. But at the same time, I feel defensive on their behalf.

"You know, you could come to church with me Sunday and check them out for yourself." The words escape my mouth before I can wrangle them back. Stupid, stupid, stupid.

Angel rolls her eyes and stands up. "Yeah, you save me a seat. I'll be there. That's all I need—the perfect kids and Jesus. Then life would be wonderful, right? Everything would magically be fixed?"

Uh . . . shaky ground here. Not my area of expertise. "That's not what I'm getting at—"

What am I getting at?

"Katie, those people don't deal in reality. They don't know life like we do." Angel's eyes lose some of their hostility. "But when you find yourself back to ground zero, and all your little friends have disappeared, don't come crawling back to me." With a final, dismissive smirk, she heads to the locker room.

The three o'clock bell rings just as I'm stepping out of the gym shower. The steam did nothing to clear my head—or the nasty drain. Seriously, how hard is it to clean a shower? Is it just part of the health code that locker room showers must have clogged, disgusting, bacteria-breeding showers?

The longer Angel's words occupy space in my head, the more confused I get. Leaving her and her group *had* to be the right thing to do. Like I told her, I can't get caught up in that. Living on the wrong side of the law is my mom's style, not mine. It can't be mine. But what if Angel is right about the churchies and Frances? When they really get to know me, when they see what I come from, when they realize my mama sure ain't staying at the Hilton, will they still be kind to me? Still offer to save me a seat at lunch? Still offer me gum in Sunday services?

I throw on my clothes and, seeing the time, all but run out to the buses. I can barely move my arms, which makes me look oh-so-cool trying to jog.

Reaching the bus just in time to escape the driver closing the door on me, I take the only remaining seat — next to the kid I've come to know as "Bucky the BO Wonder." I inhale his offensive aroma all the way to the Valiant, where I torpedo off the bus, desperate for air that doesn't smell like gym socks and armpits.

As I step into the lobby, I find Sam hunched over the concession stand counter, inspecting some newly applied wood trim.

"Good afternoon, little missy. Ready to do some sanding today?"

Moving in, I examine what I suppose will be my work area. "Yes, sir. I was just thinking to myself, the only way this day could get any better was if it involved sanding. How do you do it, Sam? How is it I walk in here and you know just what I need?"

Sam smacks his Juicy Fruit, and I have a flashback to projectile teeth. Let's hope his teeth stay where they belong.

"Don't go worrying about your pretty little manicure." Sam runs his weathered hand over the trim and grins. "We'll get you some work gloves and get you started. Pretty soon, you'll be begging me to let you sand."

Shaking my head at the thought, I readjust my backpack. "I'm gonna put this in the office. Be right back."

He waves me off.

"Don't start without me," I yell, finding my way to Millie's office space in the back.

I settle my backpack on the floor, and curiosity gets the best of me. I listen for a few seconds for anyone in the vicinity, then make my way over to Millie's desk. I'm not gonna rifle through the desk (though the old me probably would have), but as long as I'm here, my eyes might *accidentally* roam over her workspace in search of sticky notes with information on Amy, important memos, copies of phone messages, or evidence of any more outgoing care packages. And if I find any chocolate or candy, I'll probably have to confiscate it. For evidence.

Searching . . .

Searching . . .

And nothing.

Nothing but Millie's giant calendar, which has the grand opening date circled a few times in bright red marker. I can't believe we are now only weeks away. Weeks away from possible disaster. The theatre isn't ready and Juliet is being played by a department-store mannequin. Something's got to give. Today I'm going to talk to Sam about what we can do to speed up the renovation.

An outburst of girlish laughter makes me jump away from the desk and hold my hands in the air like I'm in a stick-up. I can hear my own heartbeat, but I exhale in relief when I realize I'm still alone, and the ultrafeminine giggles are coming from the lobby.

I leave the office and follow a cloud of Chanel No. 5.

Right to Maxine.

"Oh, Sam, please, have a cookie."

Maxine is leaning over the concession counter, plying a

google-eyed Sam with bottled water and snickerdoodles.

"Hey, Maxine."

The two star-crossed love birds jump apart.

Maxine does not look thrilled to see me. "Well, well, well, if it's not our favorite school girl. Don't you have some homework to do?"

"Nope." I move in between them, picking up my work gloves. "I'm here to work. You can't say Katie Parker shirks her responsibilities. No way." There has to be a halo above my head, I'm radiating so much innocence.

Sam clears his throat. "Um . . . er, uh . . . Maxine here was just bringing us some cookies. Weren't you, Maxine?"

Maxine proudly holds out a plate of cookies, partially covered by foil. "These just came out of the oven. Take one now, everyone. I insist!"

Sam looks at me. "Ladies first."

"No, no, I insist. Age before . . . reformed rebellious foster kid."

Maxine shoves the plate closer to Sam. "Come on now, fresh, warm cookies." She bats her mascara coated eyelashes.

"Katie's worked so hard lately, I want her to have the first one, Maxine."

"No, thank you." I push them toward Sam. "Take a cookie, Sam." It will probably be your last. "They just came out of her oven."

Maxine sniffs indignantly. "I didn't say they came out of *my* oven."

My hand collides with Sam's as we make a dive for the cookies.

"Mm, good. Who made these, Maxine?" I ask, my mouth full.

"Patricia Rigglebottom. As you may or may not know, I am

the coordinator for the annual Shady Acres Harvest Ball, and Patricia is a member of the food committee. We are considering her cookies for the event, and she brought over a sample, which I wanted to share." Maxine's cheeks glow pink. "Share with Millie, of course. To get her opinion. She said she'd help me with the ball, and I thought she might be here."

"Yes, imagine running into Sam here instead. Crazy, crazy coincidence, huh?"

Maxine jerks the cookie out of my hand midbite. "Go scrub some toilets or something, would you?"

"Well, I am pleased to see you, Maxine," Sam says, his evident hope making the man look almost silly.

"Thank you, Samuel. Good to see you. I didn't know you'd be here." Maxine elbows me in the ribs. "But I would appreciate a man's opinion of these snickerdoodles. Tell me, is there enough sugar?"

"He definitely needs more *sugar*, Maxine."

I'm rewarded with a heel stamped on my toe.

Sam takes off his hat, as I've found he does in times of stress, and wipes his nearly bald head. "These cookies are fine, Maxine. Just fine. God bless the hands that made them. And the hands that brought them."

I suffer whiplash jerking my head in Sam's direction. Ew. I think my cookies might come back up.

"Well now, isn't that nice? Isn't that nice, Katie?" Maxine giggles.

Stay down, cookies. Stay down.

"I guess there will be some fine eats at the Harvest Ball this year — with you in charge, Maxine."

"Sam, you are such the gentleman. Yes, I think we'll have some wonderful food there,"

"If you would like . . . well, I was wondering . . . "

"Yes?" Maxine coos, and she and I both lean in.

"Er . . . if no one else has asked you . . . " Sam swallows. "Would you like, um . . . Oh, shoot! I gotta go! How did the time get away from me? Oh, no, I . . . uh . . . "

I don't know if you can freak out when you're a senior citizen, but that's definitely what I would call what Sam is doing. Maxine looks to me for help, but I just shrug.

"You okay, Sam?" I ask.

"Um, Maxine, thank you for the cookies. You are . . . uh, I mean the cookies were a delight. Now if you'll excuse me . . . " Sam takes off his hat, this time to tip it like an English gent, "I must . . . run an errand."

And the white-haired carpenter jets out like his overalls are on fire.

Again.

Hmm, very interesting indeed.

Maxine clutches her cookie plate to her ample bosom and her eyes narrow. "What, pray tell, just happened?"

"I don't know. He did the same thing a few days ago."

"Left? Left at this particular time?" She consults her rhinestone-crusted watch. "At four thirty?"

I pause. How much do I tell? I don't want to get poor Sam in trouble. "Yeah, I guess."

"Something doesn't smell right here."

"I totally agree. I think you have way too much perfume on, Maxine."

"No! I mean with Sam."

Oh. Right.

"Well, for one thing, the poor guy was trying to ask you out for the Harvest Ball, and—"

"Shh!" Maxine waves her hands in front of my face. "I think I hear Millie."

Sure enough, my foster mom, juggling bags of supplies from the hardware store, appears at the door and knocks on it with her foot to get our attention.

Maxine puts the clutch of death on my arm. "Don't say a word. You got me, Sweet Pea?"

Bang! Bang!

"Not a word." Maxine's voice sizzles as she backs up and opens the door for her daughter. "Millie, dear! What a wonderful surprise to see you here!"

I intercept Millie and take some of the bags out of her hands. She catches my eye, waiting for me to translate her mother's odd behavior. Yeah, that'll be the day. There isn't a decoder ring in existence that could explain that woman.

"This is my theatre, Mother. Of course I'd be here. What are you doing here?"

Maxine falters, but she plods on. "You were going to help me with the Harvest Ball, remember? I have so many decisions I have to make by tomorrow, and I desperately need your help."

"Okay, Mom. Sure." Millie runs a hand through her hair. "Katie, I don't know what Sam wants you doing today. Is he around?"

"He had to go, but he didn't get to show me exactly what to do. He had to run an errand."

"Again?"

Maxine's eye twitches, and I rub a hand over my grinning mouth.

Millie sighs. "I don't have a clue what he wanted you to do, so why don't we all take a seat in the theatre and watch the rehearsals and discuss the gala."

We enter the theatre to find the cast gathering their belongings.

"See you tomorrow. And Stephanie, make sure you let us know next time you have a hair appointment." Bev turns away from the actors and holds her script over her face, rambling incoherently.

Millie rushes to the flustered director and puts a gentle arm around her. "Bev, is everything okay here?"

"I don't know, Millie. To be honest, I don't know if we're going to be ready for the opening."

"But you *have* to be." Millie's voice rises in pitch.

"We need practice, practice, and more practice, but Romeo is often late due to baseball practice, our Nurse had to be out last week when her son had the chicken pox, and today Stephanie is leaving to take care of her split ends. It's just not coming together."

"Here, Katie." Maxine scoots in, grabs Bev's script and shoves it into my hands. "Here's your job for today—Juliet."

"Wh-wh-what? No way! I can't go up there. I—"

"Oh, it would be *such* a help." Relief softens Millie's face. "You can read her lines, can't you?"

"Read her lines? Oh, this girl reads like a dream. Millie, have I not been telling you what a beautiful job she does for me on Tuesdays? When she reads, the story just comes to—"

"Hey, Millie, did you know Maxine brought cookies for S—" Maxine shoves a snickerdoodle between my teeth. "*Oomph.* Nebbermindh."

"Katie, we could really use your help."

Bev pleads without saying a word, and I embrace the inevitable. The unavoidable.

"*All* right. Let me see the script."

Bev squeals and returns to the stage to stop her cast from leaving.

"Come on, Millie. Let's park it in a seat and discuss the Harvest Ball."

Maxine wraps a bangled arm around her daughter and steers her away from where I'm standing. And fuming. My foster grandmother takes one final look and winks in ornery satisfaction.

"Break a leg, Toots."

Chapter thirty~five

"MY BOUNTY IS AS BOUNDLESS as the sea, my love as deep; the more I give to thee, the more I have, for both are infinite."

"I have no idea what you just said, but Rocky seems entranced by it."

Startled at the sound of James's voice behind me, I fling my script across the room in a spastic motion and nearly fall off the bed.

"Oh, my gosh." I hold my racing heart. "James, you scared me."

On this early Sunday morning, James takes in the scene before him: me standing on my bed, a silk flower tucked in my hair. And Rocky, a shirt tied around him like a cape, sitting at attention, waiting for his next command.

"You're kinda scaring me too. I did knock, but I guess you didn't hear me." He pats his dog on the head and walks across my bedroom to pick up my projectile script.

"Here you go." James reads the cover. "Ah, *Romeo and Juliet*. Of course. Great stuff."

I know if I looked in the mirror right now my cheeks would be feverishly red, and my neck would probably be broken out in weird splotches like it does when I experience total, utter humiliation.

I sit down on the bed, very aware of how ridiculous I look (not to mention how I've shamed the family dog). "I . . . um, still have the script Bev gave me when I stepped in for Stephanie at rehearsal last week."

And I like to dress up your dog and call him Romeo, and together we put on plays. Sure, that makes perfect sense. Because who doesn't like to perform Shakespeare in their free time?

"Hey, I've been meaning to talk to you about that." James pulls out my desk chair and sits down, like he has all the time in the world. Like he doesn't have to leave for church soon. "I heard you were some kind of wonderful on that stage."

My blush intensifies. "I was wonderful?"

James chuckles. "That's the report I was given. I hear you can 'wherefore art thou' with the best of them. And you saved the practice."

I was wonderful.

"Katie?"

"Oh, yeah. Right. Well, it was no big deal. You know, just glad to help out."

James rolls his chair in closer to me, his face serious. "Even Maxine was bragging on you, and she's a hard sell—believe me. I've been trying to win her over for thirty years."

We share a smile, and I begin to relax.

"Maybe next semester you can see about getting out of art and into drama. You'd probably enjoy that." James taps his fingers on his knees. "And maybe you could talk the teacher into letting Rocky audition for a play too."

I launch from my seat on the bed and pull on the shirt until

Rocky is free of it. "No animals were harmed in the reading of this script." I smile sheepishly.

James shakes his head and grins. "Katie, I . . . " He clears his throat. "I want to tell you how proud I am, how proud Millie and I both are of the job you've been doing at the Valiant. I know it's a lot of work, and you haven't complained a bit."

My fingers follow a ring pattern on the quilt. "No problem."

"And we're also really excited about your math grade coming up. It's hard asking for help, and you've been very open minded about Frances and tutoring."

Yep, that's me. Miss Open-minded. Not a judgmental bone in this body.

Coming to his feet, James puts a hand on my shoulder. "You're doing a great job, Katie. I don't get to be around as much as I'd like, but I want you to know I see it." James nods thoughtfully. "I see how hard you try. I know it hasn't been easy for you, and I really admire how you've hung in there."

I blink a few times to relieve my stinging eyes. "So I'm through with my punishment?"

"Not on your life. Do you know how many people we've gone through, trying to find someone who can stand Maxine long enough to read to her for an hour or two?"

"The number must be in the hundreds."

"Yeah, well, we'll never know. I think Maxine must eat them alive because they're never heard from again."

I pretend outrage. "But you send me over there?"

James laughs. "Even Maxine doesn't eat children . . . yet."

"No, she just tortures them."

James pauses on his way out the door, his hand on the knob. "I thought you didn't like Rocky."

"He seemed to have the depth I wanted to see in the part of

Romeo. And he works cheap."

"Well, if you and Rocky can break away from rehearsals, break-fast is ready. I fixed my world famous omelets this morning."

"I don't know. We're kind of at a pivotal scene here."

Shaking his head at his dog's discarded cape, my foster dad exits stage right. "Katie, you do have issues."

"Right back atcha, big guy."

I double-check my hair in the mirror, slip my feet into some funky heels, and descend the stairs, ready to grace the Scott break-fast nook with my presence.

James stands at the stove, his navy tie hanging loose around his neck. He adds more eggs to the skillet and winks in my direc-tion as I walk past him to join Millie at the table, where she sits drinking coffee and ignoring her toast.

"Hey, Millie."

She partially drops the paper she's reading. "Good morning, sweetie. Did you sleep well?"

"Yeah. Sure."

"That outfit looks great on you. Pink is your color." Millie smiles over her coffee cup, but it doesn't quite reach her eyes.

"Here we go, one Spanish omelet coming up." James flaps his masterpiece onto my plate, and Millie's nose goes back into her paper.

I study the chef. "Are you eating with us?"

His eyes dart to Millie before meeting mine. "Ah . . . I've already eaten, actually. Got up early this morning."

"Oh, okay."

Knowing I'm not going to do it myself, James says a breakfast prayer for me and my eggs. I stab into my omelet and let it melt in my mouth. Very nice. The eggs at Sunny were solid. In the way a brick is solid.

With my napkin I daub at some cheese on my chin. "You can still sit with us for a bit, right?"

James hesitates for one very uncomfortable second. I peer at Millie, but her head is lost in the Society section.

The Scotts always eat their meals together at the table.

Something is rotten in the state of Texas.

"Sure . . . sure I can."

James refills his coffee and brings the pot with him to the table. He raises it over Millie's cup, but her hand slapping over her mug stops him from pouring any refills. "No, thanks."

He straightens and rests the pot on a place mat, his face slightly pink. James turns his head in my direction and stretches a smile across his face. "Ready for church today?"

My eyes dart between the two of them before I answer. "Yeah, I guess."

And I guess I'm sick of the frigid temperatures in this house lately. First they were mad at each other. Then they ignored one another. Then yesterday James started acting more like his old self, and Millie continued playing freeze-out.

"I heard you guys fighting last Wednesday night before church."

Who said that?

James chokes on his Columbian blend, and Millie snaps her paper shut, eyes wary.

Why can't I ever just keep my mouth shut? It's like I'm genetically mutating into Maxine or something.

Millie sighs "Katie, adults argue. That's part of life."

"It's part of marriage." James focuses his intense expression on his wife.

Oh, okay. That explains it all.

Are you *kidding* me?

"I don't understand why you don't talk about Amy." I just had to throw it out there.

Millie tenses and casts her eyes downward. "We do talk about Amy."

James picks up a fork, absently turning it end to end. "What do you want to know about Amy?"

"Anything. Everything. Where is she? Why doesn't she visit?"

It all comes out in a gush, and Millie looks at no one. James may be ready to talk to me about his daughter, but his wife is not so ready to lay it all out there.

"Amy is in Colorado. She lives there with her boyfriend, and—"

"She's in Atlanta." Millie cuts in, and James sets the fork down with a thud.

The two stare each other down for a moment and communicate on a level that doesn't include me.

"She's in Atlanta?" James growls. "Since when?"

"Since last month."

"Millie, you knew our daughter moved again, and you didn't tell me?" James jerks the napkin out of his lap as he stands, then throws it on the table.

Eyes widening, Millie sends James a warning.

"Katie, will you excuse us?" Giving my shoulder a bolstering squeeze as I rise, James helps me out of my chair.

I lumber up the stairs and land facedown on my bed. I probably just smeared my mascara, but who cares. I can't stand this. I don't *want* James and Millie to be unhappy. I thought normal families got along. What's with all this fighting? The Middle East doesn't have a thing on James and Millie right now.

Sluggishly I move to the bathroom and brush my teeth with

my Barbie toothbrush. (Hey, I never could have one as a little kid, so when Millie said, go pick out a toothbrush, Barbie it was.) I inspect my hair, today pulled on top of my head in a casual updo, and rinse out my mouth with water from a cute Snoopy Dixie cup.

Knock. Knock.

James and Millie.

If they're here to tell me they're splitting up, I am going to be so ticked. "Come in." I take a seat on my bed as my foster parents enter my domain.

"Katie, we want to apologize." Millie sits down next to me. James goes for my desk chair again.

"We didn't intend to keep anything from you, and we're very sorry if you felt left out or deceived in any way." James glances at his wife, and I wonder if the mention of deception is aimed at her.

"Katie . . . " Millie draws a tired breath. "Amy's dream was to graduate from high school and go to NYU to study acting. James and I debated over allowing her to go, and as much as we wanted to encourage her dream, after much prayer, we just knew college in New York was not for her at that time."

James swivels in the chair to face me. "We told Amy we would continue praying about her college, but she needed to find a school closer to home. Amy wasn't—isn't—as strong as you are, Katie." James shakes his head, and his eyes focus on something—another time, another place only he can see. "Besides believing God didn't want Amy at NYU, we had a lot of reasons to not want Amy too far from us. As a child and as a teenager, she was very needy, very emotional. We had her in counseling for many years; we had her on medication; we did everything. It's like Amy has danced with destruction all her life."

"We love our daughter. She means the world to us. Please understand that." Millie's eyes are pleading, and I know I'm looking at some serious mama hurt here.

"The night we told Amy she wouldn't be going to NYU, she took off in the middle of the night." James glances down at his watch then puts his tie in order.

"She packed a single suitcase, took a few of our credit cards and all of her graduation money, and rode a midnight bus to New York. She left us a note, but it was over a month before we heard from her again."

James grimaces. "And even then it was just a postcard that said 'I'm in New York, and I'm okay.'"

"Amy is just . . . "

"A mess."

Millie bristles at her husband's words, but schools her features back into a neutral mask.

"We've been on quite a chase for our daughter in the seven years since she left. Millie and I have traveled all over this country, invested thousands in trying to keep up with her, not to mention all the money we've sent to every PO box she's ever had." He glances at Millie, who studies my bulletin board.

"So why won't she come home?" I cannot imagine not wanting to come home to all this — this house, this family, those omelets. Okay, Rocky's a deterrent, but you throw him a raw steak or two, and he's out of your way.

"Amy's gotten mixed up with some pretty serious stuff. We've done everything we can to help her, but aside from being her personal bankers, she doesn't want anything to do with us."

"James, that is not fair." Millie's nostrils flare. "Amy is lost and confused, and she's not emotionally well."

"She's spoiled and selfish, and it's gone on too long."

And here we go again. I was hoping they had signed a peace treaty or something downstairs.

Millie opens her mouth to blast a comeback, but our eyes meet, and apparently, she thinks better of it. Instead my nonMom purses her lips and folds her hands in her lap. Probably so she won't deck a preacher.

"Amy has been in so many towns in the last few years we can hardly keep up with it. Well, I certainly can't." James's words fly over me and land on Millie.

She lays her soft hand over mine. "While it is definitely true Amy has never and probably will never find any success as a professional actress, we still love our daughter and have hopes for the rest of her life. We pray for her to come home and get the care and attention she needs."

"Medical attention."

I jump in before Millie reacts to James's comment. "So why don't you all talk about her? Why doesn't anyone talk about her?"

My foster dad rubs a hand over his face, and for once he looks his age. Beyond his age. "I guess . . . I guess it's hard to admit you failed as a parent. There's not a whole lot to say about it. Other than pray, we can't do anything for Amy right now."

"And I suppose people are just trying to respect our privacy by not asking about her. They used to ask about her—years ago—but I think the people in the church and the community know our daughter isn't well." Millie's voice breaks a little, and the sight of a single tear running down her perfectly made up face hurts my heart.

I place my other hand over Millie's and give it a squeeze.

Me comforting Millie. Who would've thought?

"I'm sorry we've argued in front of you, Katie. Amy is the

burden of our hearts, for both of us, and it wears on us. James and I would hate for you to be affected too."

"Sometimes we want to approach Amy's situation in different ways, that's all." James graces his wife with a quiet smile.

Millie returns his smile, but it doesn't quite ring true. Or maybe I've just been watching Stephanie with the permanent megawatt grin too long.

James glances at his watch again. "I've got to get to church, but Katie, anytime you want to talk to us about something, we're here for you. Nothing is off limits."

"Can I get the pin number of your ATM card?"

"Not on your life."

"But you just said —"

"Why don't I pray for us right now?"

James takes a hold of our hands. And as he prays for us, I open an eye and take a peek at this family I'm in. We are connected, this pastor, his wife, and I. Hands joined, I feel their strength, and with everything I am, I know these people are solid. They've become like home base, like when I used to play freeze tag. No matter where I was or who was after me, I could run to base and be safe. Amy had to know that. Yet she keeps running anyway.

"God, we thank you for Katie and for this family. We thank you for Amy, and pray if it's your plan, you would deliver her back to us, safe and sound and ready to live in your will, and be the young woman we know she can be. Lord, we pray we would not get in your way. You are in control. We pray for patience. We pray for strength. In Jesus' name, amen."

My foster parents both squeeze my hands and I squeeze back. Millie wipes at her eyes and wraps an arm around me, pulling me close. She kisses the top of my head, and I stay there, content to be close to her.

"All right, kiddos, I needed to be at the church a half hour ago, so I'd better run." James leans down and kisses his wife. He plants one on my forehead and glides out the door.

"We'll see you in a little bit." Millie calls after him, then gets a glimpse of herself in the mirror. "Oh, my. I'd better go fix my makeup."

"Yeah, if you don't powder up, the choir will disown you."

"Funny girl. Your eggs are probably cold by now. You want me to heat them up?"

"Nah. I'm good."

"Okay, then meet me downstairs, ready to go, in ten minutes."

"Hey, Millie?"

My foster mom throws a hand around the doorframe to halt herself. "Yes?"

"Are you gonna change the grand opening date of the Valiant now?"

Millie inspects her manicure. "No, I'm not. I sent the programs to the printer weeks ago. We won't be changing anything."

I swallow. "Do you think she'll be there?"

Millie's gaze is steady on mine. "Yes. My daughter will be there."

Chapter thirty-six

THE THREE O'CLOCK BELL RINGS, and I shuffle out of class and elbow my way through the pressing crowds to my locker. I mentally review my classes for the day and try to recall the ones I have homework in. This is still a new phenomenon for me—homework. Back in the day, I would have left the books in my locker and gone home to watch some television and fix dinner. When your mom hasn't once glanced at your report card, it's a little hard to muster up the motivation to do something like homework. But James and Millie are different. They're all about the homework. And obsessed with checking my grades online. (Twenty-four-hour access to my grades. That's a brand of punishment I'll never get over.) So between my grade-tracking foster parents and Frances's tutoring, I am slowly turning into a school-conscious kid. Not too sure how I feel about that yet, but slowly floating up from the bottom of the class isn't too bad.

I stuff my needed textbooks and binders in my backpack, and like the Hunchback of Notre Dame, I lumber out to the bus waiting area. I choke on some exhaust and stand next to the corner of the building under a shade tree.

Psst.

I readjust my droopy backpack.

Pssssst.

I search to my left and my right. Nobody there.

"*Psst*, over here."

An acorn beans me in the back of the head.

"Are you deaf? I'm over here!"

I peer around the corner, and there is my foster grandmother, dressed in black from head to toe, plastered to the side of the building, inches away from me.

"Maxine, *what* are you doing?" I notice she has her helmet on. And there are leaves all over it. "Did you hot glue those leaves?"

"All 106 of them. Now keep your voice down."

My eyes dart side to side, as I desperately hope no one is watching this odd scene.

"Maxine, aren't we reading today? It's Tuesday."

She shakes her head. "No books today. We have a very important mission."

"A mission?"

"Yes. Your mission, should you choose to accept it . . . "

"What mission?"

"*Ahem*, your mission, should you choose to accept it—"

"Would you just spit it out! You look ridiculous." I swipe my hand across her cheek and bring back a charcoal-colored thumb. "Is this black paint on your face?"

"Nah, it was supposed to be, but I ran out of face paint and had to smear mascara all over my cheeks."

"Very becoming." I don't even want to think about why she owns face paint in the first place. "What is this about?"

"Do you accept the mission or not?"

I hear the buses shift into gear, and out of the corner of my eye I see a yellow haze pass by. My bus. Gone. A tired sigh escapes my lips.

"Your bicycle is here somewhere, isn't it?" I am not heaving this backpack all the way to Maxine's house.

"Well, I sure didn't take the subway. Now, as I was saying, we have work to do. *Mission: Sam Is a Cheating Dirt Bag* is afoot."

"Sam is a—"

"No time for your questions." She looks around me, checking for eavesdroppers, and her voice lowers. "We must move quickly. I have received credible intel that Sam Dayberry has been socializing with another woman."

"Well, why wouldn't he? He's waited on you for an entire year, and look where that's gotten him."

"I did not ask for your sass! I am not bringing you along to think. I am taking you to work."

Warning bells clang in my head. And it's not a tiny little ring. It's like a symphony of a Wal-Mart parking lot full of car alarms, the town tornado siren, and the school fire alarm all rolled into one. I should walk away right now.

"Where are we going?" *Clang! Clang!*

Maxine rubs her hands together—her gloved hands. Great, she wants to involve me in something, and she doesn't plan on leaving fingerprints.

"You haven't said you'll accept the mission."

I exhale like a bull and stare her down.

"Do you choose to—"

"Yes! Yes! Get on with it!"

"First, we need to get you suited up."

"I am not changing."

"But we can't be seen."

"It's broad daylight! Do you really think all this black you've caked on yourself is going to make you invisible?"

Maxine picks a stray leaf off her black turtleneck and puffs up. "It's a very important mission, Katie Parker, and I don't like your attitude. We might be out until the wee hours of the morning, for all you know, Miss Smarty Pants."

I close my eyes and massage my temples. My head doesn't hurt now, but moments like these are just a breeding ground for migraines.

"Prepare for take-off."

Maxine hands me a lilac-colored helmet.

"My own helmet?" My attitude softens at her sweet gesture, even if the helmet does have what looks to be a small shrub duct taped to it.

She shrugs. "My insurance doesn't cover head trauma." Maxine tightens her own hot pink helmet. "Follow me."

I have to practically run to keep up with her, as Maxine scurries toward the back of the building, stopping occasionally to duck and survey the premises. I'm waiting for a nice drop and roll.

"You want to tell me what this is about?" My voice is low, but loud enough to carry to the crazy woman in front of me.

"It's Sam. I found out where he's been going—who he's been spending his precious time with."

"Where?" And where is this woman's bike?

"At Trudy Marple's house. That floozy. That . . . that tart! Why, she doesn't even try to color her old gray hair. And—" Maxine turns around, her face drawn in disgust. "She wears muumuus." Swiveling around, Maxine picks up the pace and leads me to a wooded area across the street from the campus.

Grabbing my hand, Maxine yanks me a few feet into the

woods, and there, propped against a giant maple tree, is Ginger, her bicycle.

Pulling some strategically placed twigs and branches off of her bike, Maxine walks Ginger out of the trees and into a clearing. At her impatient hand signal, I toss my backpack in the metal basket near the horn. I throw a leg over the seat, and following Maxine's lead, begin to pedal.

Lord, if you are real . . . or if you even answer prayers from a girl dumb enough to get on a bicycle built for two with a deranged senior citizen bent on stalking her geriatric, cheating nonboyfriend, I just want to say I can't really afford to get in any more trouble right now. So just remember this was not my idea. I can't say no to Maxine. I'm sure you know what I mean.

And we pedal at speeds worthy of the Tour de France. Through yards, fields, and a small stream I didn't even know existed; cutting across an elementary playground, past the rural fire department, and then finally into a subdivision of newly constructed homes.

"Lean!"

Maxine throws her arm up to signal a right turn, and we take it so fast, we're nearly horizontal.

I sigh with relief when the pedals slow down and Maxine allows us to coast for a moment. She directs us onto Apple Blossom Street, and the bike skids to a stop in the driveway of a gray two-story home.

"Let's move." Maxine leaps off and runs around the house toward the back yard.

My only choice is to follow her, but I'm thoroughly confused. "Is this the house?"

"No! Amateur."

When Maxine opens the gate in the chain-link fence, dread settles in my stomach like I swallowed the weighted ball from PE.

"We can't go through there! Do you even know who lives here? What if there's a rabid, angry, starving pit bull in—"

I'm yanked through the opening, and the two of us tear across the yard and out another gate.

"There." Maxine points at the back of a large brick home. "There's where the little cheat is."

We cross another large lot and close the distance between us and the object of Maxine's loathing, a red brick Colonial, surrounded by an extra tall privacy fence.

"You think Sam's in there?" I can't even see in there for the fence.

The house in her sight, her eyes narrow like a reptile's. "Yes. I know he is."

"So do you want to walk around and see if his truck is there?"

Maxine tosses her head back and laughs. "Silly child! That would be too easy. What I have in mind for us takes skill and strategic planning."

I roll my eyes.

"Plus, I think he keeps his truck in her garage when he's here." Maxine squats down, intertwines her fingers, and makes a basket with her hands. "I ain't gettin' any younger, Sweet Pea, up you go."

I look at her hands, then back at Maxine. "No, way."

She moves her head from side to side, and her neck gives a *crack* and a *pop*. "Yup, right now. Time's a wasting."

We couldn't just read today, could we? Nooo. Of course not. "Oh, all right! If I do this, then can we leave?"

"Need I remind you, Agent Sixteen, you accepted this mission."

"Agent Sixteen? Like my age? So you must be Agent One Hundred and—"

"Never mind! Just stick your foot in my hands, so I can hoist you up."

I pause to stare at Maxine like she's crazy. 'Cause she is.

"Katie, either you do it, or you'd better start figuring out a way to heave me up there, because we're not leaving till one of us gets a good view into that house."

I plant my left foot in the step she's made for me, grip her shoulder with one hand, and at her count of three, reach for the top of the privacy fence with my other hand.

"Okay, got it." I release her shoulder and pull myself up on the fence.

"You sure you have it?" Maxine calls sweetly.

"Yeah." Kind of painful though, what with the fence digging into my chest and all. I can't imagine how uncomfortable this would be if I didn't have my superturbo padded bra on today.

"Absolutely positive?"

"Yes, Maxine."

"Good, on to step two."

And she releases my feet.

I cling to the fence, my desperate legs kicking out for a foothold.

"See the tree over your head? Climb up the fence and grab onto the big branch there with the pretty red leaves on it."

"Are you out of your *mind*?"

"I'm a woman scorned, Katie."

I brave a look back, my neck constricting painfully, and see Maxine leaning against the fence, comfortable as you please.

"You're gonna have to help me, Maxine, or else all we're going to accomplish today is me hanging here." The wooden slats cut into my arms.

She pushes off the fence and sighs. "Very well. What do you need me to do?"

"Walk over my direction. No, come closer . . . closer. Perfect."

Maxine stands next to my dangling feet.

"*Oomph!*"

I step on her, adjusting my footing until I have my balance.

"That's my nose, you impertinent little cream puff!"

"Oh, sorry. I was aiming for your shoulder." But a nose will do. I stretch as far as I can overhead, my eyes on the ground below me. "Oh, nice pool she's got here."

"Humph."

My hands latch onto a thick branch, and thanks to Coach Nelson and her punishing chin-ups, I'm able to pull my body up enough to hook a leg over the branch and climb on.

"Brilliant work. I couldn't have done a better job myself."

Oh, the nerve!

"Now what? I don't see anything." Nothing except the large pool, which hasn't been covered up for the fall. Beautiful landscaping skirts the outer area, and brightly colored lounge chairs are arranged sporadically near umbrellas.

"Nothing? Are you sure?"

I look past the pool and try to see into the house. On the left seems to be a bedroom. Nothing in there. In the center looks to be the kitchen. Nope, I don't see any questionable activity. And the next window over to my right is . . .

"Oh, no."

"What? What? Tell me what you see!"

I see Sam. At least I think it's Sam. And his arms are around someone. "Maxine, it's nothing. Time to go, okay? I have homework tonight."

Maxine stomps her foot, throws her hand up to the sky, and points a finger at me. "I'm not turning back now."

"Well, I can't see too well in there. I mean, it could be Sam. I don't know." I want to go home. Or anywhere but here. In a tree. Twenty feet above some stranger's yard.

Maxine cups her hands around her mouth. "You have to climb out onto the branch. You'll be able to get a better look."

I don't *want* a better look!

"Do it!"

I place my hands farther down the thick branch, fairly confident it can hold me. Like an inch worm, I travel the branch, stopping at the point where it begins to narrow too much.

"See anything?"

My neck stretches, and I strain to focus on the dining room. I glance down at Maxine, who is frozen in her spot, her eyes riveted on me. I gulp. This isn't going to be pretty. "Maxine, he's in there."

She nods. "And he's with Trudy Marple." Her eyes are fire, and I suddenly fear for Sam's life.

"Um . . . no."

"No? Tell me what you see."

"He's dancing . . . "

"Yes?"

"With a guy."

Maxine scratches her chin. "I did not see that coming."

I patiently wait in the tree, letting my foster grandmother process the information.

"I need more information, Agent Sixteen. Give me concrete details."

I eye the tree limb. "Maxine—"

"You're a lightweight. Get on out there and take a closer look."

I close my eyes. "For the record, I was forced into this. If we get taken downtown, I will sing like a canar—"

Crack!

My head jerks toward the noise.

"Thirty more seconds, Katie, that's all I ask. I can't believe I forgot my camera."

Snap! Crack!

"Um, Maxine . . . "

"And to think that I trusted him! I shared my Burger Barn Value Meals with him. Well, never the fries of course . . . "

Pop, pop, pop!

"Maxi-i-i-i-i-i-ne!"

My world spins on its axis as the branch and I spiral out of control. I plunge down, my body upside down and sideways. My horizontal becomes vertical, and I am aware only of my own screaming. Branches slap me in the face, and limbs reach out and poke at my skin. My life flashes before my—

Splash!

My body crashes into the pool, and my skin spasms and stings at the frigid contact.

I will my wooden limbs to cooperate, and I slowly ascend through the water, paddling through leaves and dead bugs.

I break through, my head shooting above the water. Coughing and sputtering, I gasp for breath.

"What is going on?"

"Sam, call the police!"

I weakly dog paddle to the side and grab onto the edge. My throat and nose burn and—did someone say police?

"No . . . no p-p-police. S'me, Sam." I choke on water. And a bug carcass. "It's me—K-K-Katie."

Through blurred eyes, I see Sam rushing toward me, and a

teenage boy following close behind. Holding the door open is a gray-haired woman in a loud housedress, who I can only assume is Trudy Marple.

My arms hang lifeless on the concrete edge of the pool. I jerk with the shivers. So. Cold.

"Katie? Is that you?"

I reach a hand up to Sam and the boy next to him, whose mouth is wide open in disbelief. The two guys pull me up, and the cool fall air hitting my wet clothing makes me gasp in pain.

"Are you all right?" Sam's face is full of urgent concern.

"What's a girl doing in my pool? Who is she? Where is neighborhood watch when you need them?" The gray-haired woman remains in the doorway, obviously not convinced I'm harmless. I can't imagine why.

Sam picks a few leaves from my hair and draws me close to him, guiding me to the door. "Move out of the way, Trudy. Everything's okay. Just gonna get this girl warmed up."

As soon as I can move my fingers again, I am going to kill Maxine.

I shiver into Sam's side, desperate for some warmth. A smart girl would probably cozy up to the boy behind us, but I'm too frozen to appreciate the opportunity.

"Okay, here we go. Step into the house. Easy does it."

Sam's gentle voice soothes me, and I can see why Maxine is fond of the guy. Not that he's worth freefalling out of a giant oak tree for, but I like him.

We ease into the kitchen, and Sam helps me settle into a chair.

"Trudy, grab some blankets, woman. What is wrong with you?"

Trudy remains near the back door, motionless, as the boy, a sophomore I now recognize from school, jumps to do Sam's bidding.

"Are you hurt anywhere?"

I shake my head no, and Sam holds my chin, moving my head to look for wounds. Or signs of brain activity.

"Here you go, Sam."

"Thanks, Charlie."

Sam grabs a blanket and some towels from my In Between classmate and turbans my head in a fluffy pink towel.

"I'm fine. Really." I take the blanket from him and cocoon myself in its fuzzy warmth.

"Trudy, get this girl some cocoa."

Without taking her eyes off of me, Trudy snaps her fingers, points at the cabinets, and once again, Charlie jumps into action. She crosses her arms over her chest and continues her long-distance watch.

"Are you sure you're not hurt anywhere?" Sam looks doubtful.

"No. I'm just" — oh, let's see: embarrassed, mad, freezing, tired; take your pick — "cold. Thanks though. Seriously, I feel fine."

"Nothing broken?" Sam grabs my arm and flops it around.

I pull my arm back into the warmth of the blanket and shake my head. I catch Charlie's eye. Okay, so my pride's a little fractured. Can't wait to hear this story circulating around the halls of In Between High.

And where is Maxine? I risk my life for her, and she bails on me?

"Katie, this is Trudy Marple."

Trudy's chin falls in a single nod.

"And this is her grandson, Charlie. You may know him from school."

Charlie, tending to the cocoa, pushes his brown, wavy hair out of his eyes, and smiles. "So, you didn't mention how you came to be floating in Grandma's pool."

Oh, didn't I?

"Yes, any particular reason you decided to climb up my tree and belly flop into my backyard?" Trudy inches a step closer.

I juggle excuses in my head. I was chasing a squirrel? I was testing the laws of gravity for a science project? I wanted to try out a new dive I call "Belly-Buster Katie"? I can't think! How am I going to get out of this?

"Ohhh, my head . . . " I squeeze my eyes shut and conjure a moan.

Sam picks me up and has me cradled in his arms before I can add any more sound effects. "I'm taking you to the emergency room."

No! Now what? If I see Maxine Simmons ever again in this lifetime, I'm gonna—

Ding-dong!

"Open the door, Trudy, I'm taking this girl to see a doctor."

Ding-dong!

Trudy, glad to be rid of me, runs ahead of us and flings the door open.

"Maxine?"

Who?

Opening an eye, I see Maxine standing in the doorway, blocking our exit.

"Avon calling!"

For an instant Maxine's eyes go wide at the sight of me in my drowned state, draped over Sam's arms. She schools her features as if I'm of no concern. "Well, *there* you are, Katie. My goodness. One moment we're doing a little bird watching, and the next thing I know, Katie's run off, yelling she's spotted an African Hairy Woodpecker, and then—" Maxine snaps her fingers. "Poof! She was gone." She smiles at Trudy. "Kids today, eh?"

Still carrying me, Sam closes in on Maxine and growls. "Maxine, what is all this about?"

Maxine sputters. "How dare you ask *me* what this is all about! You . . . you . . . "

"What are you doing here?"

Maxine throws both hands over her heart. "What am *I* doing here? What about *you*?"

Sam takes a step closer.

"Don't you come near me! In fact, give me this girl."

With the strength of the Amazon she is, Maxine claws Sam's hands from me, and before I can catch myself, I'm flat on my back on Trudy Marple's Berber carpet.

Ow.

"Now look what you've done!" Maxine makes no move to help me up.

Sam is so lost in the brewing argument, that he, too, ignores me. I watch the dueling seniors from the floor.

"You sent Katie up that tree to spy on me, didn't you?"

Maxine's mouth opens and shuts like a guppy. "If I am associating with someone of questionable integrity, I have a right to know. I will not defend my actions!"

"Questionable integrity!" Sam's face glows beet red. "Are you out of your mind?"

"I'd like to answer that—" I chime in, but Maxine shoots me a withering look, and I clamp my mouth shut.

"Get up, Katie. We're leaving."

I ease off the floor and stand beside the fuming Maxine.

"Now, you wait just a pea-picking minute—"

"No, *you* wait, Samuel Dayberry. I've been on your trail for days. You come sneaking over here and make me think you and Trudy Marple are all cozied up. And then Katie and I happen to be in the neighborhood, and what does this child see?" Maxine throws her arm around me. "You, doing the cha-cha with some boy."

"This boy"—Sam points to a mortified Charlie—"is Trudy's grandson. And he's teaching me how to dance. Do you get it yet? Is it *clear* to you?"

Quiet descends on the room.

Maxine smiles and bats her eyelashes. "Well . . . I never meant to imply anything indecent was going on."

"I was trying to learn how to dance, so I wouldn't embarrass you when I asked you to dance at the Harvest Ball, but forget it. You just saved me from two more weeks of dancing torture. I'm through with it. And with us."

"Now, Sam—"

"Good-bye, Maxine."

"I'm breaking up with you too! Let the record show you didn't break up with me first! We broke up with each other simultaneously and—"

Slam!

The door shuts, with me and Maxine on the outside.

"An African Hairy Woodpecker?"

Maxine purses her lips. "It's the best I could do under pressure."

Despite nearly meeting my death, I feel a twinge of pity. "Sorry about Sam, Maxine. He was pretty harsh."

She laughs. "I'm an old pro, Katie. I've got Sam right where I want him."

We walk down the road, my shoes squishing with every step. "You have no idea how to get out of this one, do you?"

Maxine sniffs. "Not a clue."

Chapter thirty~seven

"CONGRATULATIONS ON ANOTHER SUCCESSFUL day of not passing out in biology."

I dig around in my lunch sack for my sandwich and scan the cafeteria. "Yeah, I've yet to be able to recreate that moment. It did get me out of class."

Frances grins. "It was kind of gross today when Mr. Hughes knocked Josh Palmer's pig off the table."

"Totally disgusting. I thought Mr. Hughes was going to start bawling."

Frances and I giggle until she's snorting.

As my friend focuses on her fries, my mind goes to James, Millie, and the Valiant. I wish I could snap my fingers and make it all better for my foster parents. I don't see any way that theatre is going to be finished by the opening. I wish Millie would just postpone it. Every day we get a little more done. But I have no less guilt.

"Earth to Katie. Hello?" Frances waves a hand in front of my face. "Did you hear a word I just said?"

"Um"—I smile sheepishly—"you said I'm the best science partner you ever had?"

"Nice try. What's up with you? You've been like this all week."

How do I explain the extent to which my life stinks right now? "Things are just really stressful at my house."

Frances steals one of my carrot sticks, which I am more than happy to share. "Like between the Scotts?"

"Yeah, but it's more than that. It's the theatre. It has to be done for the opening night, but it's just not possible. And it's my fault, you know?"

"It's not your fault. It's the fault of those people you were hanging out with. You didn't know that was going to happen."

"But it did. And I was there." I shake my head. "We're running out of time."

Frances pops another carrot in her mouth. "So tell me what you need to fix this."

I laugh, though nothing is funny. "A miracle. It would take a miracle to fix the Valiant on time."

My friend smiles. "Guess you'd better start praying for one. I mean, God is in the miracle business, you know."

"That's what I hear." Like it's just as easy as that.

"Hey, Frances."

Frances looks beyond me. "Oh, hi, Charlie."

All the noises in the cafeteria fade away and thoughts of the Valiant dissolve as Charlie's name echoes in my head. Oh, no. This is where Trudy Marple's grandson tells Frances and everyone else at In Between what a freak I am. How I climb up in trees and spy on complete strangers like a perv.

"Charlie, do you know Katie?"

Though I'm tempted to be rude and ignore him, I'm forced to turn around and acknowledge Charlie.

"Katie, nice to . . . meet you."

I clasp his outstretched hand to shake, but I don't return his mischievous smile.

"Are you new here?" He acts like we've never laid eyes on each other, as if he didn't see me facedown in a pool full of algae just two days ago.

Frances kicks me under the table. "Katie's been here a little over a month. Haven't you?"

I shake my head to clear it and remember I need to be on my guard around this guy. I sigh. I'll just get it over with. "Right. A month or so. But Charlie and I actually met—"

"In the hall the other day. I think we usually pass each other on the stairs right before second hour." He smiles. "It's good to put a name to the face."

I'm suspicious, but I return his smile. "Yeah, you too."

Charlie takes an empty seat next to Frances. "It's so easy to get lost in the *pool* of faces."

I choke on a carrot.

"Yeah, the school is getting pretty big." Frances says and offers our new tablemate a french fry.

"It's like sometimes you could *drown* in all the people here, you know?"

Frances frowns in confusion, but nods in agreement.

I glare at Charlie and give him my best evil eye. I call it Evil Eye Number Twenty-seven. It's just the right combination of eyebrow, nose wrinkling, and lip curl.

"I guess for a small town your school is fairly large. But the halls are so crowded it's like you're close enough to *dance* with someone." Score one for Katie.

"We were just talking about overcrowding yesterday at the student council meeting."

I ignore Frances and continue staring down the guy in front of me.

And then I get it.

He's not going to rat me out and announce to the world I'm a Peeping Tom. Charlie's afraid of me outing *him* for dancing with Sam Dayberry. I breathe a sigh of relief.

"Thanks for *waltzing* over here and introducing yourself, Charlie." Hey, this is kind of fun, though I'm running out of material.

His face turns as pink as Frances's wool sweater. Frances becomes engrossed in conversation with the girl next to her, and Charlie gives me his full attention. "Just remember this, Katie Parker. I have cafeteria-lady connections. You tell anyone you saw me dancing with Sam, and you will never have a hair-free lunch again."

His voice is low, for my ears only, and he barely holds on to his serious face.

I lean in. "Charlie." I snap a carrot with my teeth. "Your cafeteria threats don't scare me. I bring my lunch. If you want me to keep quiet about your little foxtrot with Sam, you're gonna have to do better than that."

He laughs quietly and considers his options. "How about I'll forget what happened Tuesday, if you will."

"Tuesday?" I force my face to go blank. "What happened Tuesday?"

Charlie stands up, waving at some people around us. "I'll see you around, Katie Parker."

His smile is a work of art, but I know boys like Charlie are not my type. He's smart, preppy—and totally hot. The guys who like me usually have a few body piercings and a taste for cheap cigarettes.

I focus on what's left of my club sandwich. "Later."

WHEN I WALK INTO the Valiant that afternoon I take a big, healthy breath, ready to confront Charlie's dance partner.

I find him sitting on the lobby floor, absorbed in laying some tile.

"Hey, Sam. Broken any hearts lately?"

He jerks, and a small tile shoots out of his hand. "Blast it!"

Bending down, I pick up the stray tile piece. "You were pretty hard on Maxine yesterday."

"Shh! Keep your voice down. Millie could show up any moment." He wipes his hands on his work pants and gets to his feet. "A man has to face his reality, Katie. Maxine is either going to date me or she's not, but her escapades have gone on for too long. It's not the first time someone's done her dirty work and crashed in a pool."

"It's not?"

Sam throws his cap on the floor. "I was being metaphorical!"

"Oh. Well, actually, Sam, a metaphor is a—"

"You know what I mean. She could've gotten you hurt—your neck broken. Maxine and I are a farce, and I'm done with it. I'm tired of the games. I'm too old for it."

"Sam, Maxine's totally devastated."

He picks up his hat and eyes me warily. "You don't mean it."

"She talked about you the whole way home."

It's true. She described all the painful ways she was going to get even with him the entire ride back.

"What did she . . . no, forget it. I don't even want to know. We have work to do. We're way behind schedule here, and we need to focus."

I catch the glimmer of interest in his eyes, but let it go. He's right. We are not going to be ready for the opening of the Valiant at the rate we're going. It's something that's been keeping me up at night.

"Sam, what are we going to do? The theatre isn't anywhere near ready for opening night. We have a week and a half left, and I'm scared it's not gonna happen."

His hand rests on my shoulder. "We've worked hard here, Katie. You've done a fine job. You need to be proud of what you've accomplished."

My hand sweeps the theatre. "It's not good enough. Isn't there anything we can do? Work more hours? I could stay longer."

Sam shakes his head. "We may be running behind here, but I happen to know the Big Guy is right on schedule."

"James?"

"No. God."

"Whatever! Look around you. All I see is the theatre's nowhere near finished. Do you have any idea how this is going to break Millie's heart? She thinks Amy's coming next week, did you know that?"

"All we can do is our part. Whether the theatre gets done or whether Amy Scott comes back home is out of our control." Sam's patient eyes meet mine. "I've been praying for God's help. Have you?"

I swallow a rude comment. "No," I sigh. "I haven't prayed about this." I really don't think I'm qualified.

"You want to help, girl, then you start praying." He gives my nose a tweak. "Tonight."

Dragging my feet, I follow him into the theatre. The conversation turns to school and church as we return to a painting project started last week. I pour some red paint in a tray, and with small brush strokes begin to touch up a damaged mural on the wall. Sam works beside me, filling in a gold Art Deco sun which completes the picture.

I load my brush with more paint. "Can I ask you something?"

"Is this about Maxine?"

"No."

"Then shoot."

"Why doesn't James ever come to the Valiant?"

Sam finishes a sun ray before answering me. "I've known James all his life—love him like a son. And that man can preach the Word like nobody else. But somewhere along the way, I think he got so busy ministering to others he didn't stop and minister to himself. James and Millie are dealing with their hurt in their own ways."

"Do you think Amy's coming?"

He draws his brush back and surveys our work. "It's not for me to say."

"But what if she doesn't?"

With a weathered hand, Sam points out a spot I missed.

"Sam, the theatre isn't going to be done on time, is it?"

He sets his brush down and wipes his brow with the back of his sleeve. "Have a little faith, Katie."

My words come out sharp and condescending. "Just like that? It's that simple?"

"Kid, it's all we've got."

I leave Sam and go to the bathroom to wash out my brushes, my mind on overload. Sam makes this faith business sound so easy. My algebra teacher makes math sound easy, but my report card tells a different story. Some things are just beyond me.

When I return to the theatre, Sam is nowhere to be found. I take the opportunity to grab a juice box and a pack of peanut-butter crackers and sit down to watch the *Romeo and Juliet* rehearsals.

"What's here? a cup, closed in my true love's hand? Poison, I see, hath been his timeless end . . . "

"No, Stephanie, quit smiling. This is the serious part, remember? We talked about this last week. You just woke up to find your true love's body next to you, and he's dead. Dead, Stephanie, okay?" Bev runs a hand through her short hair and paces back and forth next to the stage. "Imagine you just broke your flat iron. Think how upset you'd be. Got it?"

Stephanie nods, her ponytail bobbing enthusiastically.

"Pick it up from your last line."

Stephanie thinks for a moment. "Poison, I see, hath been his timeless end . . . um . . . um . . . Don't tell me. I know this."

I finish her line. "O churl! Drunk all and left no friendly drop to help me after? I will kiss thy lips; haply some poison yet doth hang on them."

Laughter behind me makes me jump.

"You know you've been spending too much time here when you can quote the lines better than the actors."

I smile. "Hey, Millie."

Maxine appears behind her. "How's it going, Sweet Pea?"

"I think we're making some progress." I hope my expression is more believable than my voice.

Millie smiles. "Good. I know you are. We've made some progress too—on the Harvest Ball. We finally have the menu set and all the decorations purchased."

"Yup." Maxine drops into a seat. "This event planning has been hard work."

Millie looks to the ceiling and blows an exasperated sigh out her lips. "I think I'll go touch base with Bev."

Maxine twirls a ring around her finger, looks behind us, and begins to absently hum a little tune.

"He's here somewhere."

My foster grandmother faces forward with a jerk. "I have no idea who you are referring to."

"Yes, you do. Sam—he's in the building somewhere. But he's probably avoiding you."

Her ruby red lips purse together in a haughty pout. "I had hoped we could be adult about this, but I can understand him being too devastated over losing me to stick around." Maxine's eyes roam the theatre. "Seeing me would probably bring him further pain, and I do so hate to see a grown man cry."

"You are an angel."

Maxine lays a hand over her heart. "I believe it's Romeo who says, 'Live and be happy.'"

"Prosperous."

"What?"

"Romeo says, 'Live and be prosperous.'"

Maxine studies my face a moment before giving a careless shrug. "Whatever." She takes a nail file out of her giant gold purse and works on her nails. "No matter. That ship has sailed."

"So who will take you to the Harvest Ball this weekend?"

"Oh, Katie, my dear. The burden of being Maxine Simmons is that there is only one of me for all of my gentlemen admirers. Maybe one day you'll understand."

"You can't find a date, can you?"

"Not even if I paid cash."

A plan begins to brew in my head—bits and pieces of ideas swirling around.

"Maxine, maybe you just gotta have some faith."

"Girl, I got faith. What I need is a date."

Chapter thirty~eight

"WHATCHA WORKING ON?"

Totally bored, I pop my head into James's study. He's been holed inside for hours.

His chair creaks as he swivels to greet me. "Wow, don't you look nice. Tell me again how you got roped into going to the Harvest Ball?"

I take a seat in a worn leather chair, settling my black skirt over my legs. "I volunteered to help."

James grimaces. "And I thought you were such a bright girl."

"Very funny. I think it will be fun. And besides, Millie needs some help."

"It's very nice of you to go."

"Plus, since I'm grounded for life, this gives me a chance to break out of the house." I look over James's shoulder and catch a few words on the computer screen. "Working on your sermon?"

He leans back in his chair and sighs. "Yes. It's not coming together like I thought it would. Sometimes it's like that. One week the sermon will almost write itself, and other times I'm still struggling with it as I take the pulpit."

"What's it about? Maybe I can help you." I grin. "I did get an *A* on my persuasive essay in English last week."

"I saw that on the refrigerator. Does your teacher always put giant smiley face stickers on your papers?"

My face warms. "No, but Millie does."

James laughs. "It was a good essay. Definitely deserving of a spot on the fridge."

"See, so maybe I could help you out. What's the topic? If it's about how God thinks every teenager should have a cell phone, you can use some of my material."

"Ah, no. But what an interesting topic—God's thoughts on you going cellular." James drags a hand over his evening stubble. "Actually I'm planning on teaching about forgiveness."

"Oh."

"Yeah. Heavy topic."

"And what are you going to say about it? How about 'forgiveness: you should do it.'"

"Very catchy. I thought I'd go a little more in depth though. I'll probably talk about how God's forgiveness is ours for the asking. That Christ died on the cross for all of our sins so we would be forgiven."

"Last Wednesday night Pastor Mike said a lot of people ask for forgiveness, but then don't let it go." My eyes are glued on James. "You know, like they go through the motions of asking God to forgive them, but then they hang on to their guilt. He said it can really weigh you down."

James laces his fingers and studies his hands.

"But what do I know? I'm new to this." I jump out of my chair, my skirt flouncing. My work here is done.

"Just can't get anything past you kid."

I stop in the doorway and turn to find James watching me.

"Many will try, James. Few will succeed." I smile, not sure what to do with this awkward moment I've created.

He unclasps his hands and relaxes them on the chair. His face is thoughtful. "You know, I wasn't sure about you."

I pop my gum. "I hear that a lot."

"No, I mean . . ." He shakes his head. "I'm botching this up—kind of like my sermon. What I'm trying to say is . . . I wasn't certain I wanted a foster child in my home—at my age and with my track record as a parent. Millie and I . . . well, Amy isn't a success story for us—yet." His eyes hold mine. "I didn't know if we—if *I*—was qualified to be a parent again."

"I think you're doing an okay job. At least your omelets are good." And I mean it. I think James has come a long way. We both have.

I take a step out the door, then a thought occurs to me. "Hey, James . . . Maybe kids are like parents—we don't pick them, you know? We just gotta work with what we've got." I think of my mom and how there were good times too. I remember the Christmas I got a puppy. How we sang Destiny's Child songs in the car. Watched *Gilmore Girls* reruns together.

"Yeah, God picks them. And you want to know something cool?" His mouth turns up in a smile. "We requested a boy foster child." He laughs at my disgusted face. "Millie and I specifically asked for a boy to be placed in our home. But when the call came, we knew we couldn't walk away from you."

I clear my throat and stare at the floor, not wanting James to see my eyes tearing up.

"That, Katie, is God."

When I reach my bedroom, I shut the door and settle onto my bed. Bowing my head, I close my eyes and try to think of all the prayers I've heard since I've been in In Between. All the pretty words. All the churchie phrases.

But nothing comes to me. Nothing that sounds right.

I stink at this talking to God stuff.

And then another idea hits me. I jump off the bed and sit at my desk. Reaching into a drawer, I drag out the stationery from Mrs. Smartly and lay it out. With pen in hand, I stare at an empty sheet of paper for a full ten minutes.

> ~~Dear Most Gracious Heavenly Father,~~
> ~~Lord, I praise you and thank you~~

Um . . . no. *So* not working. I crumple up the paper and try again.

> ~~Dear Heavenly Father,~~
> ~~Lord, I come to thee today and offer thou~~

Definitely not. Sounds like Shakespeare just invaded my body.

Life would be a lot easier if I could just shoot the Big G-Man an e-mail. God seriously needs a Yahoo account. I wad the stationery in a ball and aim for the trash can across the room. It bounces off the wall and lands three feet in front of me. Oh, forget it.

I grab a new sheet of paper. Time to just get real.

> *Dear God,*
> *It's me, Katie.*
> *Look, I don't have all the fancy words for this, so*
> *I'm just gonna spit it out. We really need your help.*
> *I know I haven't been the model child here, but I*

have really been trying. Somehow, someway, the
Valiant needs to be ready for the opening. I know
it's all impossible, but well, you do have that whole
God thing going for you. Look, God, Millie and
James need this. And I guess so do I. These people are
important to me.

Please help. You're my last shot.

~~Later.~~ *Amen.*

"ARE YOU SURE SAM said he would be here?" I wring my hands and eye Frances.

"Yes, he promised me. You should've seen me. I deserve an Oscar for that performance. I told him with both of my grand-fathers living so far away, I thought of him like a grandpa."

"And then you told him you would be here helping out."

"Right." Frances's face glows as she reenacts the story. "I said, 'Sam, it would mean the world to me if you would come to the Harvest Ball and dance with me.'"

"And what did he say?"

Frances's voice goes deep. "He said, 'I don't know, girl. I think I'm going to be busy that night.' So I gave him the face." Her expression changes to a tragic pout. "And I said, 'If my grandfathers were here, they would be at the ball to dance with me. Sarah Jane Patterson always dances with her grandfather at the Harvest Ball.'"

I frown. "Kind of a lame story, Frances. I was hoping you'd be a little more original. Like tell him Julia Roberts was going to be here. Or how it was one of the residents' dying wish he come tonight. Maybe tell him they were giving away door prizes — overalls and tool belts."

"I'm telling you, it's gonna work. I had him in the palm of my hand."

Suddenly we're surrounded by a haze of heavy perfume.

"Well, Sweet Peas, you're not being paid to stand there and chitty-chat." Maxine, in a silky lilac formal, joins us at the refreshment table.

"We're not being paid for anything. We're volunteers." I arrange the napkins in a fan, resisting the urge to fold them into swans.

Maxine digs in her beaded clutch and pulls out her lipstick. "What do you think about our theme?"

I read the banner over the entry of the activities room. *A Night of Fall Foliage.*

"Yup." Maxine blots her lips on a napkin. "I voted for *All Dried Up*, but nobody went for it."

"You look very pretty, Mrs. Simmons."

"Thank you, Frances. I wasn't sure about the color, but old Cecil Tucker just told me I look like Jessica Simpson."

"Are you sure he didn't say Bart Simpson?"

Maxine whacks me on the shoulder with her purse. "I don't need your sass. Now get back to work. Ask people if they need anything—cake, punch, hearing aid batteries." Maxine walks away in her purple stilettos, mumbling something about a disco ball.

I clean up some crumbs and stray trash on the table. "Nice music."

Frances and I pause to listen to the twenty-piece orchestra.

"What's up with the bubbles?" I pop one with my finger.

"It's setting the mood."

"When you have an eighty-five-year-old saxophone player tooting out Nelly's 'Grillz,' setting the mood is the least of your worries."

The orchestra transitions into a number that sounds like an old Mariah Carey song, and the lights dim. A man in a navy suit walks past me, closing in on the pigs in a blanket.

"Sir, can I get you some punch?" I fill his glass. And then nearly drop it. "Sam?"

Sam Dayberry tugs on his collar and his eyes shift nervously. "Hello, Katie. Frances."

I can't believe what I'm seeing. It's like *Extreme Makeover: The Sam Dayberry Edition*. "I didn't recognize you without your hat."

His face turns as red as the watered-down punch. "You've seen me without my hat. At church."

"But not like this. Not with a suit and tie."

"You look so *GQ*." Frances gives me a pointed look when the disco ball flickers to life.

It's go time.

"Um, Sam . . . this is my favorite song. Would you like to dance?" Frances looks longingly at the dance floor.

"I don't know. I just got here. Maybe I could have some of these hot dog thingies here first."

I jump into action, placing myself between Sam and the appetizer table. "No, you guys go ahead. Frances has been looking forward to a dance all evening."

Totally defeated, Sam grabs a cup of punch and throws it back. He reaches for another.

"You don't want Frances to miss her favorite song."

"Oh, all right." Sam offers Frances his hand, and the two step onto the floor.

I search frantically for Maxine. Where is she? I know Sam isn't going to stay long. With no time to lose, I run into the kitchen calling out Maxine's name.

No sign of her.

I check the ladies' room, the men's room (you never know), the parking lot, and the outer hallways of Shady Acres. I sprint back into the dance hall, catching Frances's attention, signing to keep him dancing.

A blur of lavender whizzes by and heads for the orchestra.

"Maxine!"

She continues her pursuit of the conductor.

"Young man, I specifically told you I didn't want to hear any eighties music tonight. It was just brought to my attention you played Bon Jovi in that last set."

"Maxine!"

My foster grandmother halts, her finger poking the conductor in the chest. "What is it? I'm handling some urgent business here."

"Maxine, Sam's here."

A single eyebrow lifts. "Katie, my dear, I really don't care. I let that man go like a stretched-out girdle."

"I saw him dancing with someone."

Her lips twitch, and she bares her teeth like a pit bull. If Maxine were a cartoon, steam would be coming out of her ears.

Satisfied the bait is taken, I make a beeline for the dance floor and give Frances a thumbs up. Frances stops her waltz with Sam, grabs a woman from a swaying couple nearby, and pushes her into Sam's arms. With some magical words to the poor woman's partner, Frances takes the guy's hand and leads him away.

That. Was brilliant.

I hear the clicking of Maxine's heels before I see her come tearing through the crowd. Her eyes lock onto Sam and the lady in his arms.

I tap Maxine on the shoulder. "Cecil Tucker looks like he could use a dance."

Maxine follows the direction of my pointing finger, marches over, and grabs a dazed Cecil by the collar. She charges onto the dance floor, her friend limping behind her. Despite the slow, drifting chords of the violins, Maxine jerks Cecil to her, chest to chest. She stomps a purple shoe to the floor and leads a helpless Cecil into a tango.

This calls for snacks. Grabbing some nuts and punch from the refreshment table, I settle into a chair, ready to watch the drama unfold.

I don't know who's the worst dancer: Cecil or Sam. Both look like they took lessons from The Tin Man.

Maxine bends herself backward over Cecil's arm, and he's forced to dip her. Right into Sam.

"Oops, excuse us." Maxine giggles. "I thought Cecil and I were the only ones in the room."

The band brings the song to a close, and Sam says something to his partner and she glides away.

I drop my plate of nuts and leap into action, desperate to catch Sam before it's too late.

Dodging a walker and an old lady breaking out some Usher moves, I rush the dance floor and plant myself in front of Sam.

"Don't go." I have to catch my breath.

"What?"

"I said, don't go." I plaster a smile on my face. "I saw you dancing with Frances. And . . . it's my turn!"

My entire dancing experience consists of square dancing lessons in fourth-grade PE. I'm afraid it's all I've got. I hook my arm through his and reel him into a very awkward Cotton-Eyed Joe.

"Katie, I don't know anything about dancing, but this doesn't seem to go along with the music."

Kick and step two, three, four.

"Sam, you *have* to talk to Maxine. She's miserable without you."

The orchestra continues their rendition of some slow Elvis song. I keep one eye on Maxine, who is still holding Cecil hostage with the tango.

"She's not miserable without me. She doesn't need anybody." Sam stumbles over my fast-moving feet.

"No, she's devastated. Just look at her." Maxine is cheek-to-cheek with Cecil. "Well, maybe look at her later . . . "

"Katie, I'm not in Cecil Tucker's league. He's a war vet. The guy only has one leg. He gave up a limb for our country. I can't compete with that."

"You're not even trying." I spot Frances and shake my head, letting her know things are not going well.

"I'm here, aren't I? I took dance lessons from a sixteen-year-old boy, didn't I?"

"Good point."

"If she wants me, she's gonna have to come and get me. I'm tired of dating in secret, and I'm sick of chasing Maxine Simmons around like a lost puppy. I have my pride, and I'm done."

That man loves Maxine. I know it.

With a little modified two-step, I pivot Sam around so I can connect with Frances again. With my eyes bulging and my head jerking, I send out a mayday and motion her over.

"Oh, look. Here's Frances, ready for another dance." And I pass Sam off to my friend. I follow the sound of Cecil Tucker's labored breathing and tap his shoulder. "May I cut in?"

Cecil's eyes light up at the opportunity for escape, and he quickly disappears into the sea of senior citizens.

"What did you do a thing like that for? I was just getting warmed up."

I grab Maxine's hands and lead us in a terrible imitation of a slow dance. "Maxine, you are being ridiculous! What do you think you're doing cha-cha-ing all over the place with that man? Do you realize you're just hurting Sam? Not to mention, I seriously doubt Cecil Tucker will even be able to get out of bed tomorrow."

Maxine takes the lead and spins me under her raised hand. "Hurting Sam? I'm the victim here. Me!"

"You should try talking to him." I roll up in Maxine's arm, only to be spun out and released.

In time to the music, Maxine clutches my outstretched hand and pulls me back in. "I don't want to talk to him. I have nothing to say."

"You're just afraid he won't talk to you."

A bubble lands on her nose. "There is that."

"Maxine, just go ask him to dance."

She gasps and throws me into a fierce dip. "I will do no such thing! I am a lady."

I'm going to have whiplash. "It's the twenty-first century. It's okay for a lady to ask a man for a dance."

She pulls me upright. "Not for one of my generation."

I try to regain the lead and steer us a few steps closer to Sam and Frances. "You carry an iPod and have Coldplay as your cell ringtone. I think you're a little more advanced than the rest."

"I am too delicate and refined."

"I've seen you pick your wedgie in public."

Closer. Closer. Just a couple more feet and Maxine and Sam will be back to back.

"Frances, *now*!"

Frances and I throw our partners at each other. Maxine stumbles into Sam, who catches her with open arms. The two stand in a loose embrace. And just stare at one another.

Then Sam pulls Maxine closer and whispers near her ear. Clutching her hero, Maxine sends me a sly wink, then the two begin to move to the waltz. Maxine leads.

"Look, they're talking." Frances sighs and collapses into a seat.

"We were brilliant." Our hands meet in a high five, and we sit and watch all of our hard work pay off.

Sam and Maxine tear up the floor for another hour until the orchestra calls last song, and the two glide across the floor in not-so-perfect rhythm.

"Never thought about ending 'I Believe I Can Fly' in the splits." Frances tilts her head to get a better look at Maxine.

"There they go." I watch Sam hold out a hand and lead his lady off the floor. I hope when I'm old and gray I'll have someone to help me out of the splits.

"Sam said to tell you he's walking Maxine to her door and not to worry about her."

I stare at Frances. "When did he tell you that?"

"The last time I went out there and snuck him some punch. I guess a guy gets thirsty keeping up with Maxine."

Frances and I bus some tables, pausing now and then to raid the leftovers on the hors d'oeuvres table.

"Whew, is it over?" Millie appears at my side, untying a stained apron.

My eyes dart through the room, but Sam and Maxine are gone. "Where've you been, Millie? You missed a good party."

She laughs and blows a few strands of hair out of her eyes. "I've been in the kitchen all night. I kept thinking I'd get to come out and watch the dancing, but just as soon as I'd get to a stopping place, there would be another food crisis."

Millie lays an arm across my shoulders. "I didn't miss anything, did I?"

Frances and I share a tired look, and I look away to avoid a giggling fit.

"No, nothing." Frances puts on her poker face.

"Did Mother get a chance to dance with anyone tonight?"

"Yeah." I smile. "Maxine got her chance."

Chapter thirty~nine

"THESE TESTS ARE TERRIBLE."

Mr. Walker throws his stack of Algebra II exams on his desk. He shakes his head. The only thing worse than a Monday is getting a big fat *F* on a Monday.

I doodle little hearts on my notebook and swallow bitter disappointment. I studied my buns off for that test. Frances drilled me for hours like she was the Coach Nelson of quadratic equations. I didn't expect to set the curve or anything, but I thought I got at least a letter grade above failing. Studying is *so* overrated.

"Apparently, you don't think algebra is important. Obviously it doesn't matter to you people that you need this math credit to graduate."

Hey, I'm all about those credits that lead to a diploma.

"Reviewing was just a waste of class time. Half of you didn't even take notes when I discussed what would be on the test."

The class is so quiet I can hear myself breathe.

Mr. Walker passes the tests back, walking through the aisles and slapping exams on desktops.

"When I review, I expect it to be taken seriously."

Other than tattooing the answers on my forearm, I couldn't have been any more prepared.

"I want to praise one student for investing the time and effort into studying. This person is to be commended for making the highest grade, a *B+*."

Gotta be Simon Pensky, the one who always pulls the highest grade and is totally obnoxious about it. Last week he offered to help me study for a quiz: "I can tutor you, Katie. I'd be glad to show you what I know." And then he made these hubba-hubba eyebrows. I nearly barfed on him. I thought about showing him what *I* knew — courtesy of Trina.

Mr. Walker tosses a test on my desk, face down, and my stomach turns.

"This person could teach the rest of you a thing or two about studying."

I flip my test over. My heart stops.

"Congratulations, Katie. You made the highest grade."

It's me? He was talking about me. I think I'm going to hyperventilate. The shock — it's too much. This has to be a miracle. They'll want to put me on the evening news, like those people who see Jesus in tortillas.

The red *B+* leaps off the page, and I can't take my eyes off of it. I must be dreaming. These things don't happen to me. Katie Parker does not set the curve. I flip through the exam, almost certain it's a mistake.

But it's not. I made a *B+*. Oh, my gosh — I *am* smart! I can't wait to tell Frances and the Scotts. This baby's going on the fridge.

The bell rings, and Simon, the dethroned math whiz follows me out. "Hey, Katie, good job on the math test."

He stands a little too close, and I give him my best Stephanie-as-Juliet smile. "Thanks. I guess I don't need you to show me all you know—about math." I waggle my brows.

I breeze past him, resisting the urge to stomp on his foot as I go. Trucking it down the corridor, I push my way through the crowded hall and hold onto my test like it's a winning lottery ticket. I walk past my locker and take a right. There's a stop I need to make before I head off to lunch. It's something I've been trying to scrounge up the courage to do, and now I feel like I could do anything.

Stalling before a glass door, I pause to collect my thoughts, rehearse what I'm going to say, and check my hair in the reflection. Not bad. A good hair day *and* I aced an algebra test.

I swing open the door and make my way down the hall until I come to the office I need. I clear my throat. "Mrs. Whipple?"

The counselor sits with her back to me, facing the window, but makes no response. Maybe she's meditating. Or thinking of more ways to torture innocent students.

"Mrs. Whipple?"

She abruptly spins away from the window and slams her hands on the desk. "What do you want?"

I can do this. I can do this. I'm a card-carrying smart girl now. "I was wondering if I could talk to you about next semester, I—"

"No, go to class." She wipes her hands on her calico skirt, and I can tell I've interrupted snack time.

"Pastor and Mrs. Scott were going to come and speak to you about next semester, but I thought I would save them the trip."

Mrs. Whipple drums her chubby fingers on the desk, weighing her options. "Fine. Just make it quick. I have important things to do, and the sooner you spit it out, the sooner I can tell you no and get back to work."

From the looks of the crumbs on her mustache, I would guess that important work involves a package of Chips Ahoy.

Here goes nothing. "As you know, I'm in Art. I think I have a decent grade in there, but I happen to be really bad at it." During the pottery lesson last Thursday, my vase came out looking like a shoe. An elf's shoe.

"Your lack of artistic abilities is not my problem, Miss Parker. You couldn't hack band, and now you want to bail out on art?"

A million sarcastic comments screech in my head, but I plaster a pleasant expression on my face. "But I think we're on the right track with the arts, ma'am."

"If you're here to ask me to sign you up for office aid next semester, you are flat out of luck."

Okay, who marries people like this?

"No, actually I'd like to be put in drama." There. That wasn't too hard. I've been in here two minutes, made my request, and so far I still have my head attached.

"Drama?" She laughs.

"Yeah, I know. It surprised me too. But I'd like to try it."

"You come in here, barely passing the tenth grade, and think I'm gonna do you favors and change your schedule? For the third time in six weeks, I might add."

I nod. "Yes, please."

"Miss Parker, I don't have time for this. You want to be taken seriously? Then you do something to earn it. The transcript you transferred in with sure doesn't scream out responsibility and seriousness." Mrs. Whipple jiggles her mouse and begins typing.

"But my grades have gone up."

"Humph." She doesn't even look up from her computer screen.

I lay the test on her desk and slide it over. "Maybe you'd like to take a glance at this."

With an eye roll and a smirk, Mrs. Whipple grabs the algebra test. Her face changes to a frown. "Well, my, my. What have we here? A *B*?

"*B+*." Thank you very much.

She shoves it back to me. "I don't think this proves anything."

"Yes, it does. I made the highest grade in the class. Me, Katie Parker. Top score." I point to her computer. "Pull up my grades. Go ahead."

Mrs. Whipple hesitates, but she punches some keys, and within a few seconds my quarter grades are on the screen.

"Hmm. Interesting."

"See? They've gone up. A lot. I've really been working hard, Mrs. Whipple. I think I've found something I might be interested in, something I might be good at. I won't ask for another schedule change." Actually, I don't know if I'll be any good, but after watching all those rehearsals of *Romeo and Juliet*, I definitely know what *not* to do.

"Even if you get in drama and can't memorize a single line?"

"I won't say a word to you."

"Even if they put you in a boy's role, glue on facial hair, and make you wear a wig?"

"I'll say thank you."

"I don't know . . . " She eyes me.

"Even if I get in there, get stage fright, and pee my pants during every performance, I will stick it out."

"Now that would be worth the price of a ticket." She sighs and grabs a pen. "Fine. But if your grades go down or if I hear of any trouble out of you, I'm sticking you in a double block of PE with Coach Nelson."

Yes! I'm out of art. "Thank you, Mrs. Whipple." I almost want to hug the old bag. "Um, while I'm here, I want to report a really mean teacher. In fact, I think she's a tad bit abusive."

"Who?"

"Coach Nelson."

"She's my sister."

Right then.

THE AFTERNOON SUN HITS me as I descend the steps of In Between High and make my way to the bus stop.

A horn honks, and soon I'm hearing my name called over the rumbling bus engines. I search the parking lot, and there, circling for a parking space, is James. I throw my hand up in a wave, and he pulls up to the curb. Rocky hangs his head out of the passenger window, and his tongue flaps out the side of his mouth.

I run up to James's truck. "Are you lost? You know this isn't In Between Community Church, right?"

He grins. "Get in. I thought I'd pick you up today and spare you a ride on the bus."

Could this day get any better? Not having to ride the stinky bus is just the cherry on top.

The truck smells like a convenience store pine air freshener, but I gladly hop in, shoving the mongrel to the middle. He promptly plants his paws on my lap and sticks half his body out the window.

"So what brings you out here?" I try to push the dog off with no luck.

James navigates through the parking lot, which at three o'clock is worse than any reality-show obstacle course.

"I thought I'd take the afternoon off, spend some time with you, and watch rehearsals. See if Sam needs me to drive a nail or two."

James and I swap smiles. Yup, this guy's really making progress. I believe we have me to thank for that. Clearly I bring out the best in people. Why, Mrs. Whipple was practically begging to assist me today.

"I also thought we'd drive through the Burger Barn and get some ice cream cones."

"Some chocolate mint would hit the spot." James should pick me up more often.

We pull through the Burger Barn drive-thru and get two double scoop cones. Rocky whines at my ice cream. "Not a chance, flea bag."

James hands me some napkins. "We'll have to eat it quick. Millie put me on a diet this weekend, and ice cream isn't on it."

"So basically you're picking me up just so you can have an excuse to have dessert."

He grips the steering wheel. "Katie, I'm a man who hasn't had sugar in three days. I'm prepared to stoop pretty low."

James takes the long way to the theatre, driving until there is no trace of his ice cream. I'm still working on the second scoop when we arrive at the Valiant.

I jump out of the truck then reach back in to grab my backpack. The dog makes a dive for my unprotected cone. "Rocky!"

The mutant mutt sits in the seat, licking his chops and what's left of my ice cream, and looking disgustingly pleased with himself.

When the three of us walk inside the theatre, both Sam and Millie look shocked to see James.

Millie hugs her husband. "Honey, what are you doing here?"

James winks at me. "My schedule happened to clear up for the afternoon. I'm here to help, so put me to work."

Millie takes James's hand and leads him into the theatre. She talks faster than the speed of sound, updating him on all things Valiant.

Sam and I work side by side, painting walls until my hand cramps around the roller brush. The gold paint covers the last of the graffiti, and as I step back and look at it, my heart lightens.

"Thank God that's gone."

"You can say that again." Sam picks up the paint trays. "You better clean up. It's nearly time for you to go home."

I wipe my hands across my painting shirt, clearing the gold off my fingers. "Nope. I'm staying. Millie said we could stay a few more hours tonight."

"How did you manage that?"

I tell Sam all about my improved grades, then leave to wash out my roller. Watching the paint rinse out into the sink, I smile just thinking about the day. Good things do happen to me. My life has officially stopped being a series of catastrophes.

"Katie!"

I ignore Sam's voice and continue scrubbing the roller. Just a few more seconds.

"Katie!" This time it's Millie.

Throwing the supplies into the sink, I shut off the water and dash into the theatre.

"What? What's wrong?" My feet skid to a halt on the tiled floor, and I freeze at the sight in front of me.

"You have some visitors."

There, filling the theatre, stand Pastor Mike, his wife, and everyone from Target Teen. They're decked out in work clothes, many of them carrying brushes, hammers, drills, and tool boxes.

Pastor Mike steps forward, wearing his Jack Sparrow grin. "Did somebody order a miracle?"

"I did." My arms break out in goosebumps. "I ordered one."

"Well, we were in the neighborhood. Thought we'd drop by and see if you needed any help."

My mouth is open, and I'm just standing there, staring at every single one of them. I can't stop shaking my head, and my eyes well up like I've just been crowned Miss America. They did this for me. And the Scotts. All those things Angel said about the churchies replays in my head.

She *was* wrong about them. I can permanently delete those doubts.

Frances breaks through the crowd, her parents close behind her. "Let's get this party started."

I hand her a paintbrush and give my friend a quick hug. Yes, me. Hugging. Sam and Millie start assigning jobs. Soon the Valiant is filled with the sounds of tools, hard work, and laughter. And progress. The hours fly by, but every few minutes I have to stop and look around, in awe at the transformation happening around me.

"You got yourself some good friends." Sam hands me a bottle of water.

My hair is damp with sweat, but I don't care. "The Valiant . . . it's going to be finished on time. I know it."

"See? Faith. I told you it would work." He puts his work-gloved hand on my shoulder. "Did you pray like I asked you to?"

"Yeah." I nod. "Could be just a coincidence though."

"Girl, there are no coincidences. We got about seventy people here who can testify to that."

"We're gonna make it, aren't we?"

Sam takes a swig of his own water and wipes his mouth. "You see, Katie, it's kind of like me and Maxine." His eyes crinkle beneath his cap. "I never had any doubts."

Chapter forty

OPENING NIGHT. IT'S FINALLY HERE.

Maxine and I sit in the front row of the Valiant, and I can't take my eyes off the place. I can't believe it. The churchies worked with us all week, putting in some long, exhausting evenings, and it was only a few hours ago we hammered our last nail and painted our last stroke. The Valiant looks like something out of an old movie, with its cool Art Deco style. It's like the theatre has come to life.

I wish I could say the same for Millie.

She's been a bundle of nerves all day. I thought she would be excited over our progress and the way the theatre was transformed this week. But she's been zombielike since this morning, staring off into space and not saying much. Could be all the paint fumes she's inhaled lately. But I know that's not it.

"Where's my daughter?" Maxine blows a bubble and shifts in her seat to look behind her.

"Probably checking her cell phone." Millie's been doing that constantly, checking for messages or missed calls. It's a safe bet she's expecting Amy to call. So far, nothing. As excited as I am for the play and for the town to see the Valiant, my stomach flutters when I think of Millie. What if Amy doesn't show up? It will ruin everything for my foster mom.

Maxine holds up her new watch, something she dug out of a cereal box this morning. "The little Power Ranger is on the four, and the big Power Ranger is on the eight. She should be out here by now. Work is over. If it's not fixed by now, it's too late."

It's a little more than two hours until show time, and Bev has a few of the cast members on stage practicing some of the scenes for the last time. I hope the actors are as ready as the theatre is. Stephanie's death scenes have improved I think. Our Juliet may not be ready for the Oscars, but at least she's not overcome with giggling fits every time she has to stab herself.

We've all been here the entire day. I'm exhausted, but also totally wired. After working like a dog, it's hard to now sit still and just relax.

"Okay, now take it from Romeo's entrance. I really want to nail this scene." Bev's voice is hoarse, and her words come out in squeaks.

Romeo, already in costume in a pair of really horrible purple tights, approaches Juliet's bedroom window. (Tights? No wonder Stephanie couldn't stop laughing.)

"But, soft! what light through yonder window breaks? It is the east, and Juliet is the sun. Arise, fair sun, and kill the envious moon, who is already sick and pale with grief . . . "

If the moon is sick, it's probably from having to look at Romeo's buns squeezed into a pair of spandex pants.

Romeo continues the wooing of his lady, and I lay my head back on the chair and allow my eyes to close.

"See how she leans her cheek upon her hand! O, that I were a glove upon that hand, that I might touch that cheek!"

I open an eye at the sound of someone entering the theatre doors. A guy wearing an *In Between Times* ball cap makes his way to the stage. He and Bev have a quiet conversation, then he gets out a camera and starts snapping photos. It's just like Hollywood and the Red Carpet—the press is here for the premiere.

Stephanie, perched in a second story window with her chin on her hand, notices the flash and begins to pose, totally breaking character. I smile to myself. The girl's waited a long time for this moment. Her photo op has finally arrived, and I imagine she feels a little like I did when I got the *B+* on my algebra test. *Ah, finally! What I've been working for!*

The photographer stands in one of the theatre seats and snaps a few. "Romeo, could you turn your head this way just a bit. Perfect, perfect."

I lean into Maxine. "Maybe I should tell him Maxine Simmons is in the house. Let him get some pictures of a real star."

Maxine's hand forms a rock 'n' roll sign. "Vegas forever, baby!"

"Okay, practice for another thirty minutes, then I want everyone in costume. Keep it going. We only have about an hour before you guys need to be ready." Bev sneezes and sits back down.

Juliet flips her hair and smiles. "Three words, dear Romeo, and good night indeed. If that thy bent of love be honorable, thy purpose marriage, send me word tomorrow."

"Those Elizabethans sure worked fast," Maxine whispers. "Juliet meets Romeo, then immediately expects the guy to cough up an engagement ring? Humph! Mr. Simmons waited a respectable week before asking for my hand."

I blink. "A week? Whoa, you and Juliet were total hoochie mamas."

"All my fortunes at thy foot I'll lay . . . "

As Stephanie delivers her lines, she gets closer and closer to the edge of the window. Like Rocky in the truck, she is practically hanging out. I know she's sitting on a ladder back there, so that can't be easy.

The photographer jumps off the chair (which I recovered myself) and squats on the floor for a different angle. The rapid fire clicks of the camera have Stephanie posing like a contestant on *America's Next Top Model.*

"Juliet, could you just lean out a little more? You're in the shadow, and I'm not getting a clear shot of you."

Bev drops her tissue box and bolts out of her chair. "No, I don't think that's a good idea. Stephanie, don't lean out any farther. Stephanie, no. You need to—"

A shrill scream pierces the air, and suddenly Stephanie is airborne.

It's like a bad slow-mo scene from a movie. Everyone is on their feet, racing toward her, but she's so far away.

I hear myself yelling, "Noooo!" And I propel my body onstage. Too late.

"Oomph! Ohhh! Urghh!"

The star of the show hits the staircase with a thud and cartwheels halfway down, only to fall off the edge.

Crash!

From the stairs, Stephanie cannonballs into a first-story canopy roof. Her body plummets through the material, leaving a giant hole. Arms and legs flailing, she soars down, down toward the stage floor.

Splat!

Landing spread-eagle in a row of borrowed shrubs.

"Owwww."

Everyone rushes the stage, circling the fair Juliet.

"Stephanie, can you hear me?"

"Stephanie, don't move!"

"Can you wiggle your toes?"

"Call an ambulance!"

"Stephanie, do you see my Diet Coke back there?"

A panicked James and Millie explode out of the lobby doors and sprint downstage.

"What happened?" Millie's raised voice ricochets through the theatre.

In two short moves James is next to Stephanie. "Are you okay? Everybody back up. Please." James kneels beside her. "Stephanie? Stephanie, can you hear me?"

Stephanie lies motionless. Absolutely still.

Okay, Lord, if she's dead, I take back every single thing I ever said about her. Even horrible actresses don't deserve to fall through a two-story set (every last piece of it).

Sam joins us on stage. "The ambulance is on the way."

James leans down, putting his ear near Stephanie's face. "She's breathing."

My own breath comes out in a *whoosh*, and I'm lightheaded with relief.

"Thank God." Millie says. I totally agree.

James tries again. "Stephanie, can you hear me?"

Not even a flicker of an eyelid.

Maxine elbows me out of the way, shoves Romeo aside, and plants herself beside James. "Stephanie, the photographer says he's ready for your close-up."

Two blue eyes pop open. "Close-up?"

The crowd erupts into sighs and nervous laughter as Stephanie attempts to sit up, looking dazed and confused.

James's arms hold her in place. "No, stay right where you're at. We gotta get you checked out."

"Oh, no." Her glossy pink mouth turns up in a smile. "My leg really hurts."

And Juliet Capulet promptly passes out.

The ambulance sirens cut through the mayhem, and everyone quiets as the EMTs file in.

Some paramedics consult with James, then hoist the limp Stephanie onto a stretcher. "We'll handle it from here."

Bev grabs her purse and shuffles behind them. "I'll stay with her until her parents get to the hospital. I'll be back soon." She shouts out some final commands for her worried cast then exits through the lobby doors, trailing behind her star actress.

The theatre gets awkwardly quiet. A few of us look around, not really sure what comes next.

"What are we going to do?" Millie's hands cover her face.

"Millie—"

"What?" Millie takes a step back out of the group, gaining some distance. "Of course I hope she's okay. But James, we have a play opening in two hours." Tears well in my foster mother's eyes, and she looks away.

The hum of the stage lights is the only sound for a full minute.

Maxine pops her gum, startling me out of my pathetic thoughts.

"You know what you have to do." Her eyes bore into mine.

"Um . . . get a broom?"

Maxine's hands latch onto my arms, and we're nose to nose. A personal space violation if I ever saw one.

"We're without a Juliet, Katie. And nobody knows this part but you."

The wave of surprise ripples among the crew.

My eyes grow large, and I shake my head. "Oh, no . . . no way."

Everyone gathers around me. They all begin talking over one another, bombarding me with encouragement, suggestions, and pleas.

No. Can't do this. They're crazy. What do I know about being in a play? My last theatrical experience was in elementary school. I'll make a fool of myself. The audience will throw tomatoes at me. They'll boo me and demand their money back.

"I can't. There's just no way." I turn to Millie. "I'm sorry. I don't know what the solution is, but it's not me."

"Katie, you'd be—"

"No, Millie." I look into every face onstage. "I'm a disaster waiting to happen. I know this. I don't want to screw one more thing up—especially something this important."

"You are not a disaster, Katie Parker. You're the girl who breezed through her math test." Millie stands in front of me and grabs my hands. "You're the girl who's been working her tail off here and at school for over a month. We know you can do it."

James puts his arm around me. "You know those lines better than Shakespeare. And we've all seen what a drama queen you are, so acting shouldn't be a problem for you."

Gee. Thanks.

Maxine sniffs with importance, tugging her skirt up like Barney Fife. "Well, I guess if you're not gonna do it, we're left with only one option." She lays the back of her hand to her forehead. "I will be Juliet."

The protests fly, and I can only stand there and smile.

"Which one of you is Romeo?" Maxine's lips squeeze into a pucker.

A few people begin to snicker. But Millie's face falls, and dropping my hands, she walks off stage.

Maybe I am an idiot. Or maybe I really don't have a backbone when it comes to peer pressure. But standing here, watching my foster mom walk away, totally defeated, through with the fight and through with her dream, I know what I have to do.

"Okay."

Millie stops.

"I'll do it."

She turns around in the aisle, a sad smile on her face. "It's okay, Katie. You're absolutely right. It's not fair to throw you into this. This just isn't meant to be."

"Millie, the girl can either 'wherefore art thou' or *I* can. Take your pick, but this show *will* go on." Maxine snaps her fingers at a lady on stage. "You! I'm ready for my costume fitting. And I'm not afraid to show a little cleavage."

"Millie, I'm in." And I am. I'll probably throw up at some point tonight, but I'm going to do this. "A lot of people worked really hard to see this place open, and we can't let them down."

James pulls me into a hug, and then Millie is there, wrapping her shaking arms around us both. A fourth party moves in, squeezing the very breath out of me, and I know without looking it's Maxine.

"*Annnd* break!" Maxine steps away, slapping each of us on the rear. "Now, little missy, let's get you in costume. While you're changing and doing makeup, I'll go over your lines with you."

I reach for James and Millie, but like a caveman, Maxine drags me behind the stage and into a dressing room.

"Okay, now you go behind that screen, and I'll pass the costume over."

A big, poufy yellow gown flies over the screen. I slip out of my clothes, forcing myself to think positive thoughts. The words from a famous literary classic come to mind, and I repeat them in my head: *I think I can, I think I can, I think I can.*

"Um, Maxine?" I step out from behind the panel. Turning in a circle, I show Maxine that Stephanie's dress fits me like a glove.

A glove that belongs to someone else and has no business being on my body.

"Oh . . . well." Maxine stares at my chest.

"Quite a bit of space here." I pat the material down.

Maxine snorts. "You could hide a small country in there."

"The dress is a little short too." I have a good five inches on Stephanie, and the same hem that covered her shoes grazes a few inches above my ankles.

"One problem at a time." Maxine scurries out of the room. She returns just as quickly, holding up a package of tissues in each hand. "Boobs in a box!"

Her hands move as fast as bee's wings, ripping out tissues and stuffing them into my bodice.

"I'll do it!" I snatch the tissues out of her grip and slap her hands away. "I am *not* that kind of girl."

Maxine is helping me with lines when Frances walks in.

"Congratulations, Juliet! Wow, you're a star."

"I *so* could've had the part." Maxine grabs me, plants a smacking kiss on my cheek, and struts out of the room.

"I can't believe this."

I laugh. *"You* can't believe it? Try being in *my* shoes." I attempt to wiggle my toes in Stephanie's heels. "My too-tight shoes."

"You're gonna be great. Millie says you have the whole play memorized."

Walking to the mirror, I begin to pin my matching headpiece on. "I don't know, Frances. I'm scared to death. The whole town's gonna be out there."

"I know you can do this."

My sigh fills the room.

"Katie, remember a few weeks ago at Target Teen, Pastor Mike spoke about Jeremiah?"

"Yeah."

"Did you read the verse he mentioned in chapter 29?"

"Well, I was gonna read my Bible. I'm sure it's a great book, but I decided I'd just wait for the movie."

Frances grins, but presses on. "It says God has big plans for you. Plans to make you a success and not harm you."

I check the clock in the reflection, panicked that I have so little time left. Don't really have any extra minutes for a Bible study right now, you know?

"So what I'm trying to say is you're here for a reason, Katie. Living in In Between for a reason. The Scotts are your foster parents for a reason. And I think you're going to be on stage tonight for a reason."

I push the final pin in my hair and look at my friend. "I'm just not there yet, okay? All I see right now is that in another hour I'm going to walk out on that stage, in a play I've never been in before, and perform one of the world's most famous parts. And I'm sick to my stomach, okay? Like so nervous I could do some serious hurling all over this hideous yellow dress. The entire town of In Between is going to be out there. And I know I'm going to totally mess up. A lot." I stop long enough to take a breath. "This could be a huge mistake. Like Lindsay Lohan as a blonde mistake."

Frances hands me a blush brush. "This isn't a mistake. And no matter what, there are people out there who care about you. And they don't really mind whether you mess up a line or have a wardrobe malfunction. That's not what this is about."

No, it's not. It's about helping James and Millie. I owe those people. And one day when Mrs. Smartly's green van swings back into town, I don't want to leave in anyone's debt.

"Thanks, Frances."

Frances tugs me into a hug.

"Um, Frances?"

"Yes?"

"You're smashing my Kleenex."

KNOCK. KNOCK.

"Five minutes until you're on, Katie. Get ready."

Bev closes the door of the dressing room, where I'm now surrounded by all the other actors not on stage. (You know, as in the actors who know what they're doing.)

My heart is beating like it's going to give out any second. My dress is too tight (well, except for the top part), and my palms are sweating. Did someone turn up the heat? It's so hot in here. I tried to drop a few subtle hints for someone to turn the air conditioner on, but no one was interested. Don't these people know who I am? I'm Juliet!

Juliet's lines chase one another in my head. Frances's words interrupt them like commercial breaks. I need a moment to clear my head. Opening the door to the dressing room bathroom, I close myself in and turn the lock. This moment calls for some heavy duty yoga breathing. My skirt gathers around me as I sit on the floor, enjoying the cool surface.

Can I do this? I mean, seriously, can I really pull this off?

God, are you up there? Do you hear me? I don't know if you're into Shakespeare, but if you are, I really hope you stop by and help me out. You know, I'm not sure where we stand. I don't have you all figured out yet. I barely have the math thing under control. But if you do have a purpose for me, and I'm supposed to be here tonight, I just want to ask you for a little help. Help me remember my lines and where to stand.

Help me to remember to not turn my back to the audience. And make sure I don't pull a Stephanie and fall out of a balcony window. And one last thing . . . please let Amy show up and make everything work out between her and the Scotts.

Knock. Knock.

"Katie, you're up."

Okay, gotta go. Bye. Er, I mean, Amen.

With my pulse racing faster than Seabiscuit, I follow Bev out into the wings.

Bev puts her hand to my back and gives me a little push. "Out you go. Break a leg."

I turn around and frown.

"No, not like Stephanie, I mean . . . oh, never mind. It's your cue."

And somehow my legs carry me onto the stage. I pause for a moment and take it all in. The lights. The stage. The theatre full of people. And even though I can't see them for the spotlight, I know James, Millie, Sam, and Maxine are in the front row, cheering me on.

I walk farther onto the stage, entering the scene. "How now, who calls?" I said it. My first line. I *can* survive this.

The crowd erupts into applause. For me. My eyes fill and chills dance along my spine. And I feel like I've just come home.

My movements grow bolder, my voice louder. I lift my chin like I'm royalty.

I *am* Juliet.

On the Valiant stage, I, Katie Parker, step into the spotlight and find Frances was right. This is exactly where I'm supposed to be.

Over a month ago I broke into this theatre.

And tonight—I'm breaking out.

Chapter forty~one

I GRAB A COLD BOTTLE of root beer, my third for the night. The production was over hours ago, but everyone involved in the play has moved to the Scotts' for a cast party. I still have Juliet's dress on, the last outfit she wears as she stabs herself. The extra padding on top really came in handy when I had to fall to the floor in a dead heap. Never mind that a few tissues slipped out and parachuted into the first row. I'm too giddy to care.

"Katie, you were wonderful. Have I told you that?"

I laugh. "Yes, Bev. Thank you." I've never had so much praise in all my life. I'm eating it like candy.

"I'm headed home; it's been a long day. But I wanted you to know you really blew me away tonight, and anytime you want to be in one of my plays, you say the word."

I just want to tattoo all her compliments on myself, so I'll never lose them. I say good-bye to Bev and go in search of my foster parents.

When I walk past the living room, I find James and some other men, discussing the theatre and watching *SportsCenter.* He dips a chip into some queso but jumps up when he spots me in the doorway.

"You're drinking kind of heavily tonight, aren't you?" He wipes the cheese off his mouth.

"I'm not the one on the diet." I elbow him in the stomach. "Don't worry, though, I won't tell on you."

"I'm so proud of you, Katie."

Sometimes I find it hard to look people in the eyes. I guess I'm not the trusting sort. But I look into the face of my foster dad, and I know this guy means what he says. James would never intentionally let me down. He's the real deal.

"I'm proud of you too." I step in closer so he can hear me above the noise. "I'm sorry about Amy. I know you're disappointed." And even though James was right all along about Amy not showing up, I hope he still thinks there's a chance one day she'll come home.

"It's okay." He nods. "We're all okay."

This tender moment is interrupted by the sound of Maxine yelling from another room. "Limbo time!"

James rolls his eyes. "All right, so not *everyone* is okay."

I search the rest of the house for Millie and finally find her when I glance outside the kitchen door. I flick the outside light on, and there she sits. By herself on the porch swing.

The creaking of the door opening sounds loud to my ears, as I interrupt Millie's quiet escape.

"Hey, sweetie." She smiles, but it's not too convincing. She needs to get lessons from Stephanie, I guess.

"Whatcha doing out here?" I take the other side of the two-seater swing.

Millie gazes at the stars, and she props her head on her hand. "Just thinking."

"About what?" My feet rest lightly on the ground, and I use my toes to move the swing.

"About how wonderful you were tonight. You know you were amazing, right?"

I shrug. "Well, I had hoped for totally spectacular, but I'll take amazing."

"I knew you could do it. I had faith in you."

I'm still not sure where I stand on this God business. I'm ready to admit there might be something to it, and I guess I hope there is. But there are still too many uncertainties for me to leap into that unknown right now. Maybe God is why I was taken out of a bad home situation. Maybe it's God who's brought me here. And perhaps God allowed me to totally rock tonight on stage . . .

. . . but this God didn't fix everything.

"Millie . . . your faith didn't bring Amy back."

Somewhere, tree frogs croak, and the cicadas chirp. And it's a long moment before Millie speaks.

"No, my faith didn't bring Amy back. But you know what else I was thinking about out here? I was thinking how I've had things all wrong lately."

Welcome to my world.

"I've been talking to you about faith and God, and here I was . . . Well, let's just say I wasn't doing a good job of pursuing either one myself."

Sometimes Christians are like Shakespeare. It's English, but a totally different version. "I'm not following you."

"I've been praying so hard for Amy to come home. For months. Years." Millie rubs her arms against the evening chill. "And I have to believe that day is going to come. But tonight I realized God has been faithful." Millie brushes a tear away. "He brought me you. Do you get that?"

No, not really.

"Katie, when I saw you standing in the spotlight, I just knew. I've been praying for a daughter . . . and spending all my time chasing after Amy. But the kid I'm supposed to be taking care of? Well, she's right here."

Millie gathers me in her arms, and just like the first day I arrived, I breathe her scent in. It was right then. And it's still right now.

Swiping at her eyes, my foster mother sniffs then laughs. "Oh, we could use some tissues."

I stick my hand in my dress and pull out a handful.

Millie laughs and kisses me on the head. "See, Katie Parker, you're just what I need."

The stars twinkle and glow above us. We watch the night sky, Millie with her renewed faith, and me with . . . well, whatever it is I have.

I do know some things for sure: I will be returning to the stage. My life doesn't have to be a catastrophe. And for right now, In Between is where I'm at.

Long live the Chihuahuas.

About the Author

JENNY B. JONES is the author of A KATIE PARKER PRODUCTION series. Though now an adult, she still relates to the trauma and drama of teen life. She is thrilled to see her writing dreams come true, as her previous claim to fame was singing the "Star Spangled Banner" at a mule-jumping championship. (The mules were greatly inspired.) The author resides in Arkansas, where, as a teacher, she hangs out with teens on a regular basis. You can visit her at www. jennybjones.com.

MORE GREAT READS FROM THE THINK FICTION LINE.

Miss Match

Erynn Mangum

ISBN-13: 978-1-60006-095-3
ISBN-10: 1-60006-095-1

Lauren Holbrook has found her life's calling: matchmaking for the romantically challenged. And with an eclectic cast of characters in her world, there's tons of potential to play connect-the-friends. Inspired by the recent success of matching her sister and new husband, Lauren sets out to introduce Nick, her carefree singles' pastor, to Ruby, her neurotic coworker who plans every second of every day. What could possibly go wrong? Just about everything.

Moon White

Melody Carlson

ISBN-13: 978-1-57683-951-5
ISBN-10: 1-57683-951-6

Heather has recently begun studying New Age ideas, but her newfound curiosity is alienating her from others, including her narrow-minded best friend, who has written her off as a witch. Isolated and lonely, Heather soon encounters fellow seekers who are far more accepting and encouraging than her Christian friends. Yet she soon learns that her "harmless" spiritual journey is anything but.

Bad Idea

Todd and Jedd Hafer

ISBN-13: 978-1-57683-969-0
ISBN-10: 1-57683-969-9

Griffin Smith is making his first interstate road trip, an adventurous rite of passage that will take him from his Midwestern home to his freshman year at college in Southern California. Soon his journey begins to take random detours, as he experiences a bittersweet reunion with his biological mother, confronts a terrible betrayal, and encounters one angry coyote.

NAVPRESS®
BRINGING TRUTH TO LIFE
www.navpress.com

Visit your local Christian bookstore, call NavPress at 1-800-366-7788, or log on to www.navpress.com to purchase, To locate a Christian bookstore near you, call 1-800-991-7747.

AVAILABLE SEPTEMBER 2007

A KATIE PARKER PRODUCTION ACT 2

on the loose

a novel

jenny b. jones